Garfield ®

THE THING IN THE FRIDGE

BY JIM DAVIS

ROSS RICHIE CEO & Founder • MATT GAGNON Editor-in-Chief • FILIP SABLIK President of Publishing & Marketing • STEPHEN CHRISTY President of Development • LANCE KREITER VP of Licensing & Merchandising
PHIL BARBARO VP of Finance • ARUNE SINGH VP of Marketing • BRYCE CARLSON Managing Editor • MEL CAYLO Marketing Manager • SCOTT NEWMAN Production Design Manager
KATE HENNING Operations Manager • SIERRA HAHN Senior Editor • DAFNA PLEBAN Editor, Talent Development • SHANNON WATTERS Editor • ERIC HARBURN Editor • WHITNEY LEOPARD Editor • JASMINE AMIRI Editor
CHRIS ROSA Associate Editor • ALEX GALER Associate Editor • CAMERON CHITTOCK Associate Editor • MATTHEW LEVINE Assistant Editor • SOPHIE PHILIPS-ROBERTS Assistant Editor
JILLIAN CRAB Production Designer • MICHELLE ANKLEY Production Designer • KARA LEOPARD Production Designer • GRACE PARK Production Design Assistant • ELIZABETH LOUGHRIDGE Accounting Coordinator
STEPHANIE HOCUTT Social Media Coordinator • JOSÉ MEZA Event Coordinator • HOLLY AITCHISON Operations Assistant • MEGAN CHRISTOPHER Operations Assistant • MORGAN PERRY Direct Market Representative

kaboom!

GARFIELD: THE THING IN THE FRIDGE, October 2017. Published by KaBOOM!, a division of Boom Entertainment, Inc. Garfield is © 2017 PAWS, INCORPORATED. ALL RIGHTS RESERVED. "GARFIELD" and the GARFIELD characters are registered and unregistered trademarks of Paws, Inc. KaBOOM!™ and the KaBOOM! logo are trademarks of Boom Entertainment, Inc., registered in various countries and categories. All characters, events, and institutions depicted herein are fictional. Any similarity between any of the names, characters, persons, events, and/or institutions in this publication to actual names, characters, and persons, whether living or dead, events, and/or institutions is unintended and purely coincidental. BOOM! Studios does not read or accept unsolicited submissions of ideas, stories, or artwork.

BOOM! Studios, 5670 Wilshire Boulevard, Suite 450, Los Angeles, CA 90036-5679. Printed in China. First Printing.

ISBN: 978-1-68415-019-9, eISBN: 978-1-61398-696-7

CONTENTS

"THE THING IN THE FRIDGE"
WRITTEN BY SCOTT NICKEL
ILLUSTRATED BY ANTONIO ALFARO
COLORED BY LISA MOORE

"THE EARLY JON ARBUCKLE"
WRITTEN BY MARK EVANIER
ILLUSTRATED BY ANTONIO ALFARO
COLORED BY LISA MOORE

"ONLY HUMAN"
WRITTEN BY SCOTT NICKEL
ILLUSTRATED BY AATMAJA PANDYA

LETTERED BY JIM CAMPBELL

COVER BY ANDY HIRSCH

DESIGNER GRACE PARK
ASSOCIATE EDITOR CHRIS ROSA
EDITOR WHITNEY LEOPARD

GARFIELD CREATED BY
JIM DAVIS

SPECIAL THANKS TO JIM DAVIS AND THE ENTIRE PAWS, INC. TEAM.

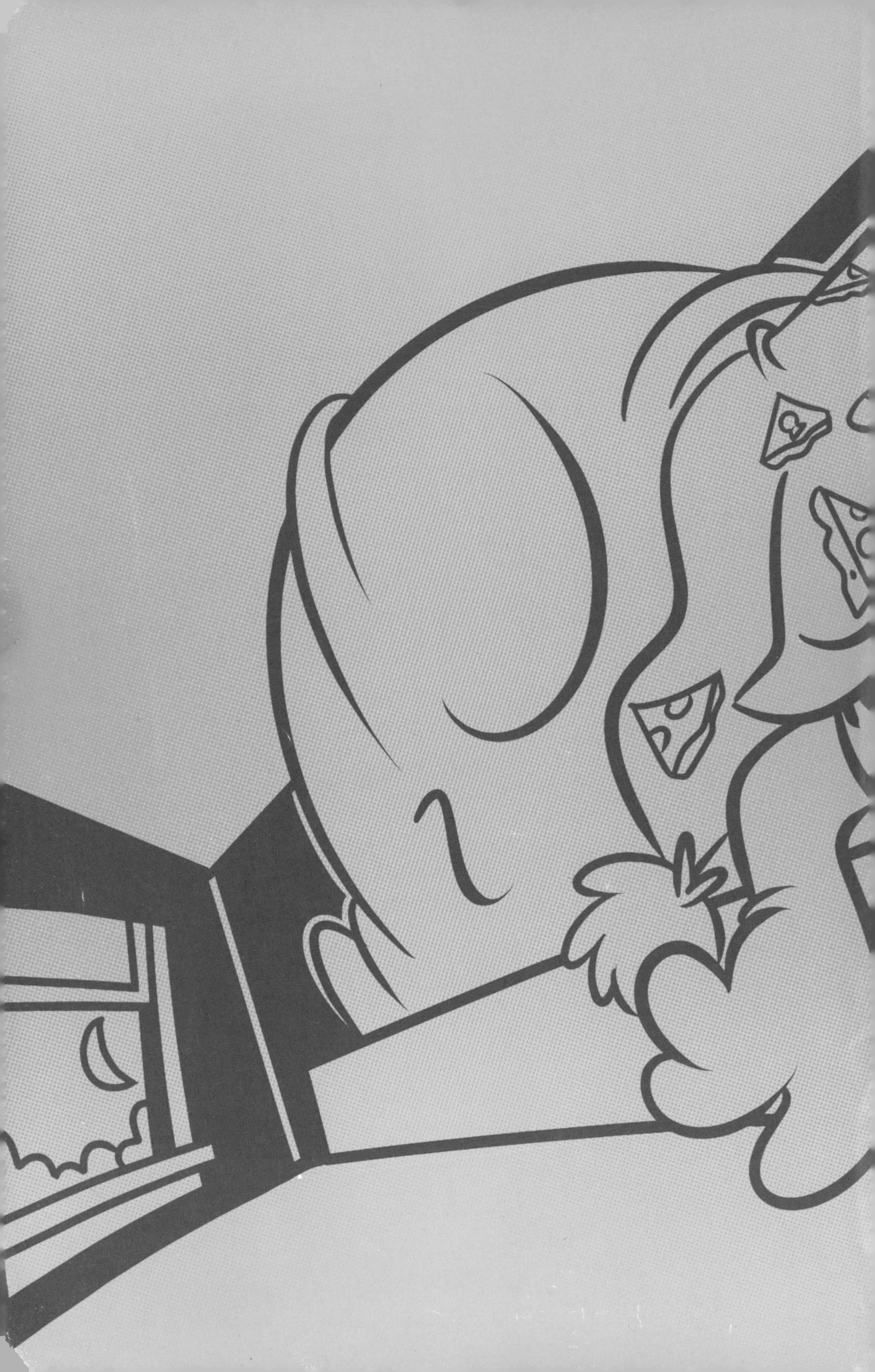

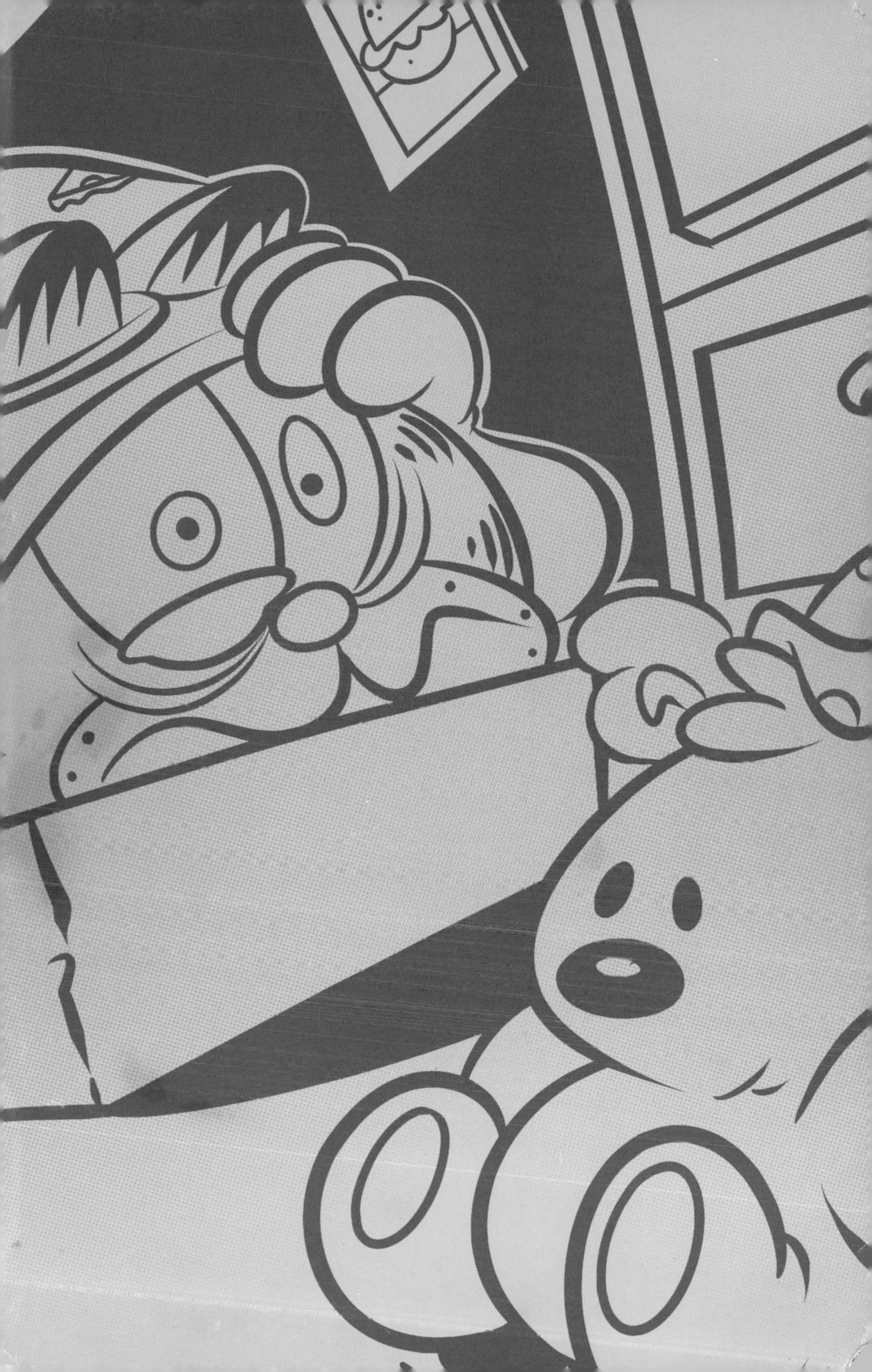

"THE THING IN THE FRIDGE"

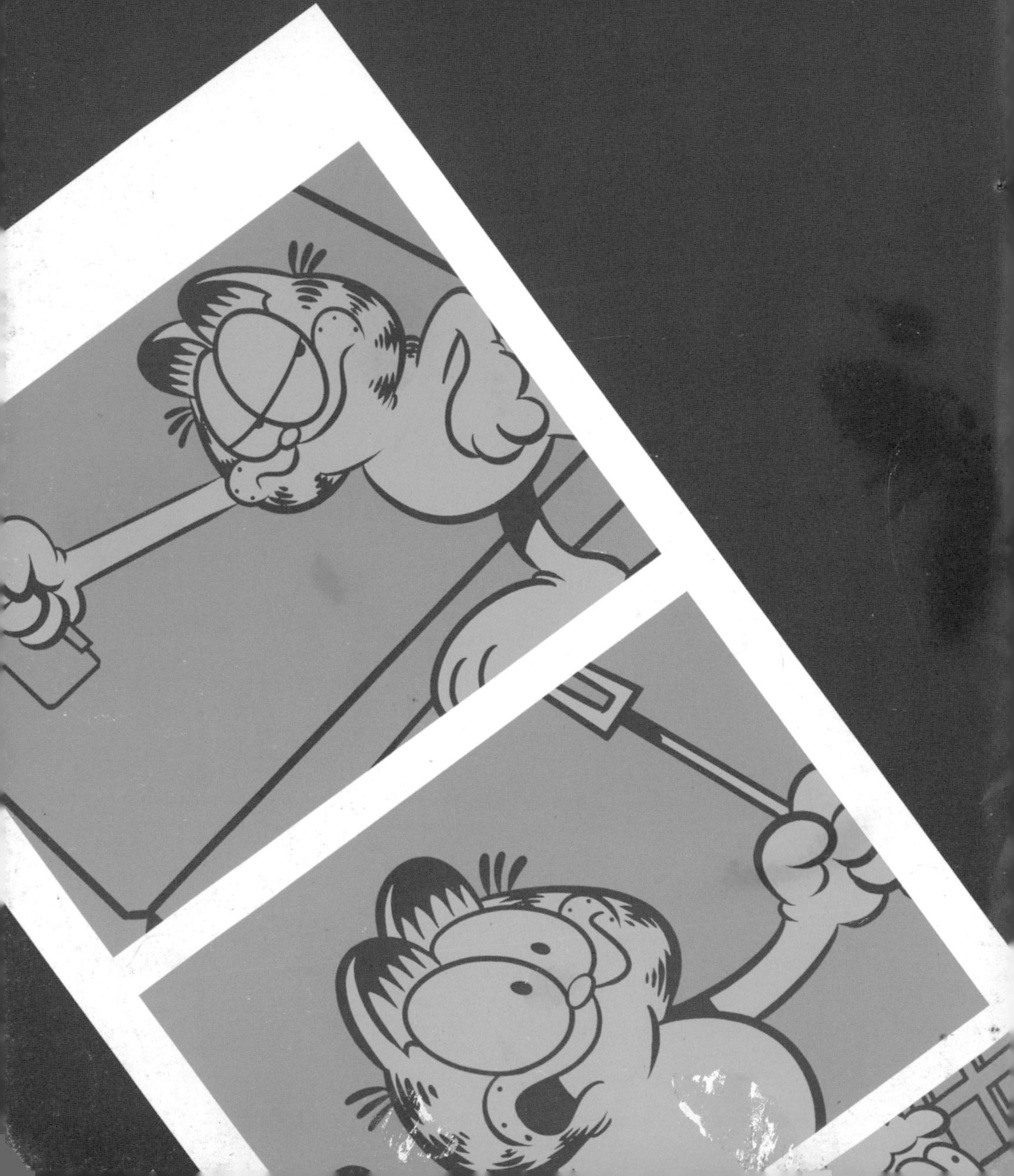

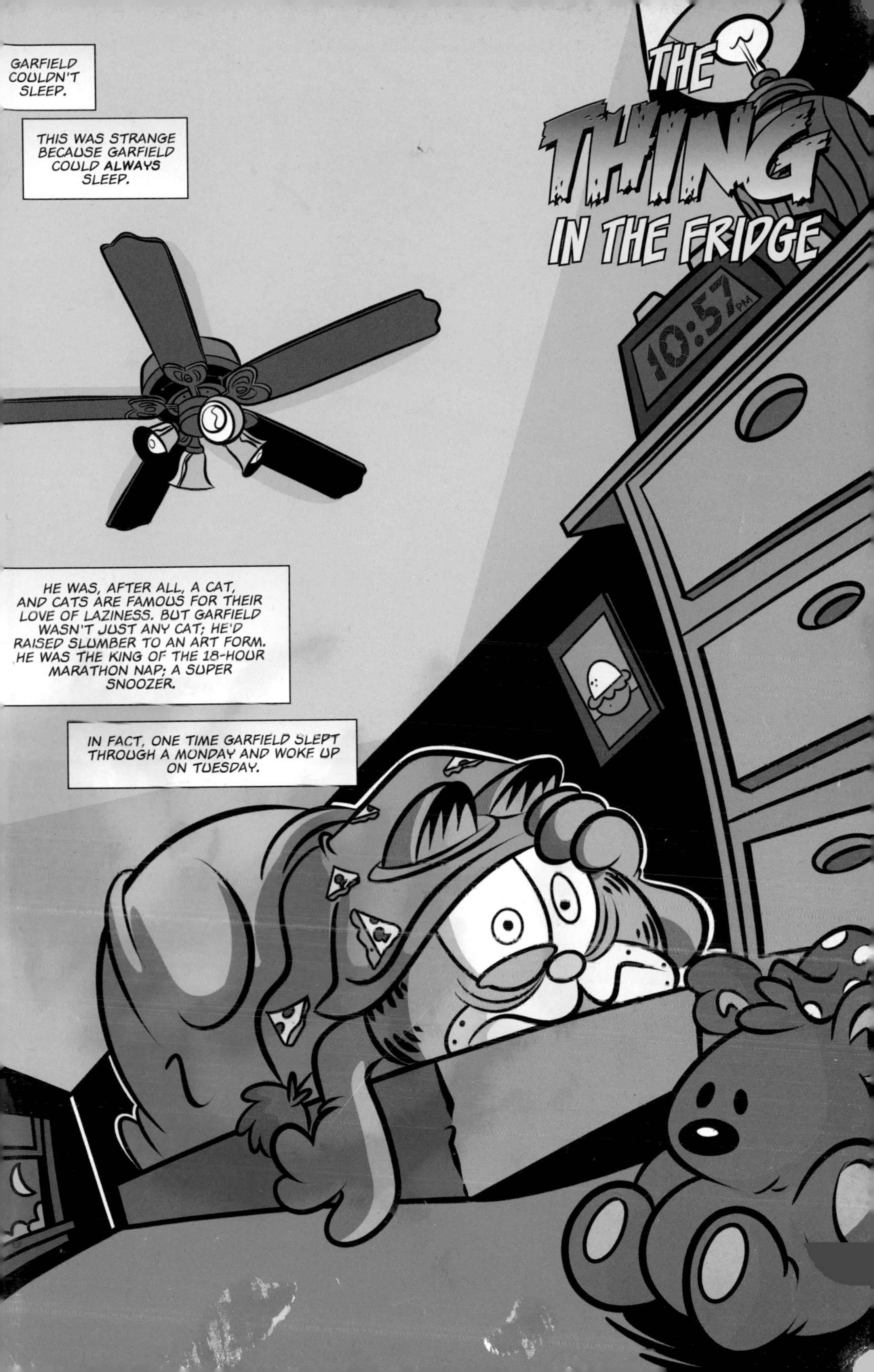
THE THING IN THE FRIDGE
GARFIELD COULDN'T SLEEP.
THIS WAS STRANGE BECAUSE GARFIELD COULD ALWAYS SLEEP.
10:57 PM
HE WAS, AFTER ALL, A CAT, AND CATS ARE FAMOUS FOR THEIR LOVE OF LAZINESS. BUT GARFIELD WASN'T JUST ANY CAT; HE'D RAISED SLUMBER TO AN ART FORM. HE WAS THE KING OF THE 18-HOUR MARATHON NAP; A SUPER SNOOZER.
IN FACT, ONE TIME GARFIELD SLEPT THROUGH A MONDAY AND WOKE UP ON TUESDAY.

BUT TONIGHT, GARFIELD WASN'T SLEEPING; HE WAS TOSSING.

TOSS!

TOSS!

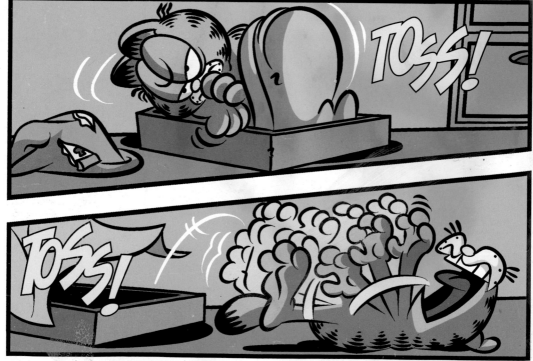

TOSS!

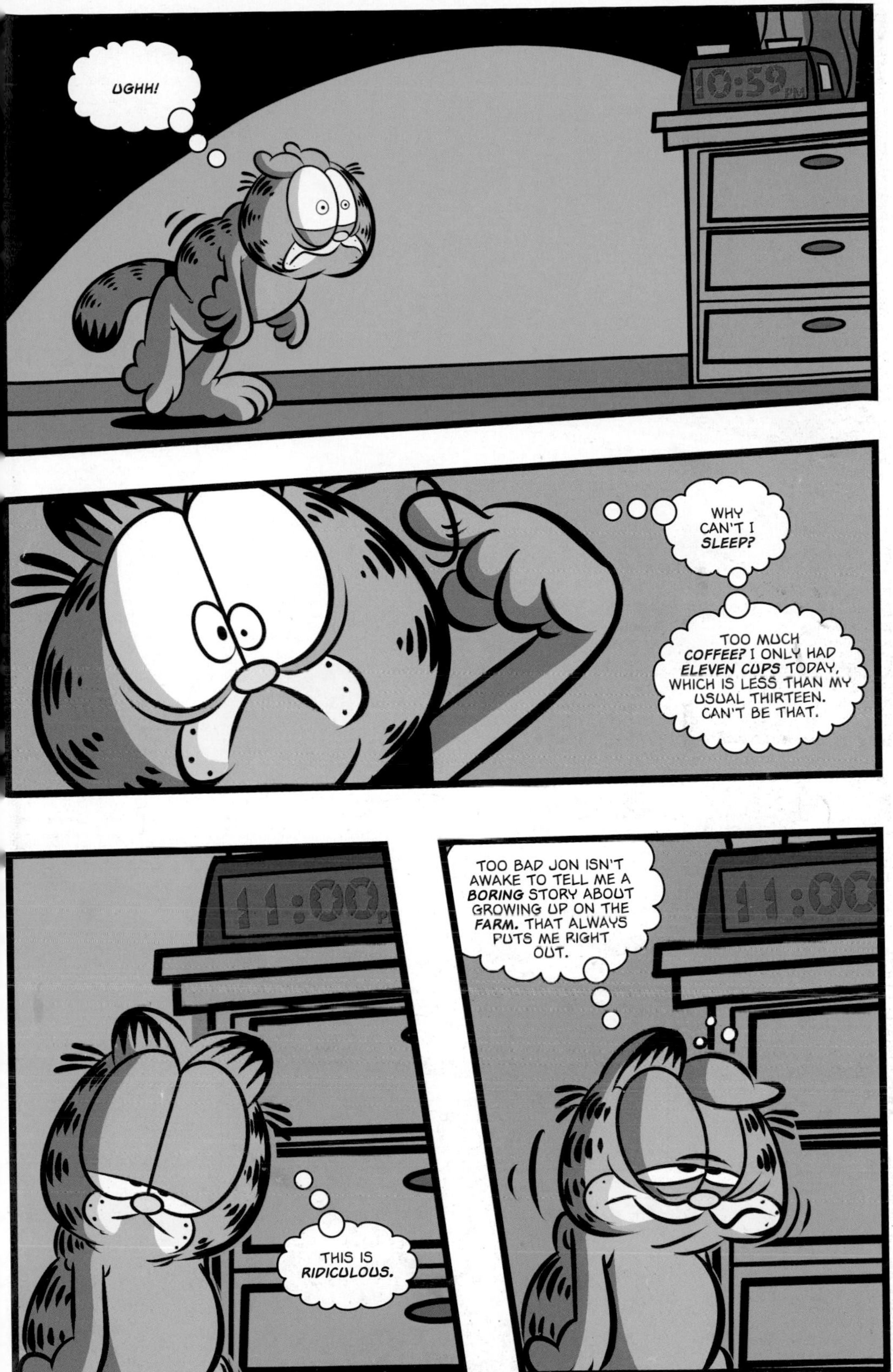
UGHH!
10:59 PM
WHY CAN'T I SLEEP?
TOO MUCH COFFEE? I ONLY HAD ELEVEN CUPS TODAY, WHICH IS LESS THAN MY USUAL THIRTEEN. CAN'T BE THAT.
THIS IS RIDICULOUS.
TOO BAD JON ISN'T AWAKE TO TELL ME A BORING STORY ABOUT GROWING UP ON THE FARM. THAT ALWAYS PUTS ME RIGHT OUT.

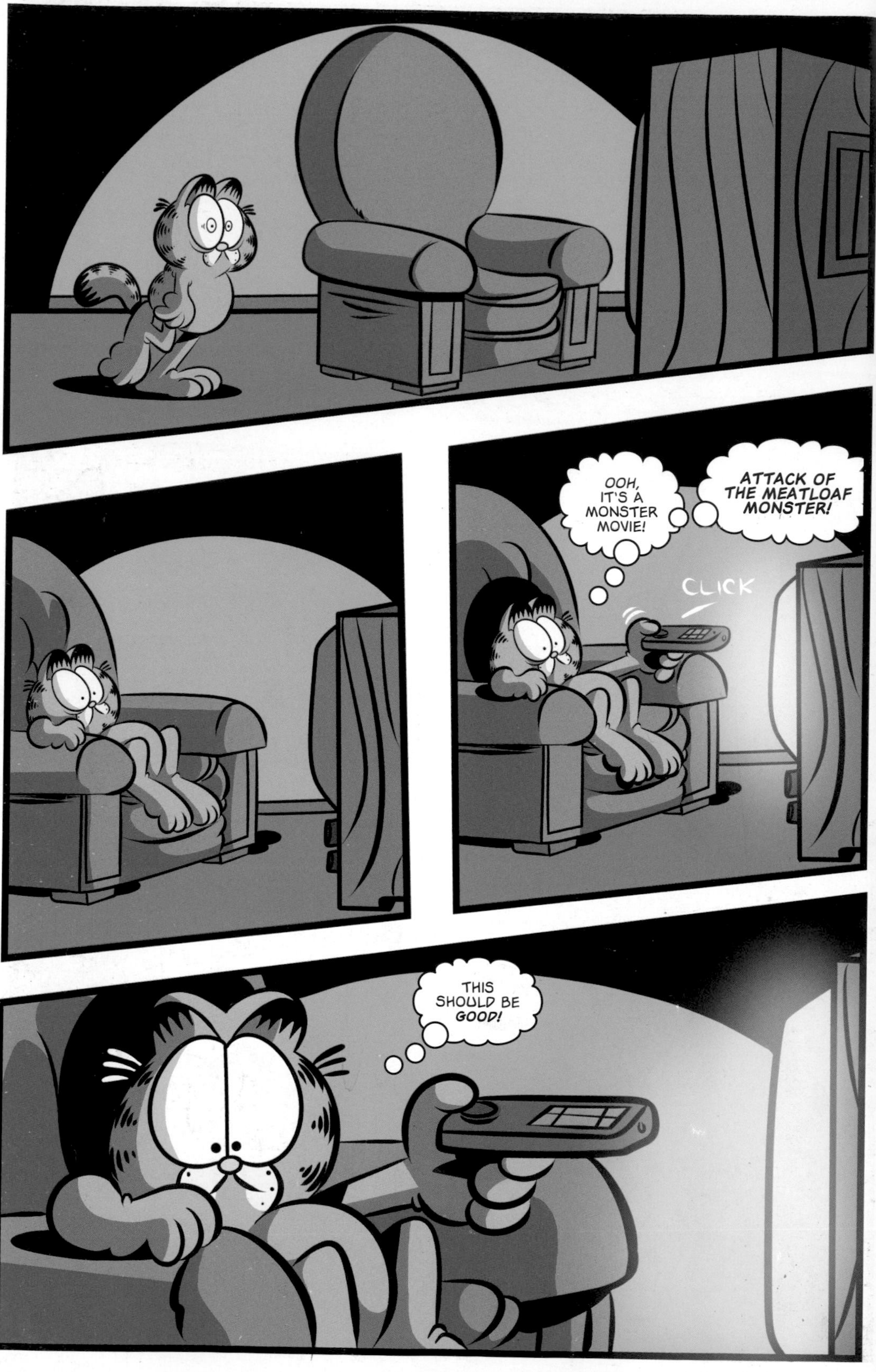

OOH, IT'S A MONSTER MOVIE!
ATTACK OF THE MEATLOAF MONSTER!
CLICK
THIS SHOULD BE GOOD!

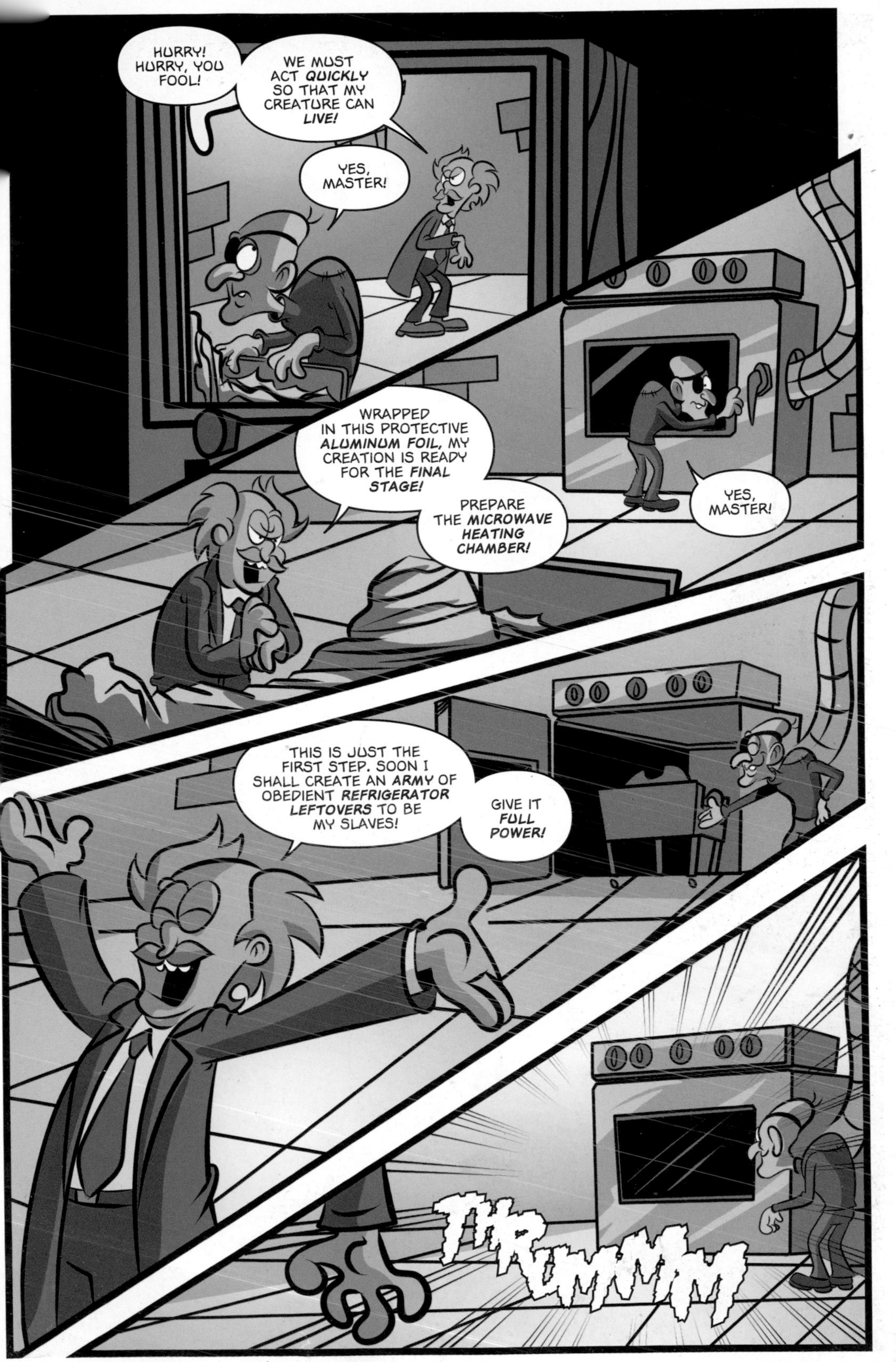
HURRY! HURRY, YOU FOOL!
WE MUST ACT QUICKLY SO THAT MY CREATURE CAN LIVE!
YES, MASTER!
WRAPPED IN THIS PROTECTIVE ALUMINUM FOIL, MY CREATION IS READY FOR THE FINAL STAGE!
PREPARE THE MICROWAVE HEATING CHAMBER!
YES, MASTER!
THIS IS JUST THE FIRST STEP. SOON I SHALL CREATE AN ARMY OF OBEDIENT REFRIGERATOR LEFTOVERS TO BE MY SLAVES!
GIVE IT FULL POWER!
THRUMMM

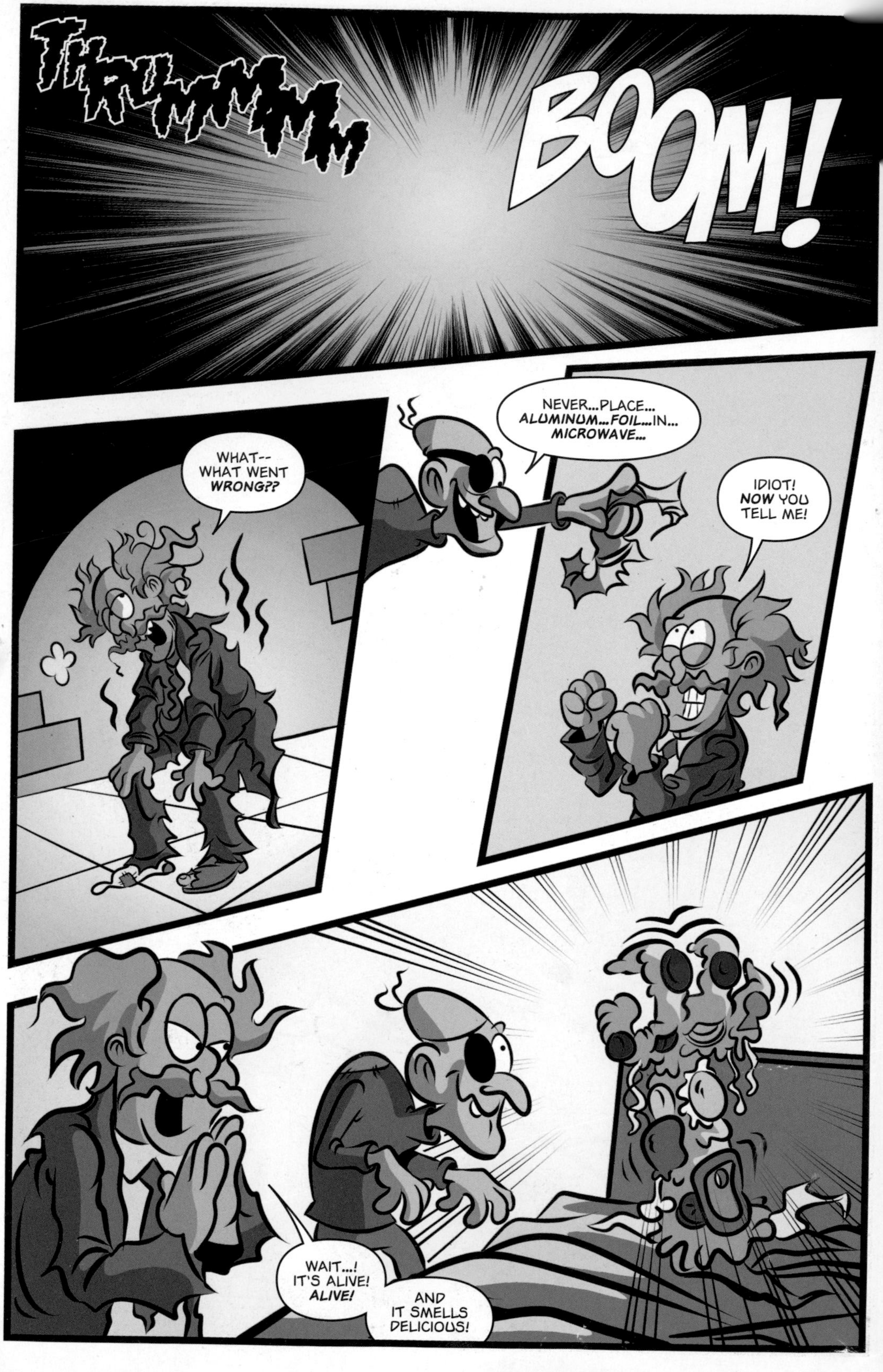
THRUMMMM
BOOM!
WHAT-- WHAT WENT WRONG??
NEVER...PLACE... ALUMINUM...FOIL...IN... MICROWAVE...
IDIOT! NOW YOU TELL ME!
WAIT...! IT'S ALIVE! ALIVE!
AND IT SMELLS DELICIOUS!

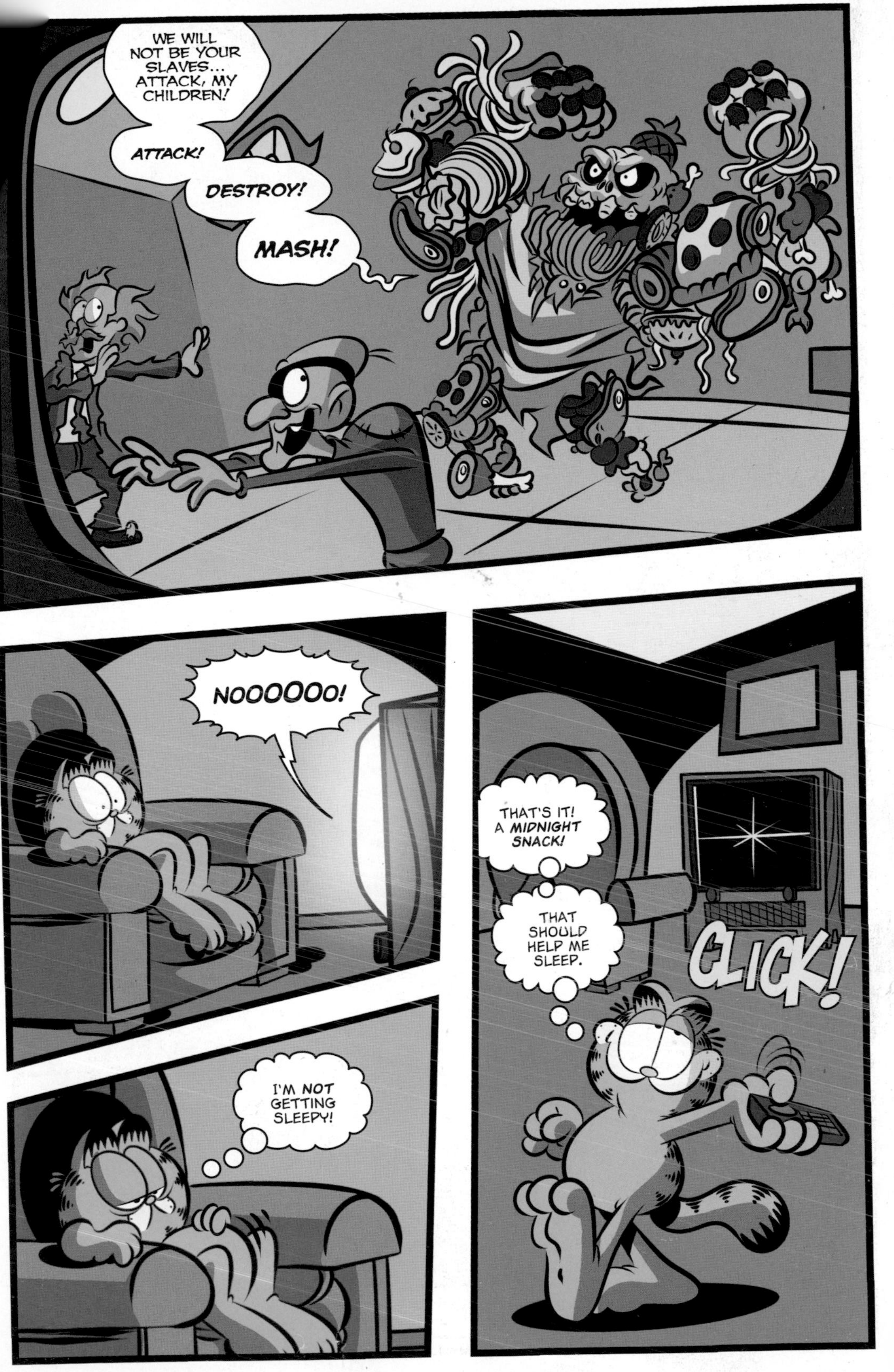
WE WILL NOT BE YOUR SLAVES... ATTACK, MY CHILDREN!
ATTACK!
DESTROY!
MASH!
NOOOOOO!
I'M NOT GETTING SLEEPY!
THAT'S IT! A MIDNIGHT SNACK!
THAT SHOULD HELP ME SLEEP.
CLICK!

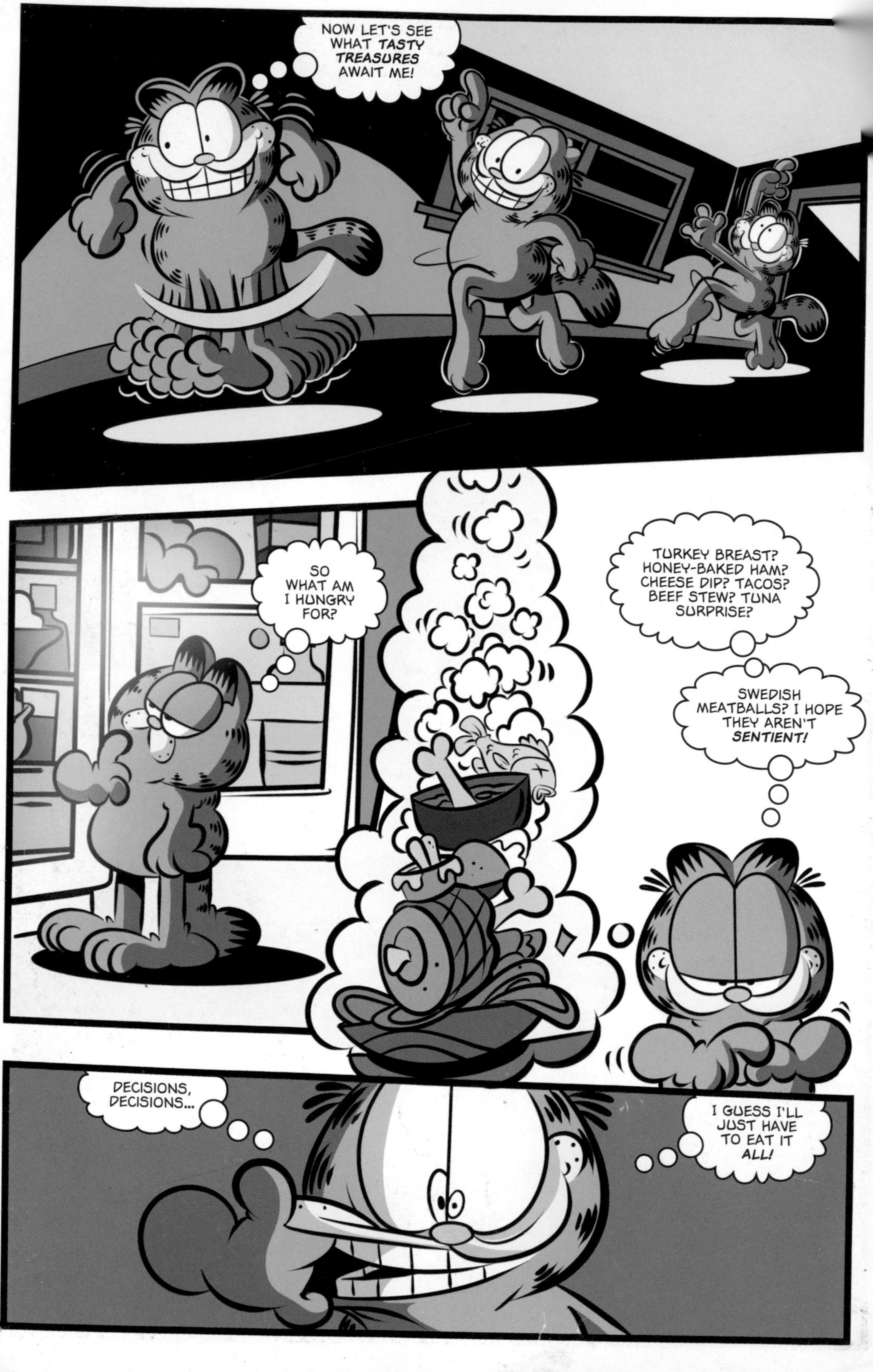
NOW LET'S SEE WHAT TASTY TREASURES AWAIT ME!
SO WHAT AM I HUNGRY FOR?
TURKEY BREAST? HONEY-BAKED HAM? CHEESE DIP? TACOS? BEEF STEW? TUNA SURPRISE?
SWEDISH MEATBALLS? I HOPE THEY AREN'T SENTIENT!
DECISIONS, DECISIONS...
I GUESS I'LL JUST HAVE TO EAT IT ALL!

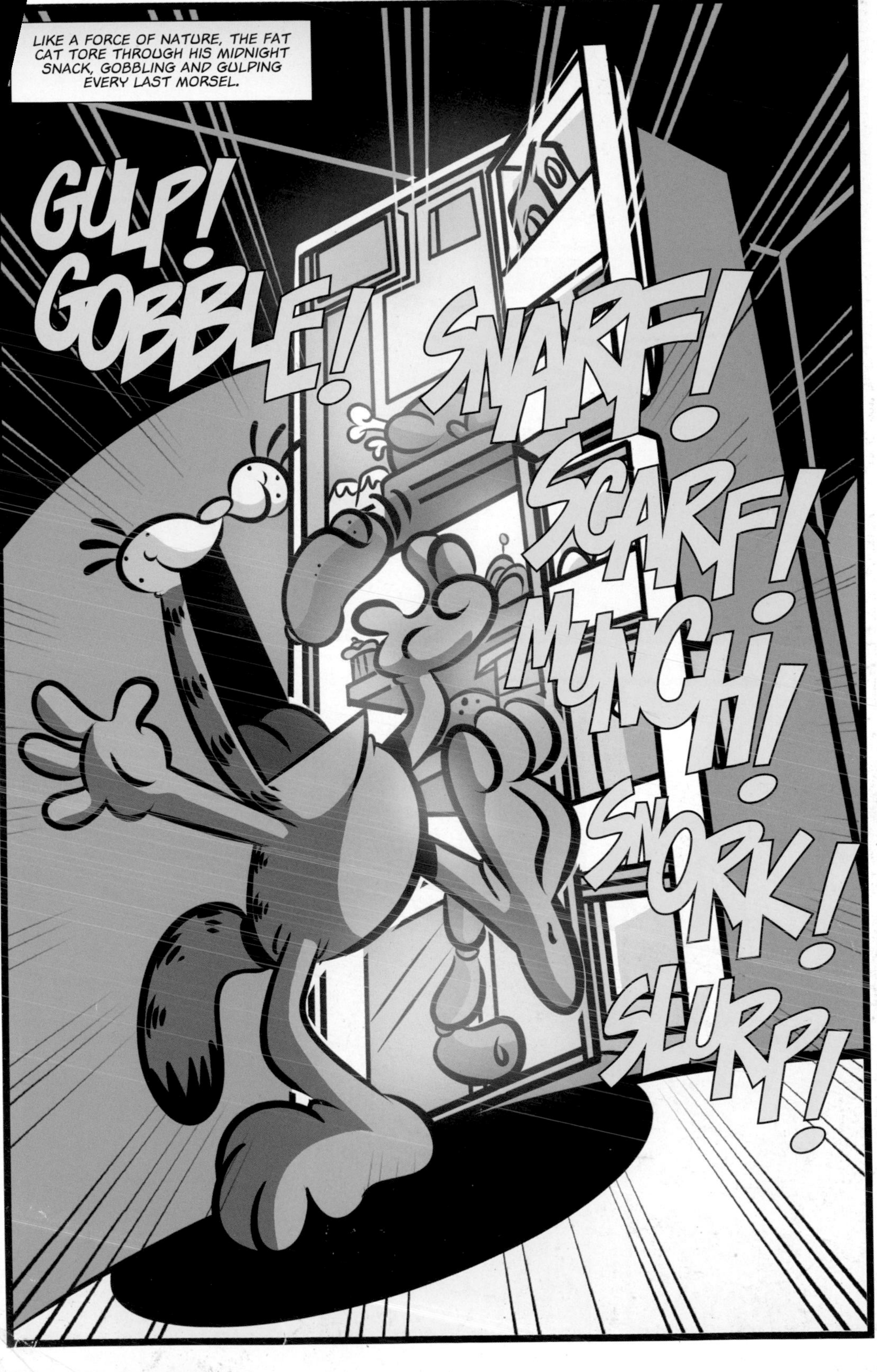
LIKE A FORCE OF NATURE, THE FAT CAT TORE THROUGH HIS MIDNIGHT SNACK, GOBBLING AND GULPING EVERY LAST MORSEL.
GULP!
GOBBLE!
SNARF!
SCARF!
MUNCH!
SNORK!
SLURP!

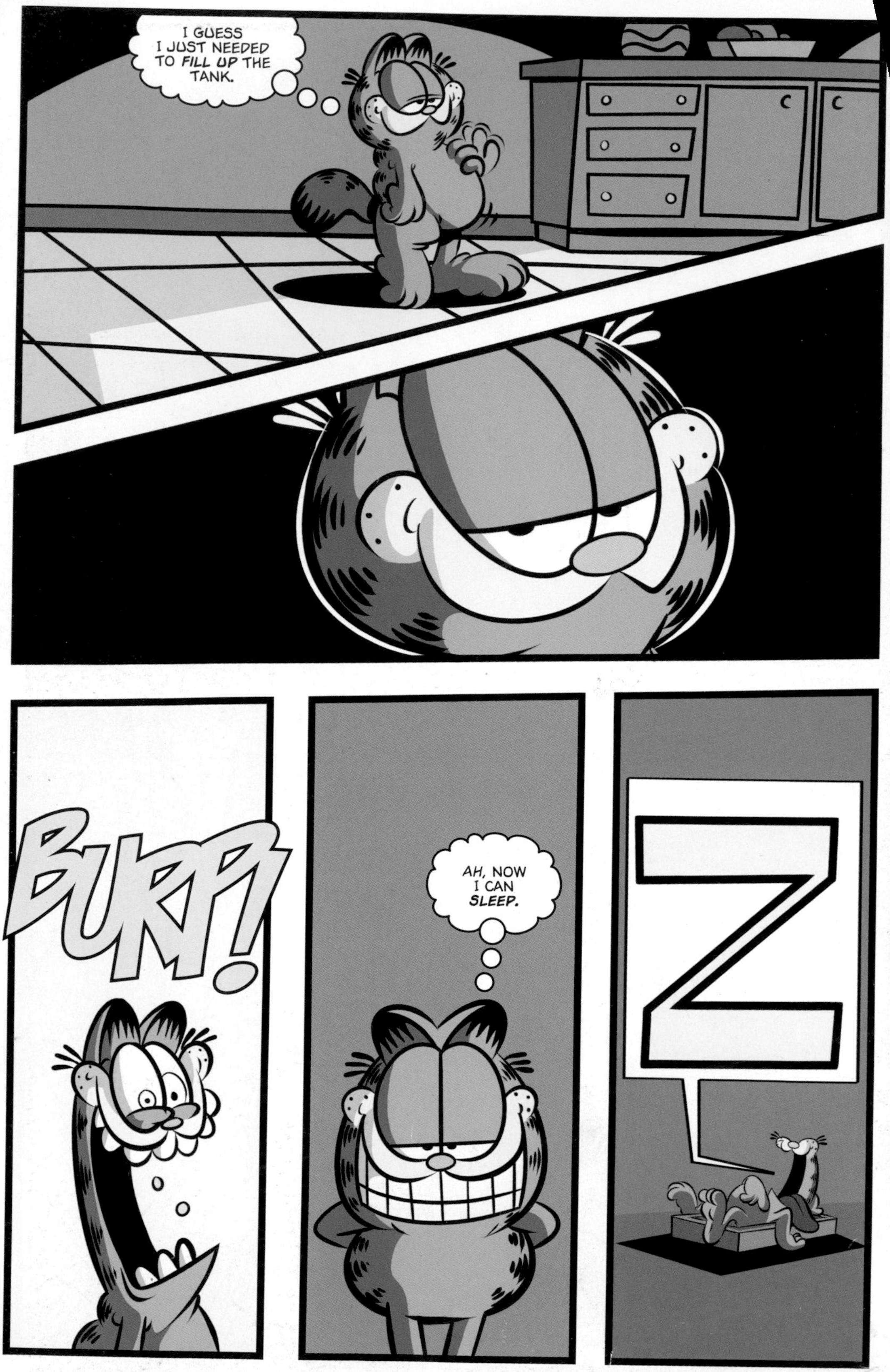
I GUESS I JUST NEEDED TO FILL UP THE TANK.
BURP!
AH, NOW I CAN SLEEP.
Z

EMPTY?!!?

THAT CAT...

I GUESS I'LL HAVE TO GO TO THE STORE *AGAIN*. THAT'S THE *THIRD* TIME THIS WEEK!

GARFIELD DIDN'T HEAR HIS OWNER'S FRUSTRATION. HE WAS HAPPILY ASLEEP. AS USUAL.

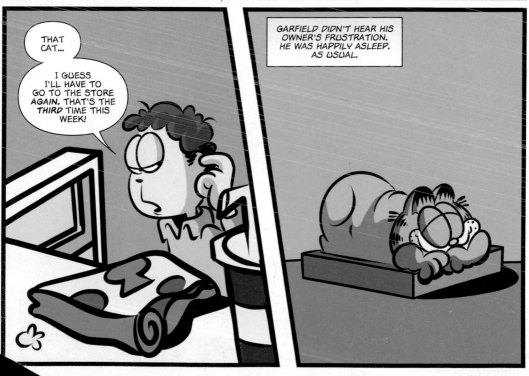

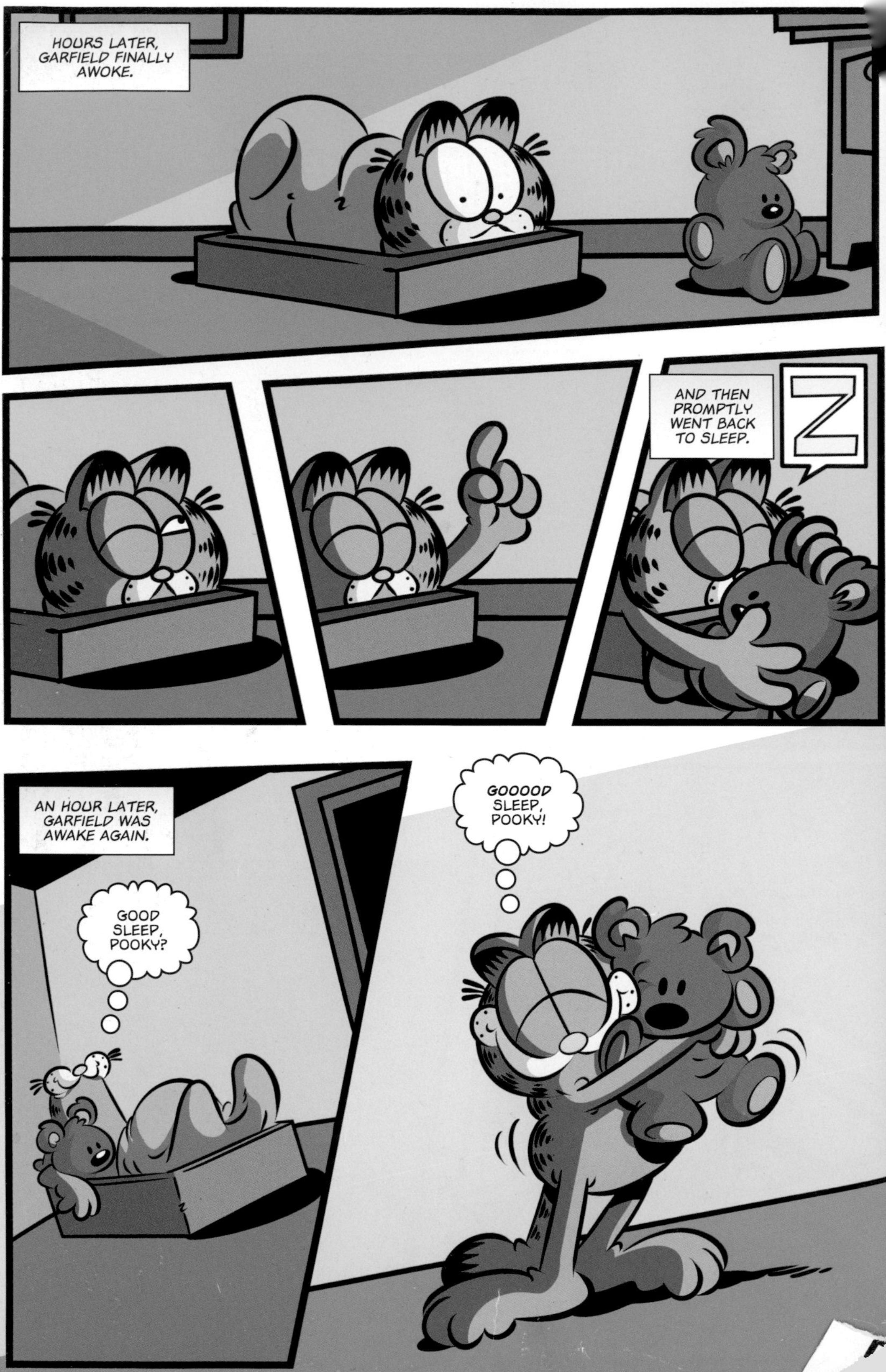

HOURS LATER, GARFIELD FINALLY AWOKE.
AND THEN PROMPTLY WENT BACK TO SLEEP.
Z
AN HOUR LATER, GARFIELD WAS AWAKE AGAIN.
GOOD SLEEP, POOKY?
GOOOOD SLEEP, POOKY!

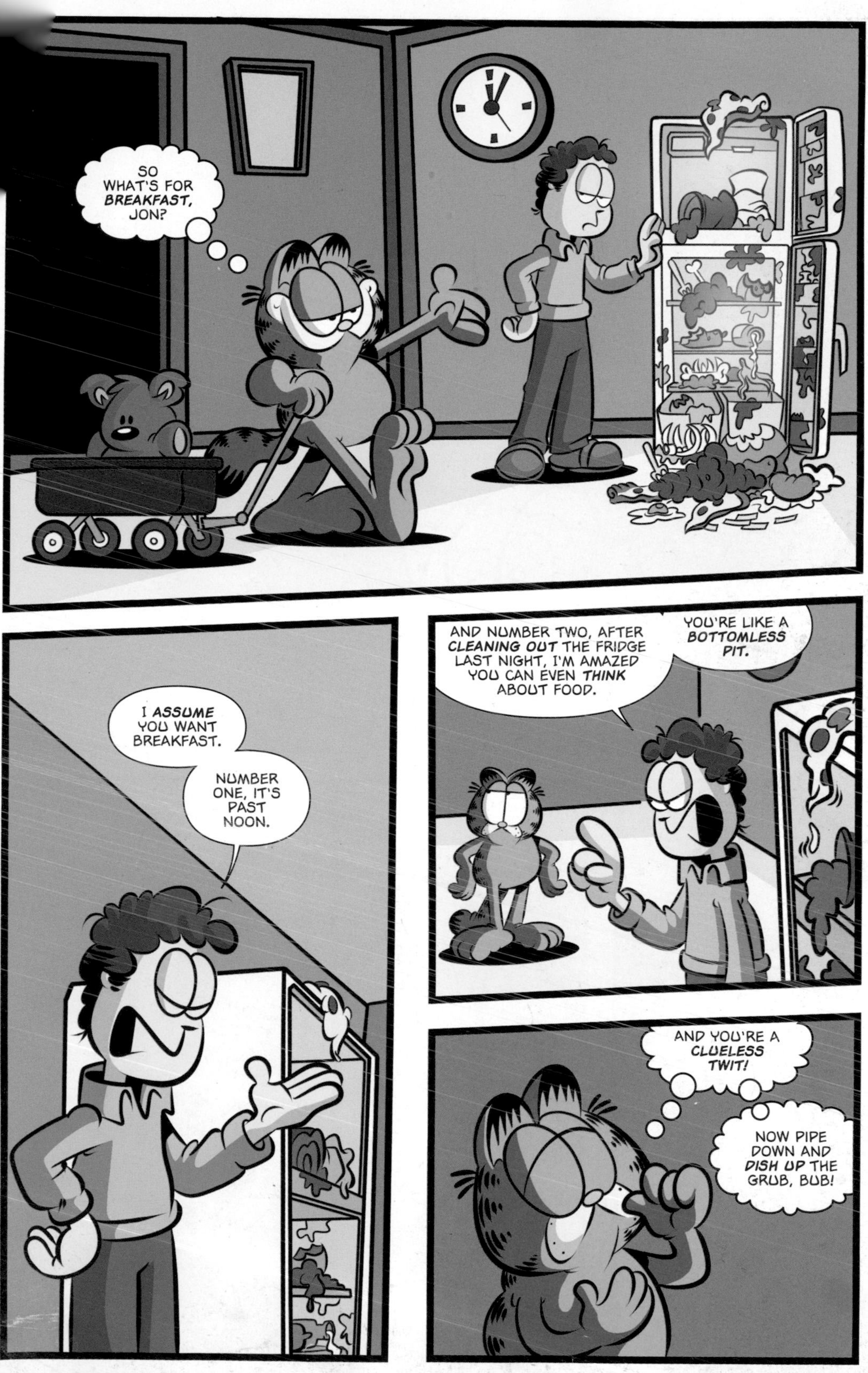
SO WHAT'S FOR **BREAKFAST,** JON?
I **ASSUME** YOU WANT BREAKFAST.
NUMBER ONE, IT'S PAST NOON.
AND NUMBER TWO, AFTER **CLEANING OUT** THE FRIDGE LAST NIGHT, I'M AMAZED YOU CAN EVEN **THINK** ABOUT FOOD.
YOU'RE LIKE A **BOTTOMLESS PIT.**
AND YOU'RE A **CLUELESS TWIT!**
NOW PIPE DOWN AND **DISH UP** THE GRUB, BUB!

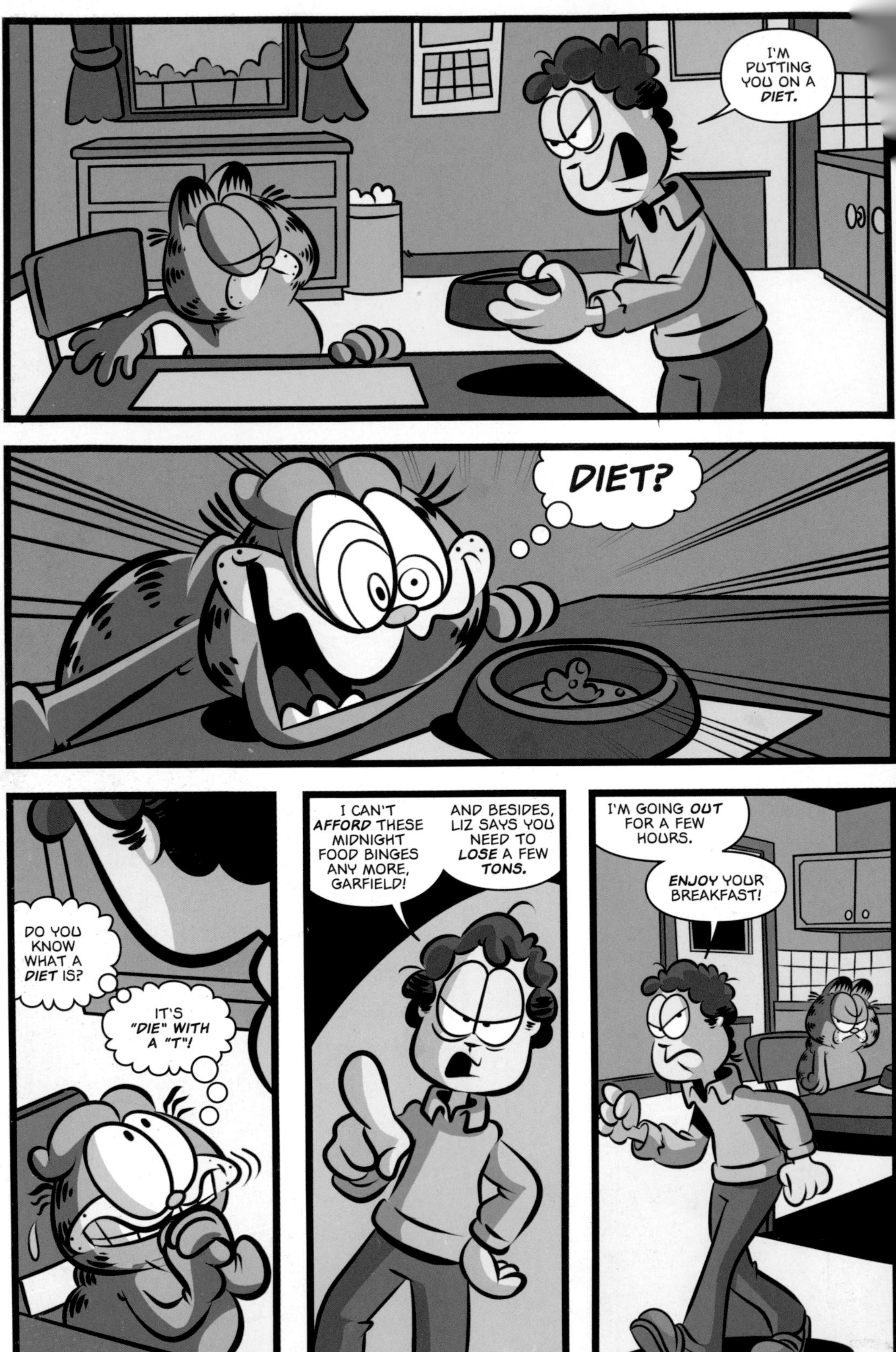
I'M PUTTING YOU ON A DIET.
DIET?
DO YOU KNOW WHAT A DIET IS?
IT'S "DIE" WITH A "T"!
I CAN'T AFFORD THESE MIDNIGHT FOOD BINGES ANY MORE, GARFIELD!
AND BESIDES, LIZ SAYS YOU NEED TO LOSE A FEW TONS.
I'M GOING OUT FOR A FEW HOURS.
ENJOY YOUR BREAKFAST!

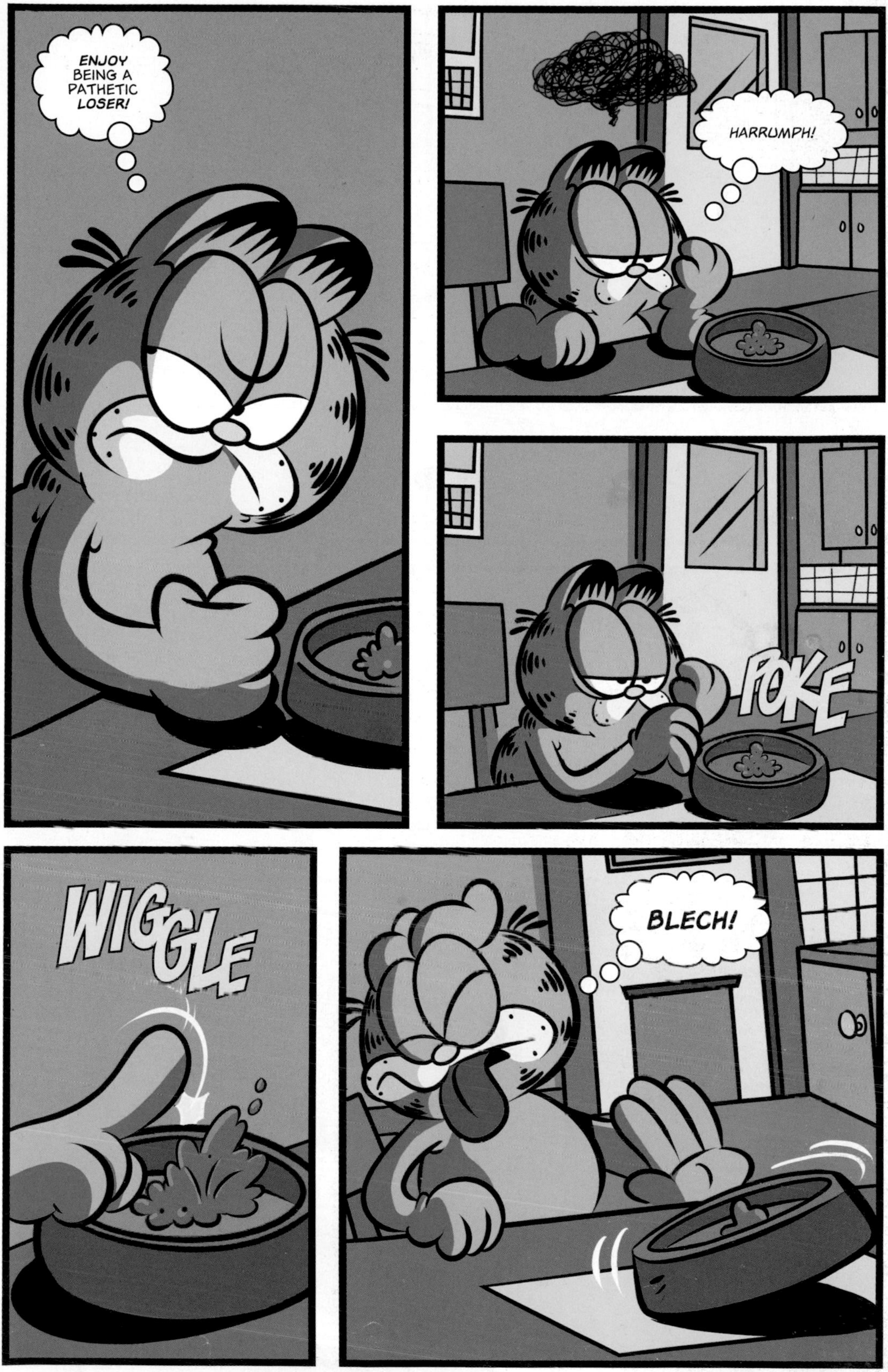
ENJOY BEING A PATHETIC LOSER!
HARRUMPH!
POKE
WIGGLE
BLECH!

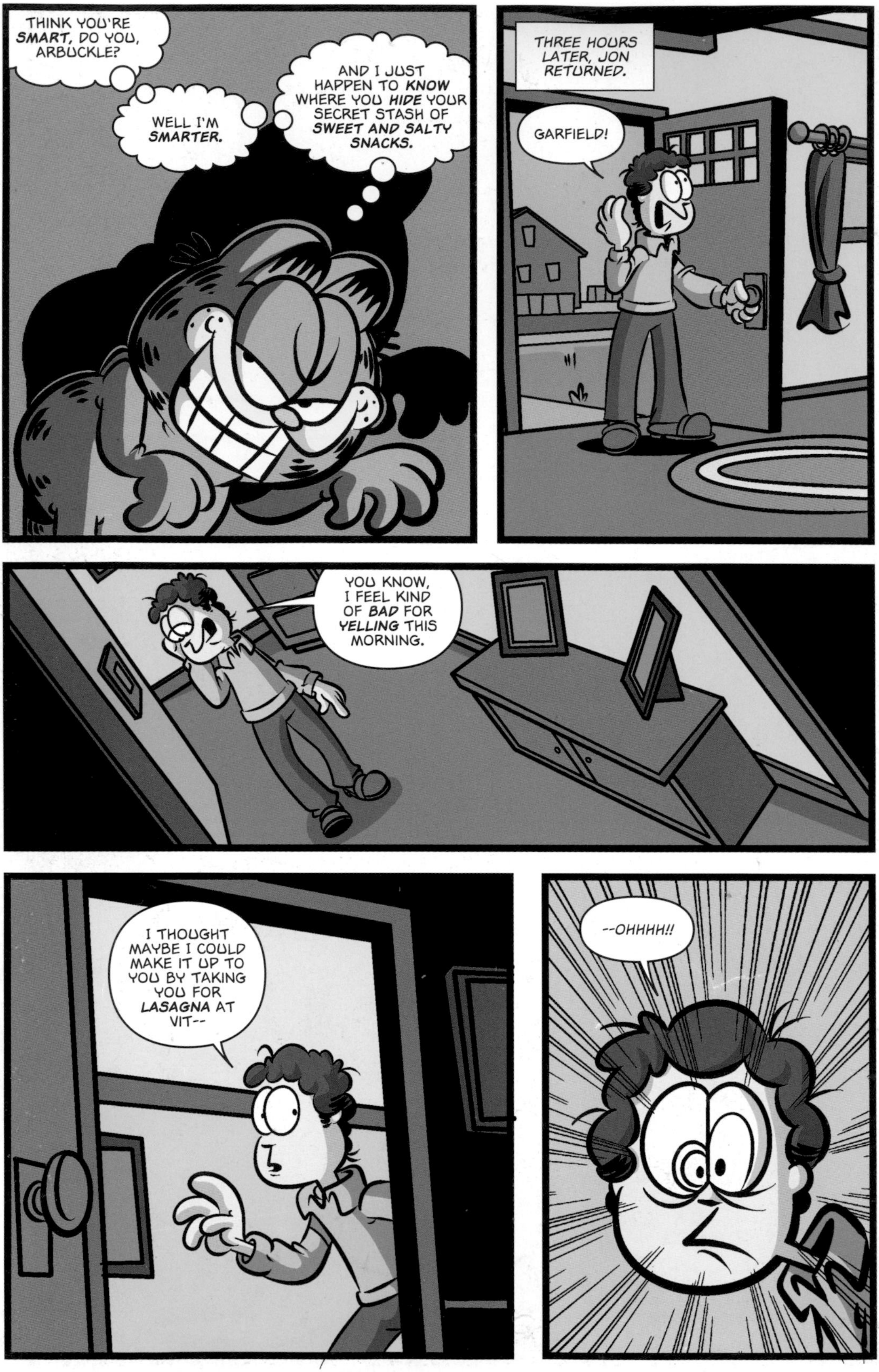
THINK YOU'RE SMART, DO YOU, ARBUCKLE?
WELL I'M SMARTER.
AND I JUST HAPPEN TO KNOW WHERE YOU HIDE YOUR SECRET STASH OF SWEET AND SALTY SNACKS.
THREE HOURS LATER, JON RETURNED.
GARFIELD!
YOU KNOW, I FEEL KIND OF BAD FOR YELLING THIS MORNING.
I THOUGHT MAYBE I COULD MAKE IT UP TO YOU BY TAKING YOU FOR LASAGNA AT VIT--
--OHHHH!!

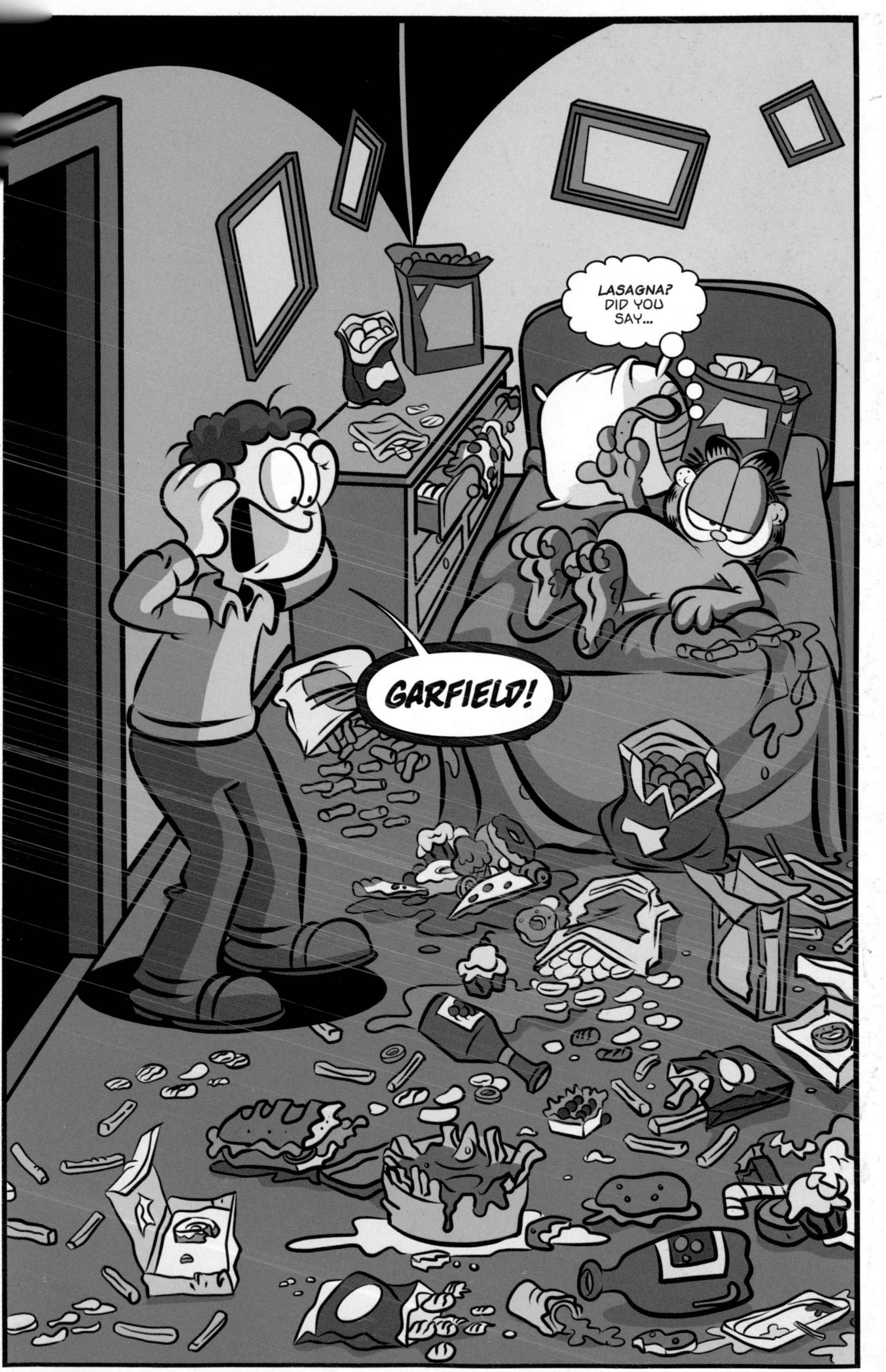
GARFIELD!
LASAGNA? DID YOU SAY...

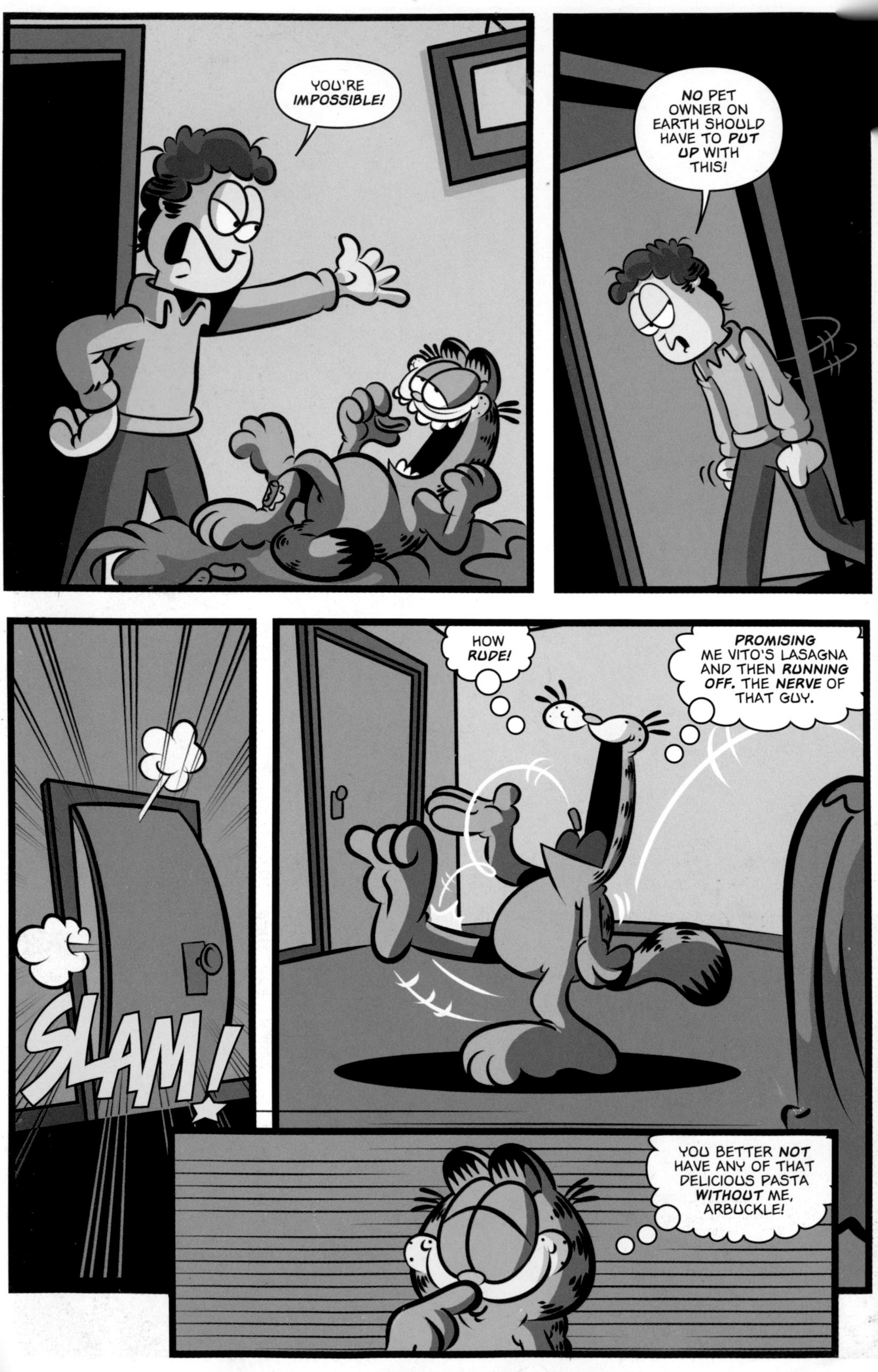
YOU'RE IMPOSSIBLE!
NO PET OWNER ON EARTH SHOULD HAVE TO PUT UP WITH THIS!
SLAM!
HOW RUDE!
PROMISING ME VITO'S LASAGNA AND THEN RUNNING OFF. THE NERVE OF THAT GUY.
YOU BETTER NOT HAVE ANY OF THAT DELICIOUS PASTA WITHOUT ME, ARBUCKLE!

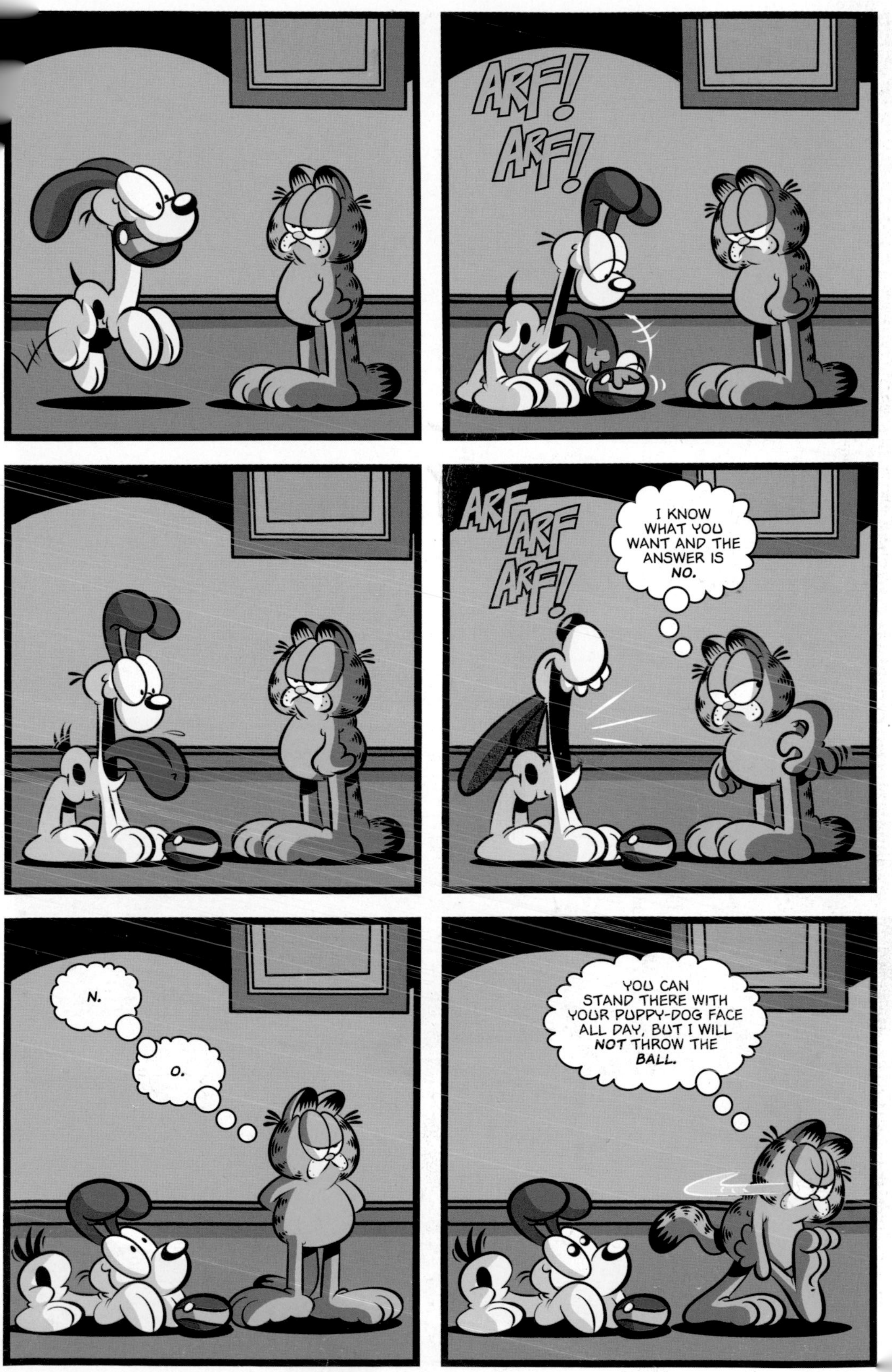
ARF!
ARF!
ARF
ARF
ARF!
I KNOW WHAT YOU WANT AND THE ANSWER IS NO.
N.
O.
YOU CAN STAND THERE WITH YOUR PUPPY-DOG FACE ALL DAY, BUT I WILL NOT THROW THE BALL.

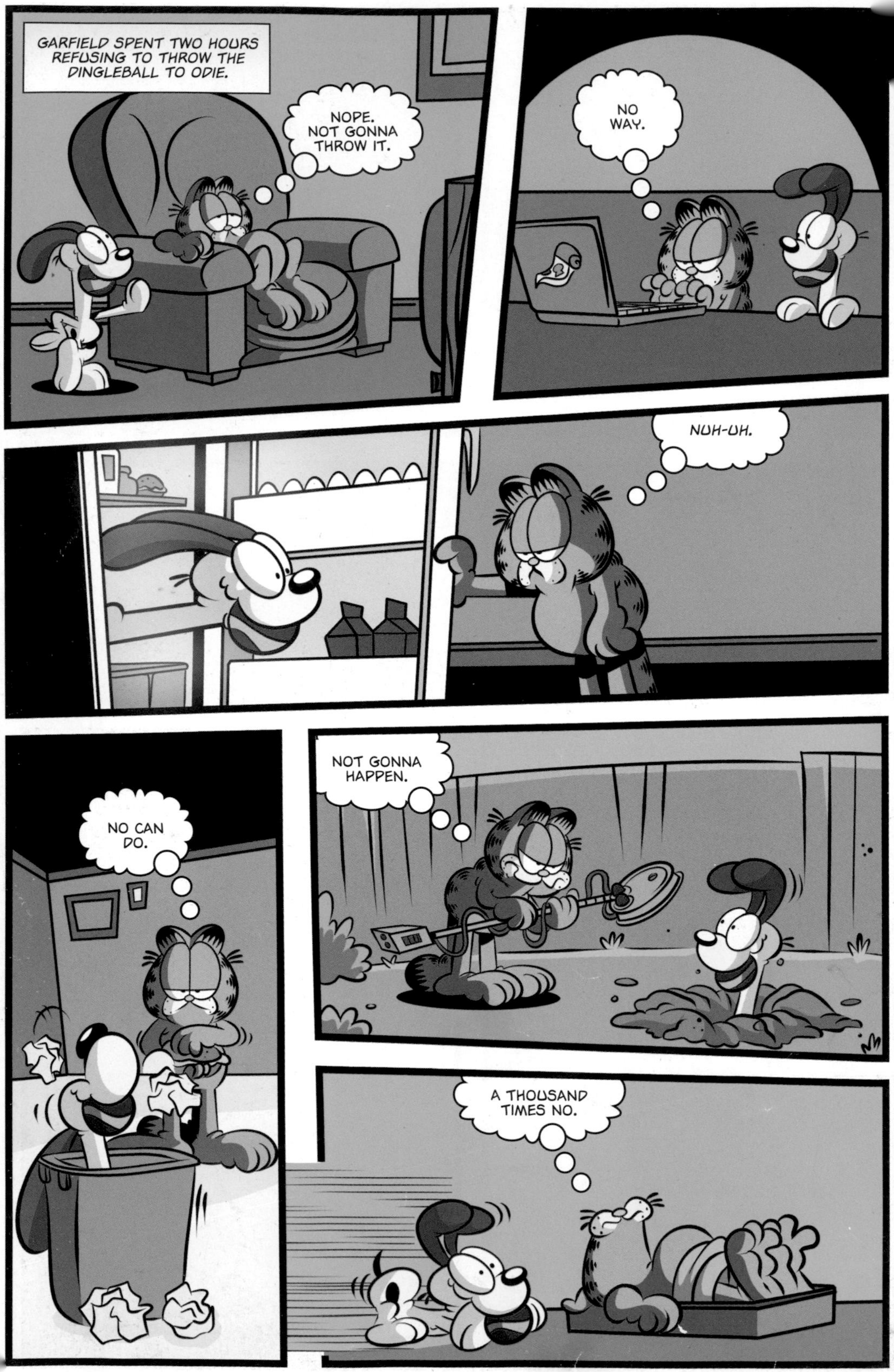
GARFIELD SPENT TWO HOURS REFUSING TO THROW THE DINGLEBALL TO ODIE.
NOPE. NOT GONNA THROW IT.
NO WAY.
NUH-UH.
NO CAN DO.
NOT GONNA HAPPEN.
A THOUSAND TIMES NO.

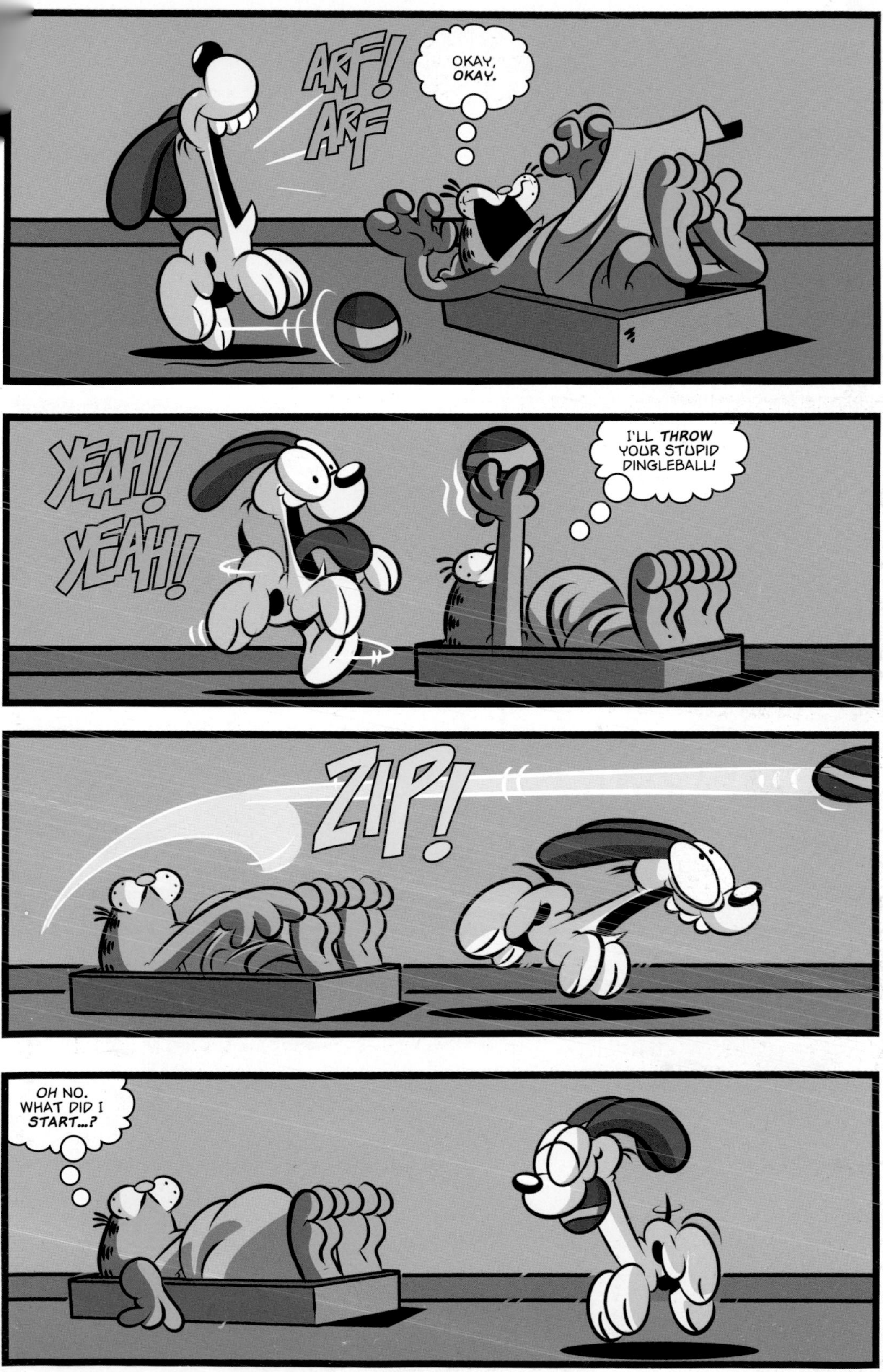
ARF! ARF
OKAY, OKAY.
YEAH! YEAH!
I'LL THROW YOUR STUPID DINGLEBALL!
ZIP!
OH NO. WHAT DID I START...?

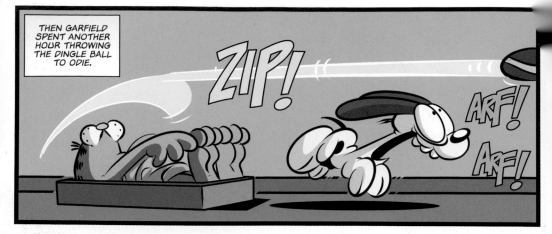

THEN GARFIELD SPENT ANOTHER HOUR THROWING THE DINGLE BALL TO ODIE.

ZIP!

ARF!

ARF!

THE ONLY THING THAT SAVED THE CAT WAS A SUDDEN NAP ATTACK.

ZZZZ

?!/?

A LITTLE WHILE LATER...

CLICK!

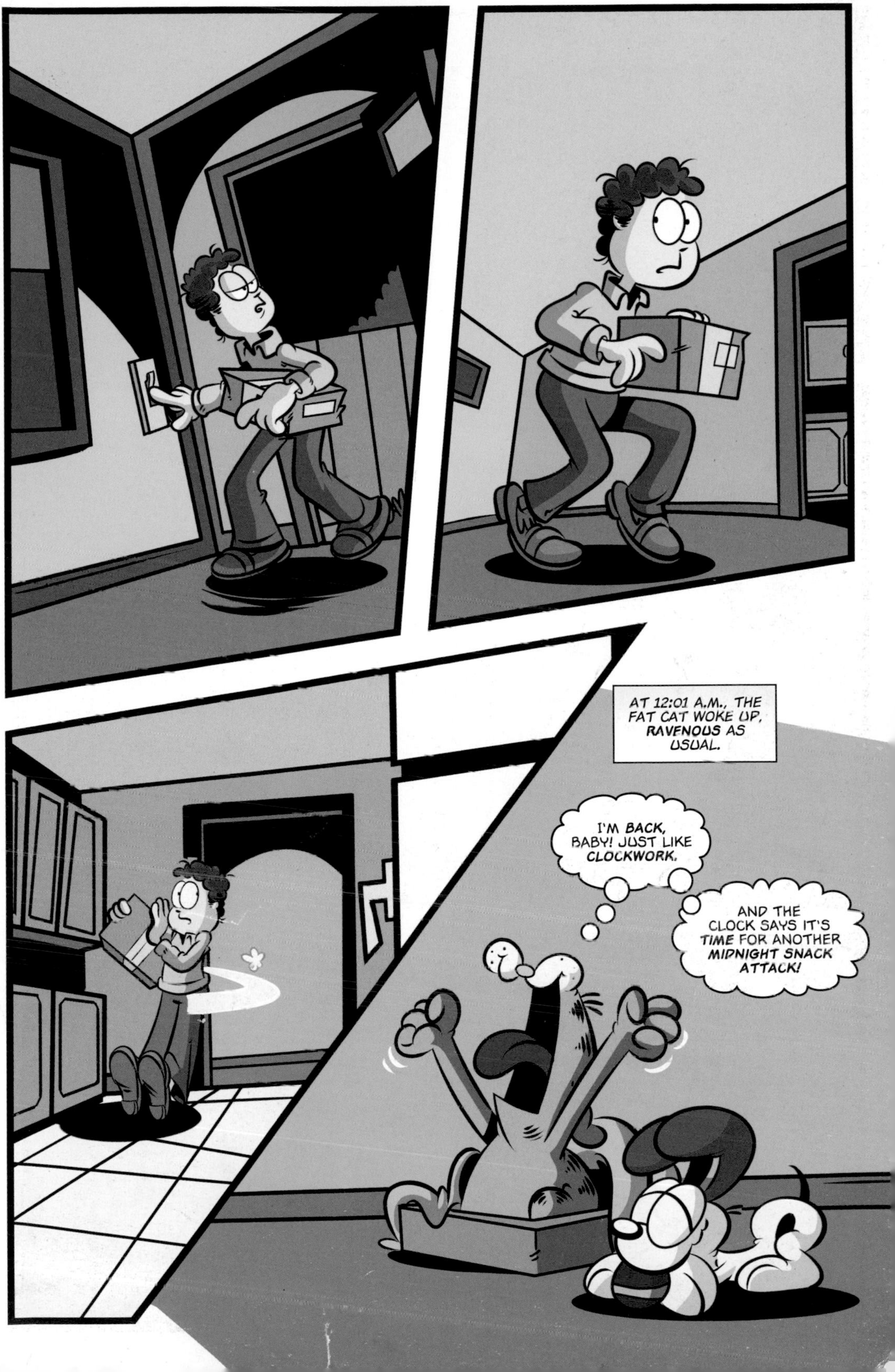
AT 12:01 A.M., THE FAT CAT WOKE UP, RAVENOUS AS USUAL.
I'M BACK, BABY! JUST LIKE CLOCKWORK.
AND THE CLOCK SAYS IT'S TIME FOR ANOTHER MIDNIGHT SNACK ATTACK!

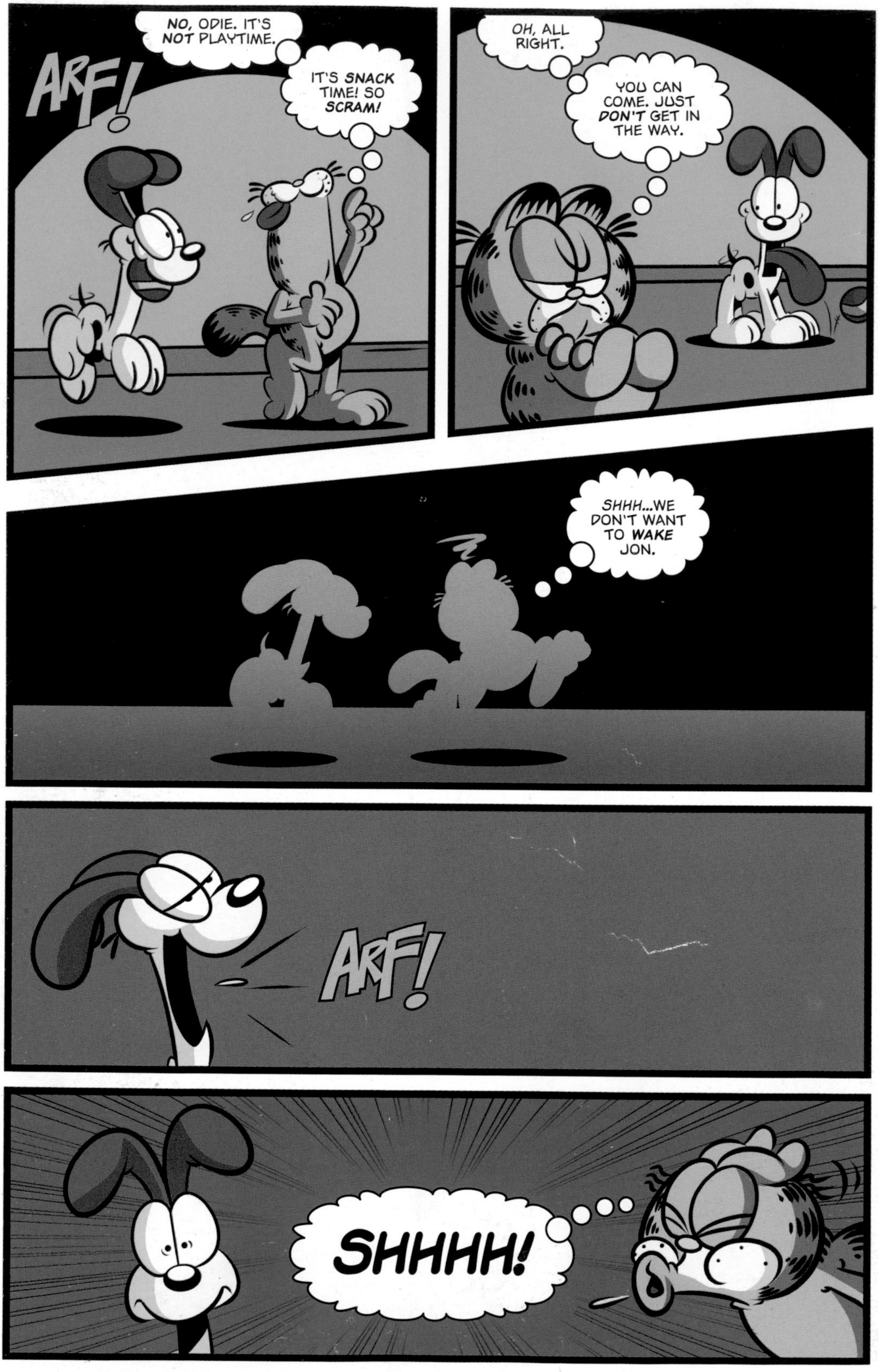
ARF!
NO, ODIE. IT'S NOT PLAYTIME.
IT'S SNACK TIME! SO SCRAM!
OH, ALL RIGHT.
YOU CAN COME. JUST DON'T GET IN THE WAY.
SHHH...WE DON'T WANT TO WAKE JON.
ARF!
SHHHH!

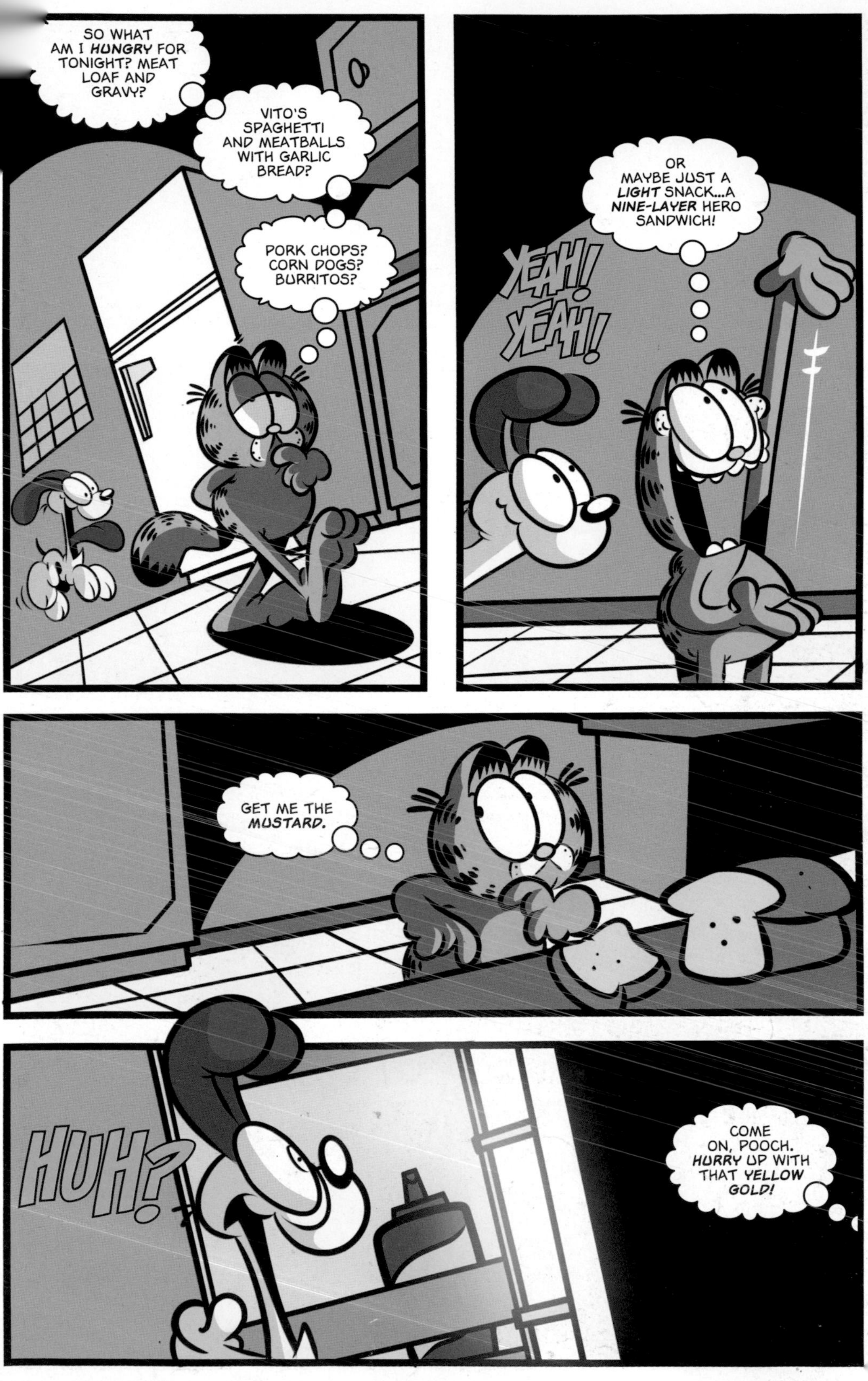
SO WHAT AM I HUNGRY FOR TONIGHT? MEAT LOAF AND GRAVY?
VITO'S SPAGHETTI AND MEATBALLS WITH GARLIC BREAD?
PORK CHOPS? CORN DOGS? BURRITOS?
OR MAYBE JUST A LIGHT SNACK...A NINE-LAYER HERO SANDWICH!
YEAH! YEAH!
GET ME THE MUSTARD.
HUH?
COME ON, POOCH. HURRY UP WITH THAT YELLOW GOLD!

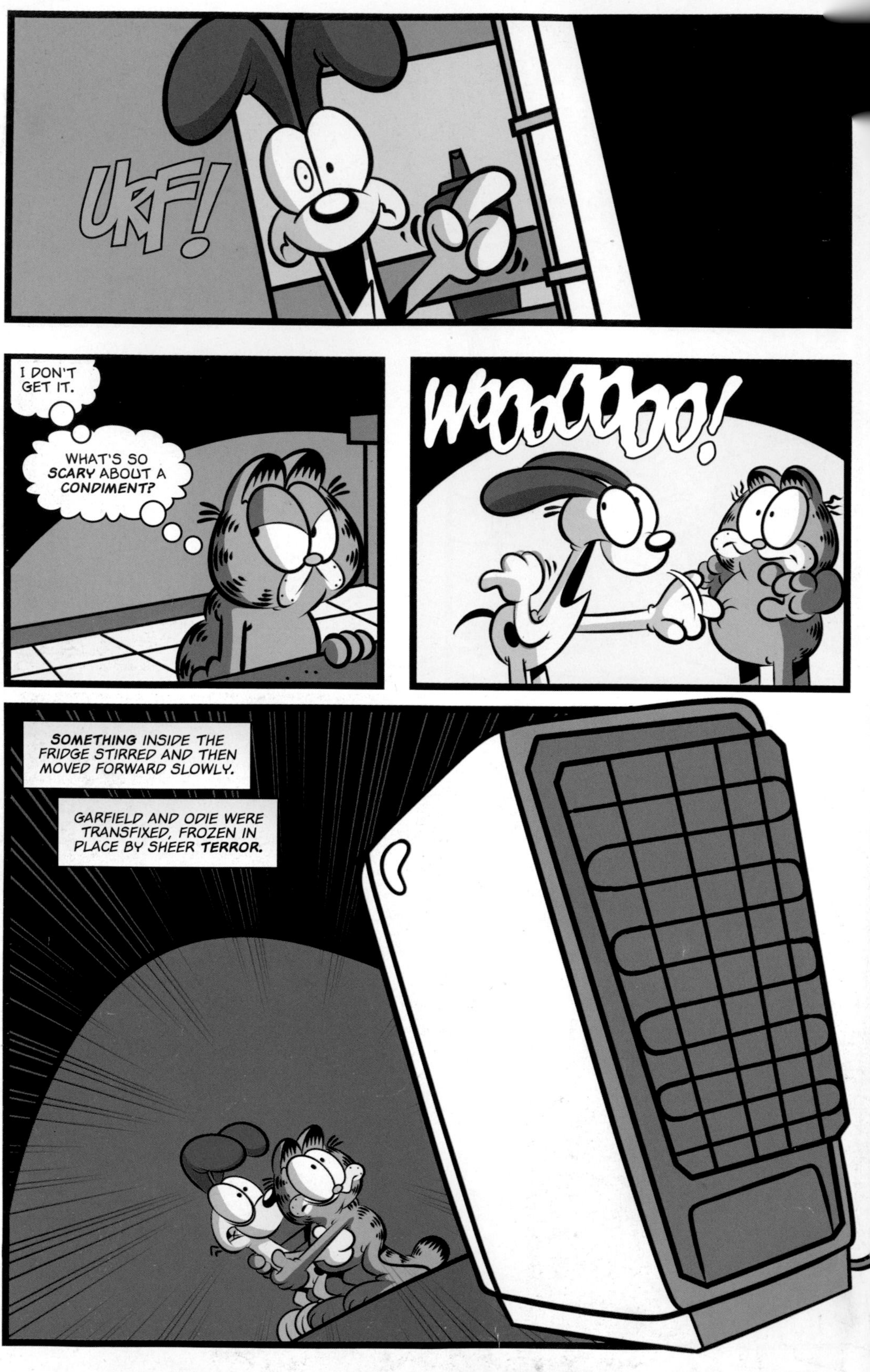
URF!
I DON'T GET IT.
WHAT'S SO SCARY ABOUT A CONDIMENT?
WOOOOOOO!
SOMETHING INSIDE THE FRIDGE STIRRED AND THEN MOVED FORWARD SLOWLY.
GARFIELD AND ODIE WERE TRANSFIXED, FROZEN IN PLACE BY SHEER TERROR.

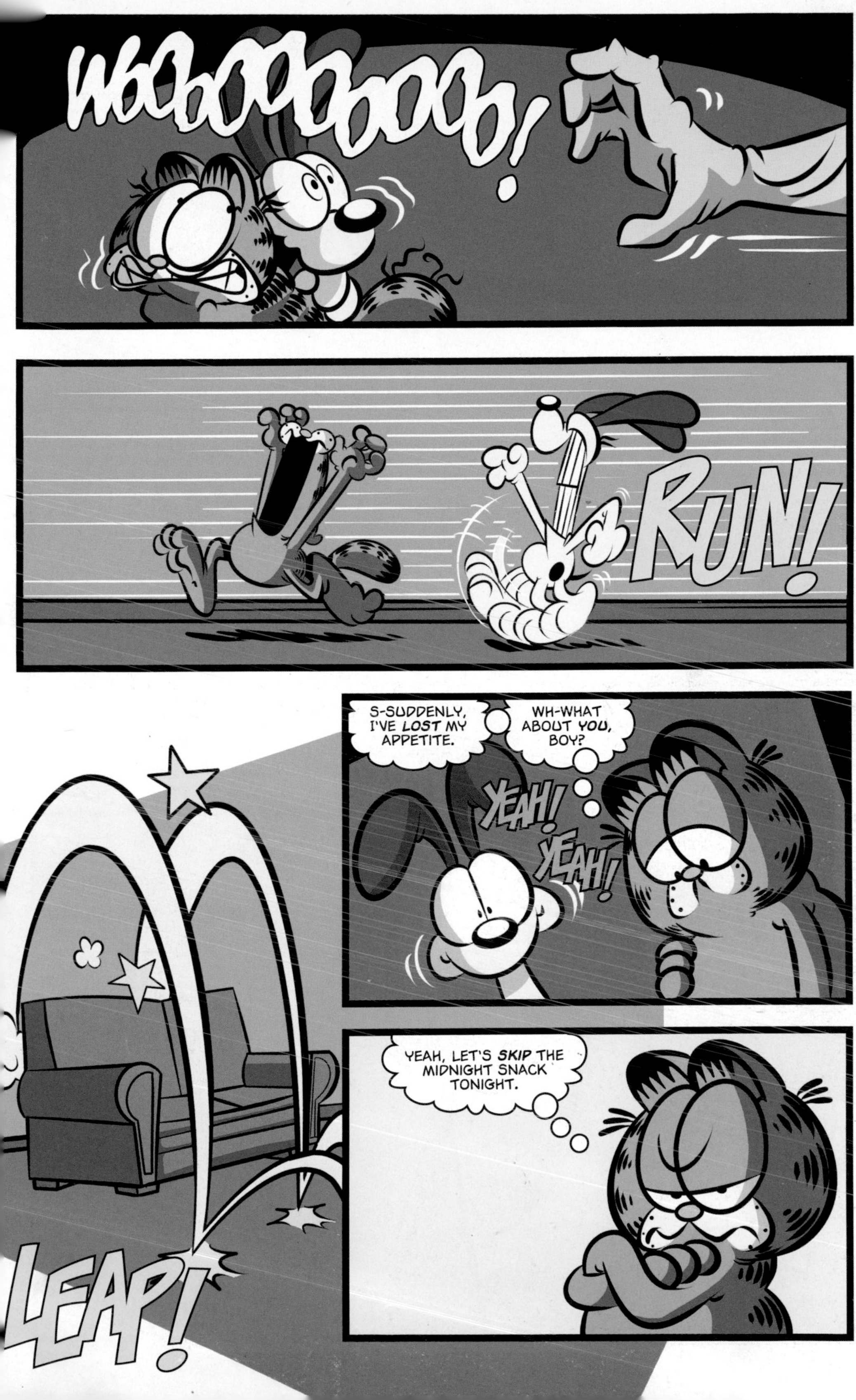
WOOOOOOOOOO!
RUN!
S-SUDDENLY, I'VE LOST MY APPETITE.
WH-WHAT ABOUT YOU, BOY?
YEAH! YEAH!
LEAP!
YEAH, LET'S SKIP THE MIDNIGHT SNACK TONIGHT.

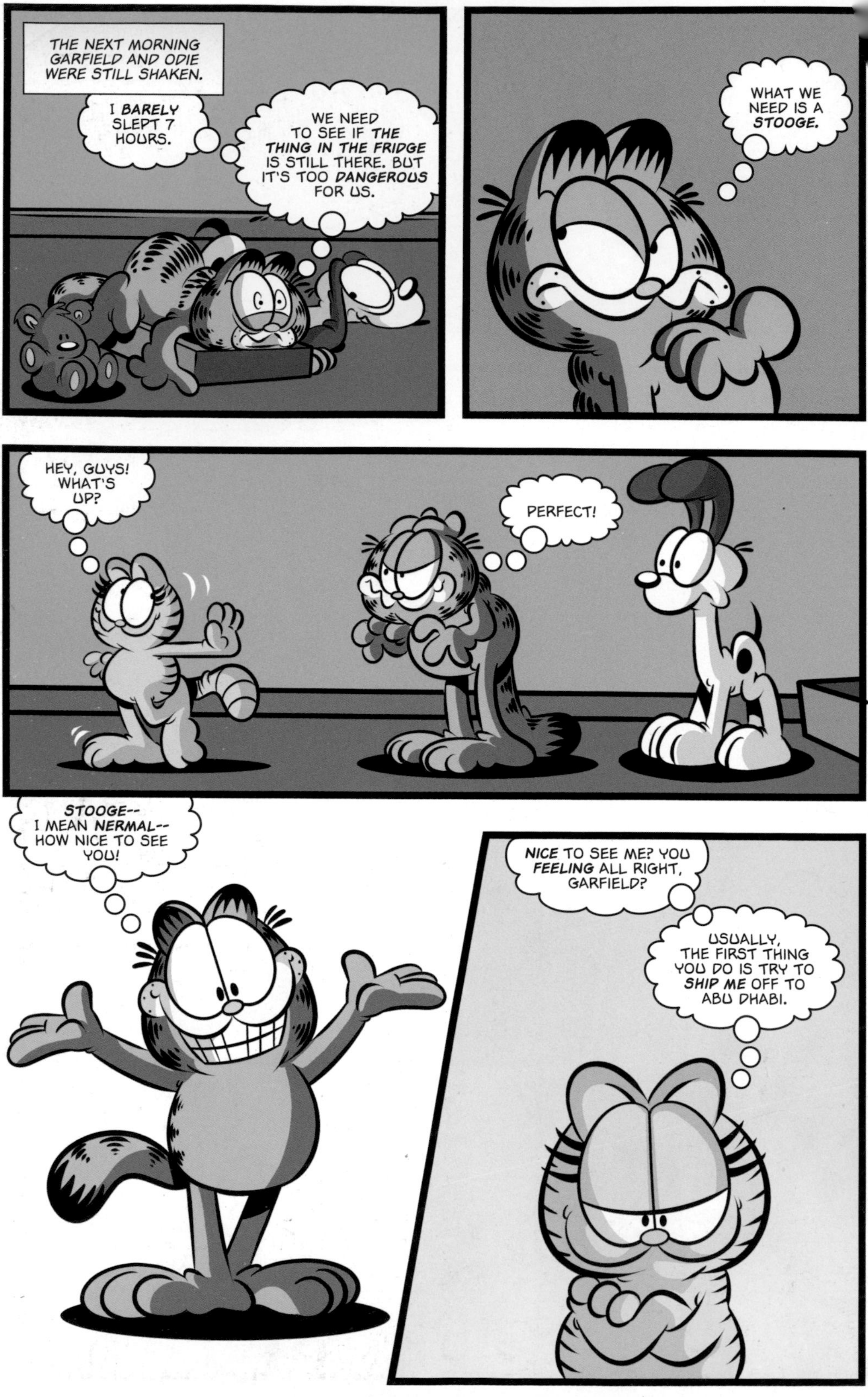
THE NEXT MORNING GARFIELD AND ODIE WERE STILL SHAKEN.
I BARELY SLEPT 7 HOURS.
WE NEED TO SEE IF THE THING IN THE FRIDGE IS STILL THERE. BUT IT'S TOO DANGEROUS FOR US.
WHAT WE NEED IS A STOOGE.
HEY, GUYS! WHAT'S UP?
PERFECT!
STOOGE-- I MEAN NERMAL-- HOW NICE TO SEE YOU!
NICE TO SEE ME? YOU FEELING ALL RIGHT, GARFIELD?
USUALLY, THE FIRST THING YOU DO IS TRY TO SHIP ME OFF TO ABU DHABI.

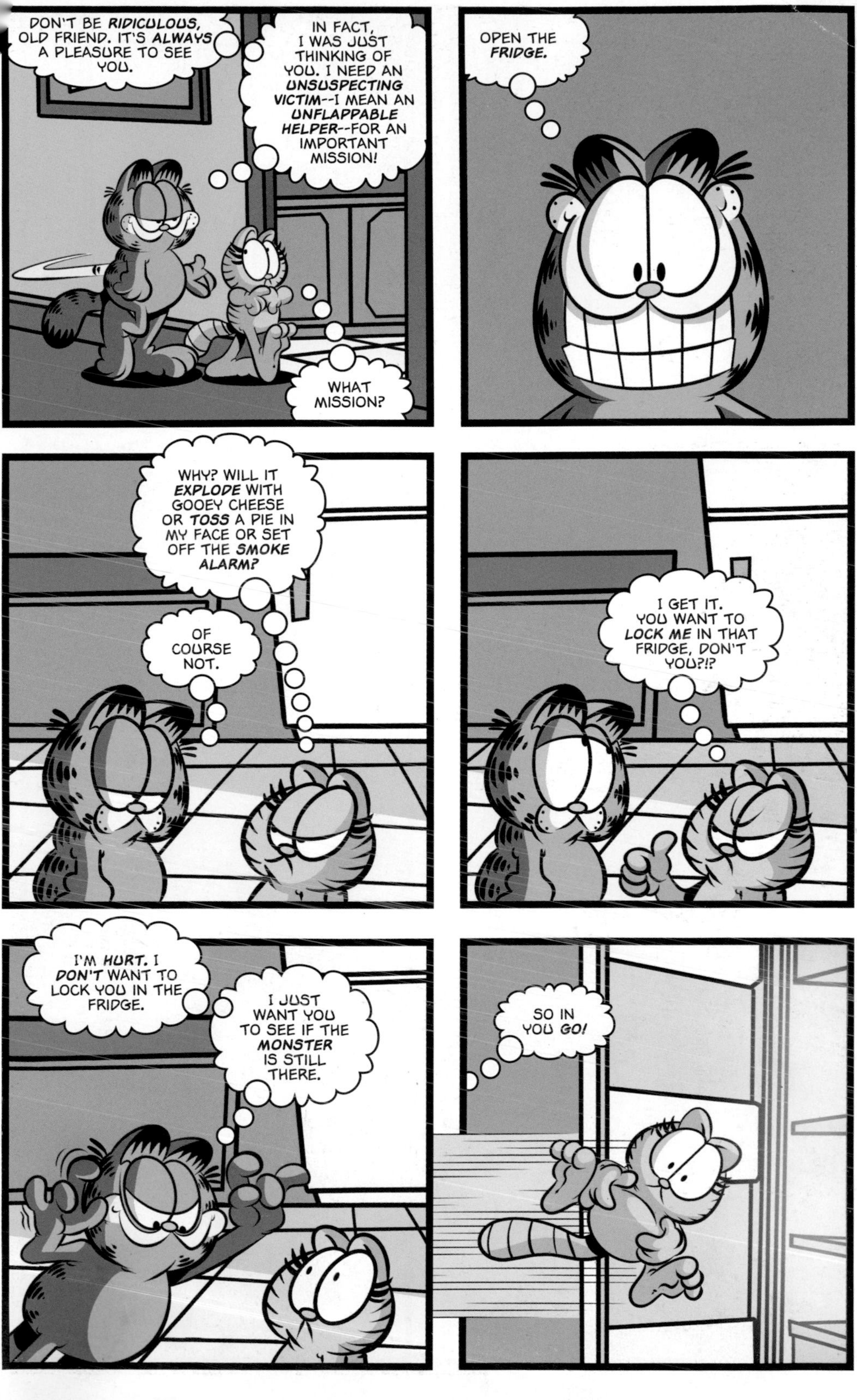
DON'T BE RIDICULOUS, OLD FRIEND. IT'S ALWAYS A PLEASURE TO SEE YOU.
IN FACT, I WAS JUST THINKING OF YOU. I NEED AN UNSUSPECTING VICTIM--I MEAN AN UNFLAPPABLE HELPER--FOR AN IMPORTANT MISSION!
WHAT MISSION?
OPEN THE FRIDGE.
WHY? WILL IT EXPLODE WITH GOOEY CHEESE OR TOSS A PIE IN MY FACE OR SET OFF THE SMOKE ALARM?
OF COURSE NOT.
I GET IT. YOU WANT TO LOCK ME IN THAT FRIDGE, DON'T YOU?!?
I'M HURT. I DON'T WANT TO LOCK YOU IN THE FRIDGE.
I JUST WANT YOU TO SEE IF THE MONSTER IS STILL THERE.
SO IN YOU GO!

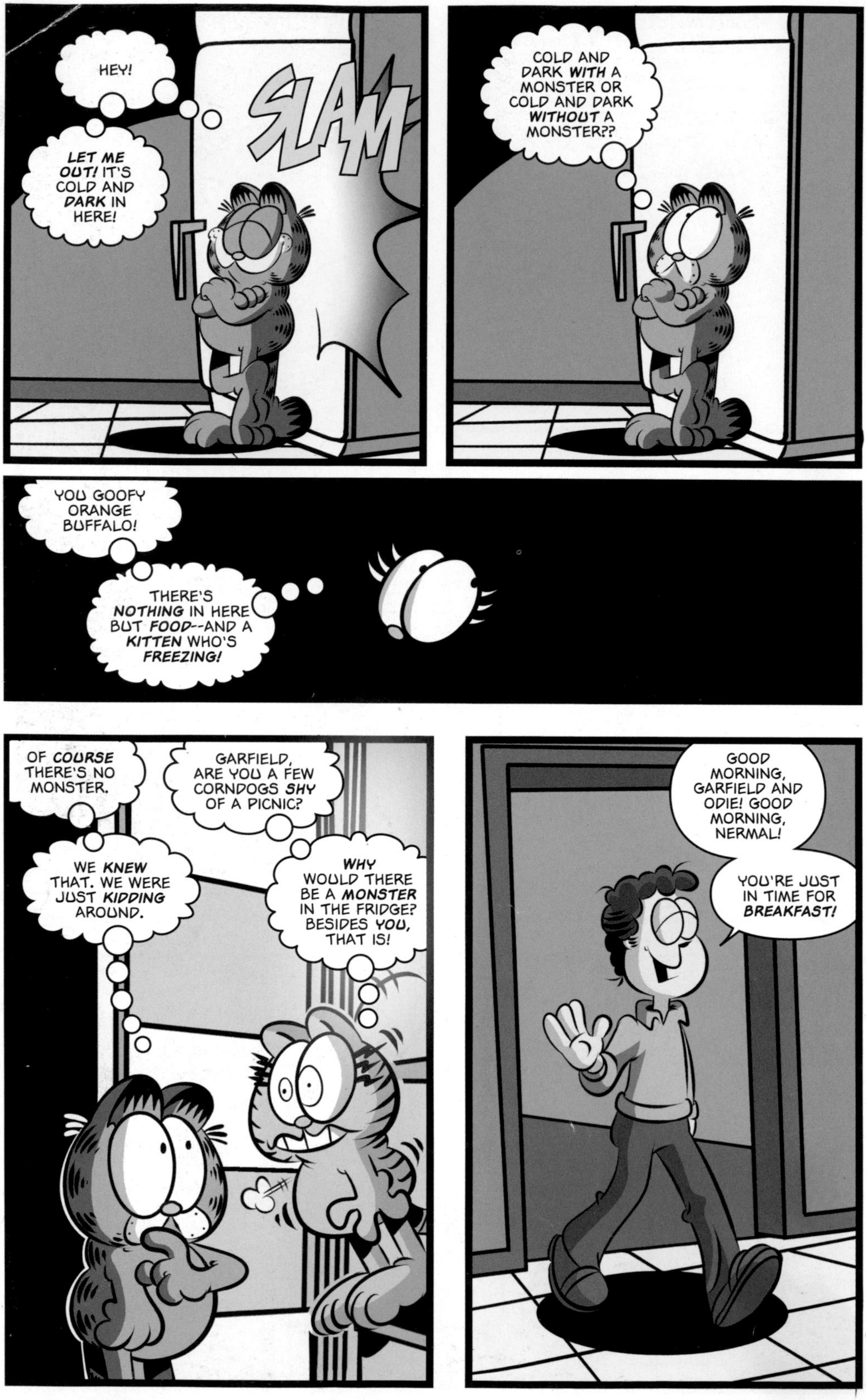
HEY!
LET ME OUT! IT'S COLD AND DARK IN HERE!
SLAM
COLD AND DARK WITH A MONSTER OR COLD AND DARK WITHOUT A MONSTER??
YOU GOOFY ORANGE BUFFALO!
THERE'S NOTHING IN HERE BUT FOOD--AND A KITTEN WHO'S FREEZING!
OF COURSE THERE'S NO MONSTER.
WE KNEW THAT. WE WERE JUST KIDDING AROUND.
GARFIELD, ARE YOU A FEW CORNDOGS SHY OF A PICNIC?
WHY WOULD THERE BE A MONSTER IN THE FRIDGE? BESIDES YOU, THAT IS!
GOOD MORNING, GARFIELD AND ODIE! GOOD MORNING, NERMAL!
YOU'RE JUST IN TIME FOR BREAKFAST!

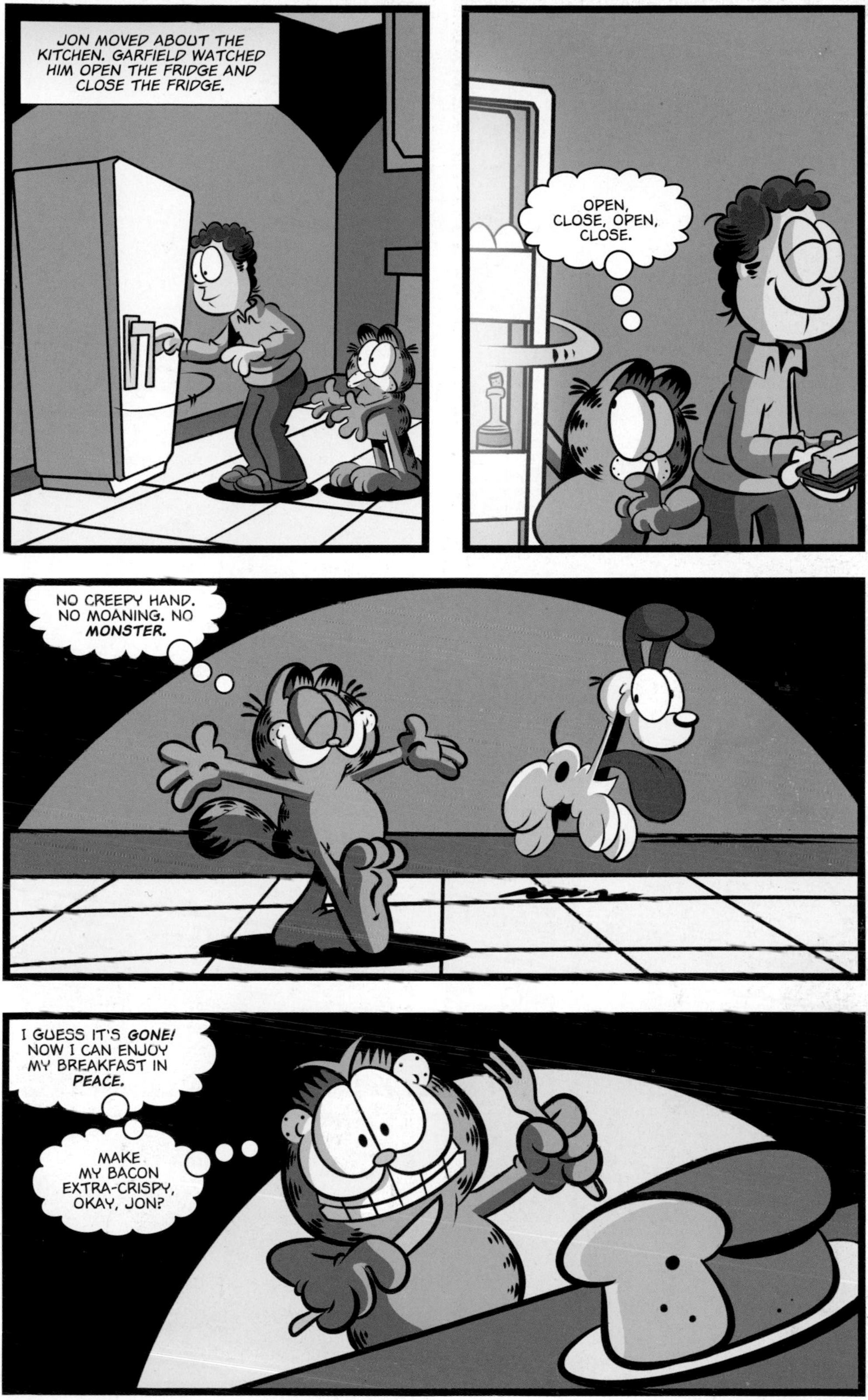
JON MOVED ABOUT THE KITCHEN. GARFIELD WATCHED HIM OPEN THE FRIDGE AND CLOSE THE FRIDGE.
OPEN, CLOSE, OPEN, CLOSE.
NO CREEPY HAND. NO MOANING. NO MONSTER.
I GUESS IT'S GONE! NOW I CAN ENJOY MY BREAKFAST IN PEACE.
MAKE MY BACON EXTRA-CRISPY, OKAY, JON?

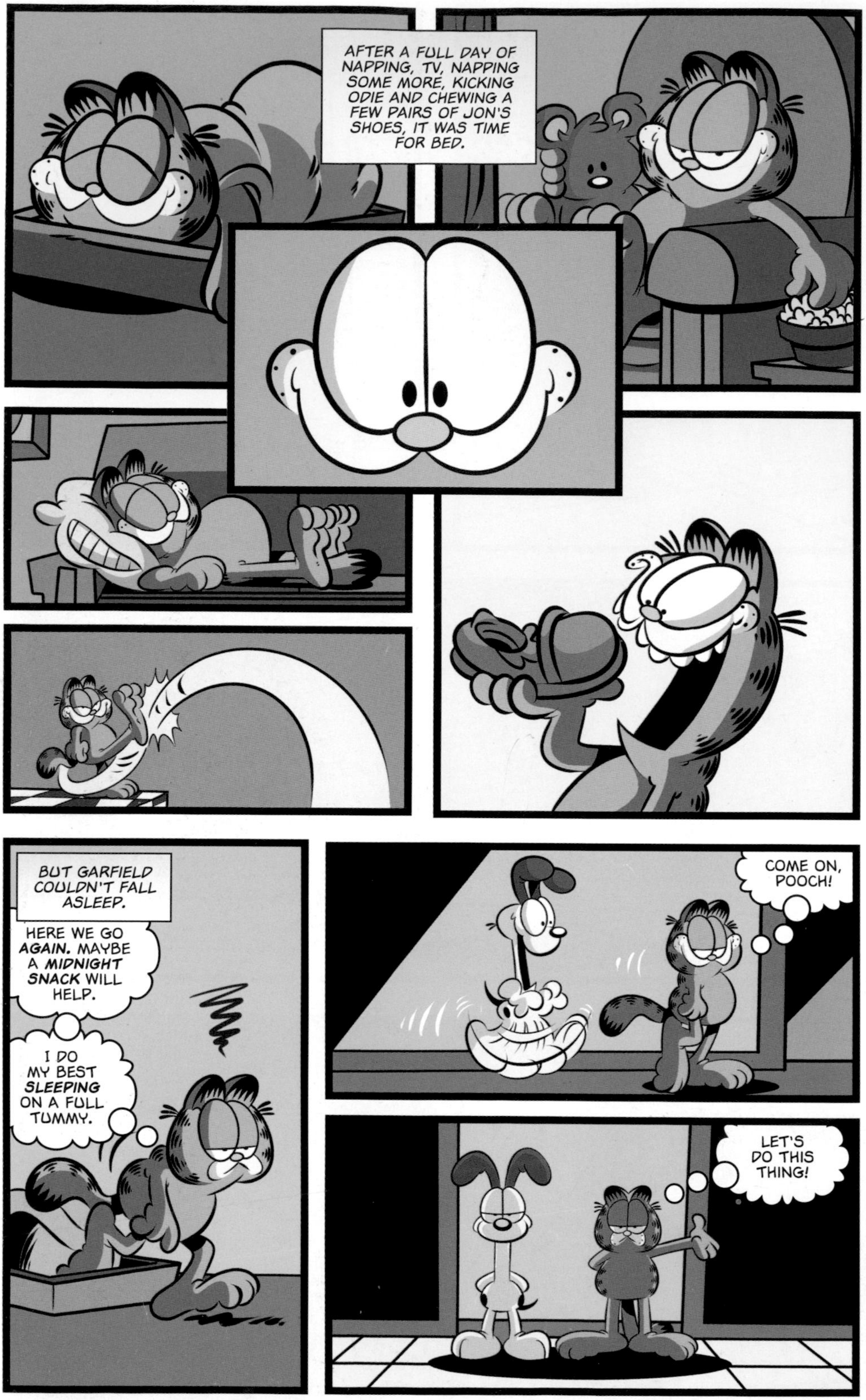
AFTER A FULL DAY OF NAPPING, TV, NAPPING SOME MORE, KICKING ODIE AND CHEWING A FEW PAIRS OF JON'S SHOES, IT WAS TIME FOR BED.
BUT GARFIELD COULDN'T FALL ASLEEP.
HERE WE GO AGAIN. MAYBE A MIDNIGHT SNACK WILL HELP.
I DO MY BEST SLEEPING ON A FULL TUMMY.
COME ON, POOCH!
LET'S DO THIS THING!

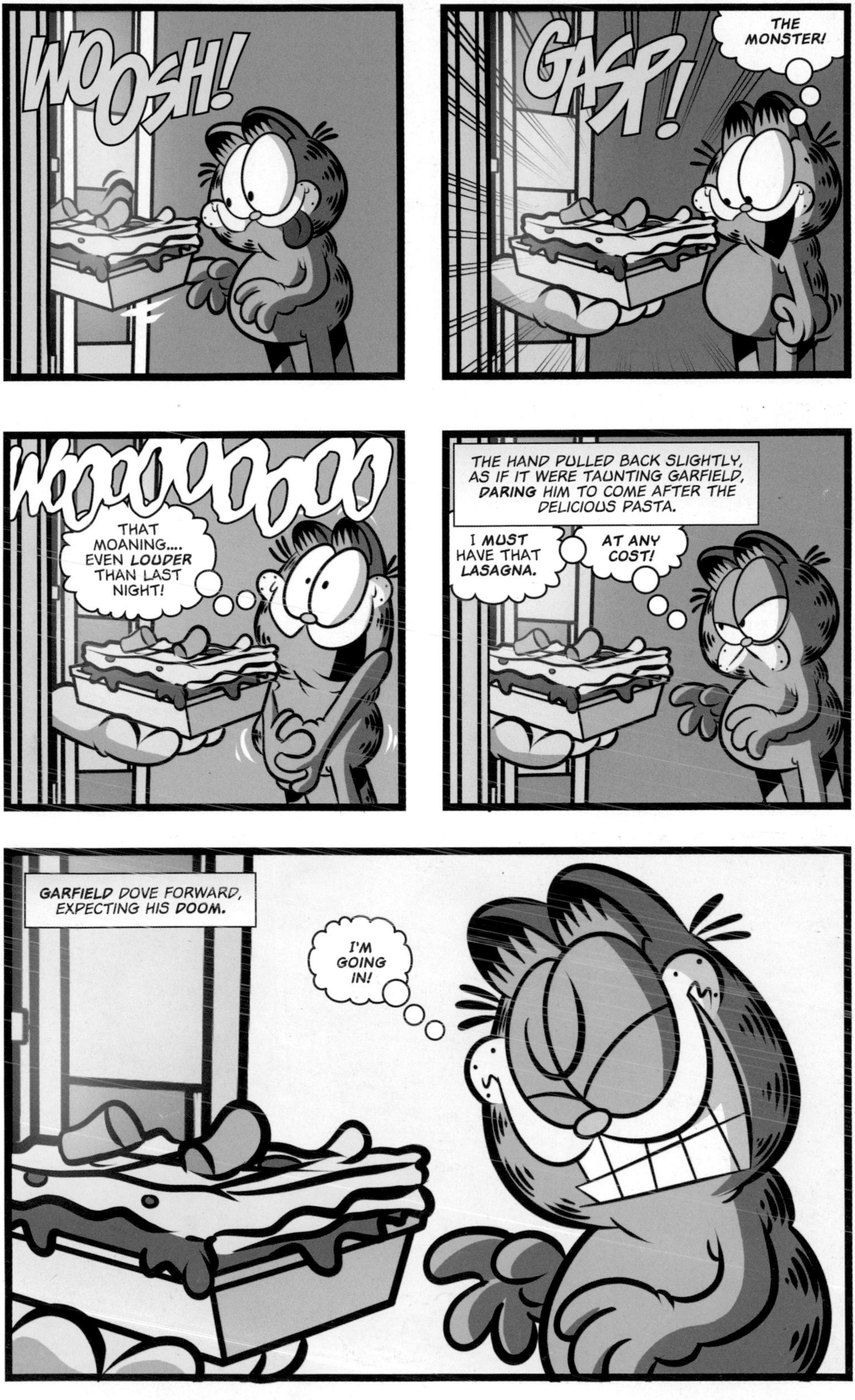
WOOSH!
GASP!
THE MONSTER!
WOOOOOOOOO
THAT MOANING.... EVEN LOUDER THAN LAST NIGHT!
THE HAND PULLED BACK SLIGHTLY, AS IF IT WERE TAUNTING GARFIELD, DARING HIM TO COME AFTER THE DELICIOUS PASTA.
I MUST HAVE THAT LASAGNA.
AT ANY COST!
GARFIELD DOVE FORWARD, EXPECTING HIS DOOM.
I'M GOING IN!

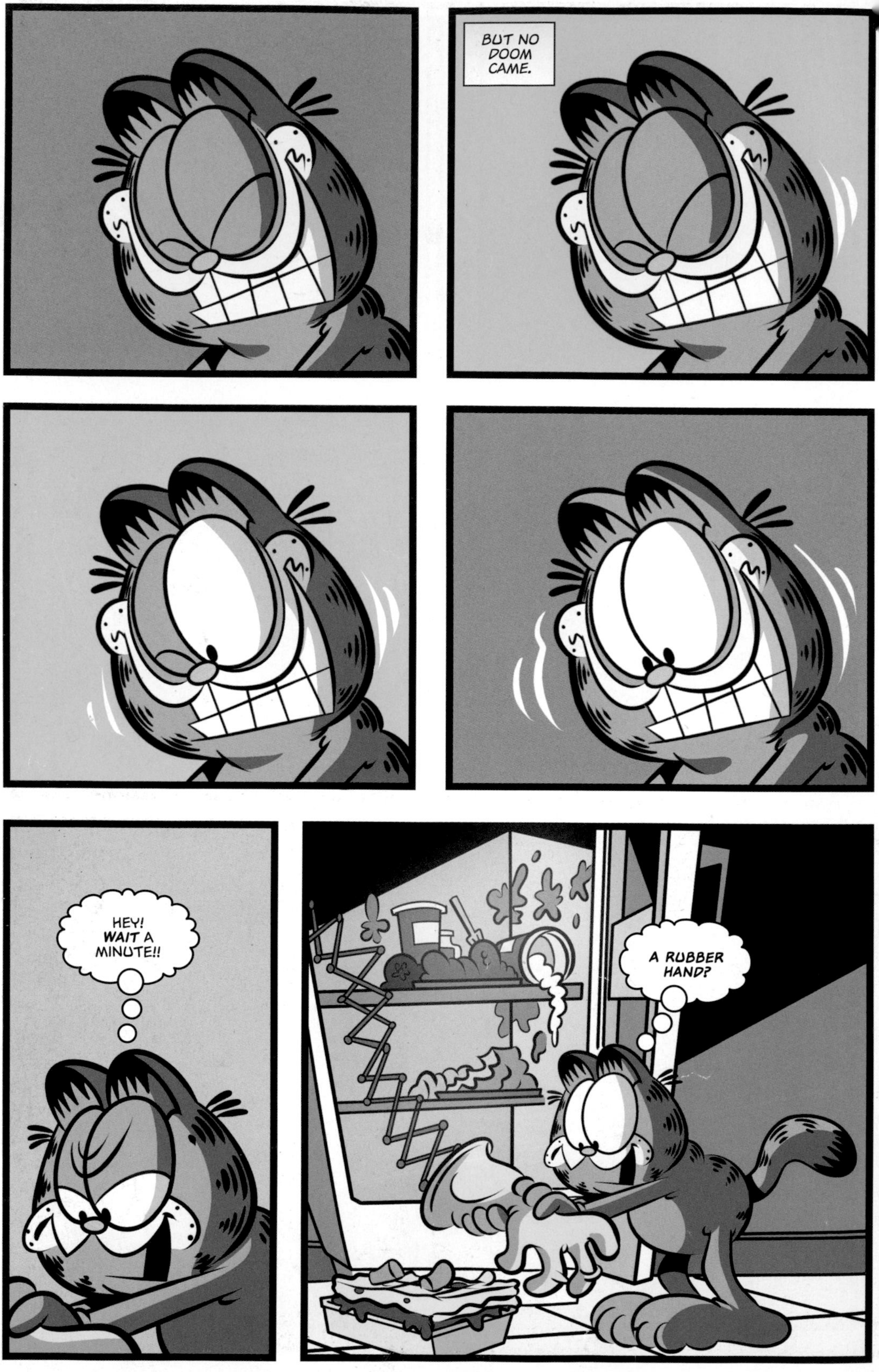
BUT NO DOOM CAME.
HEY! WAIT A MINUTE!!
A RUBBER HAND?

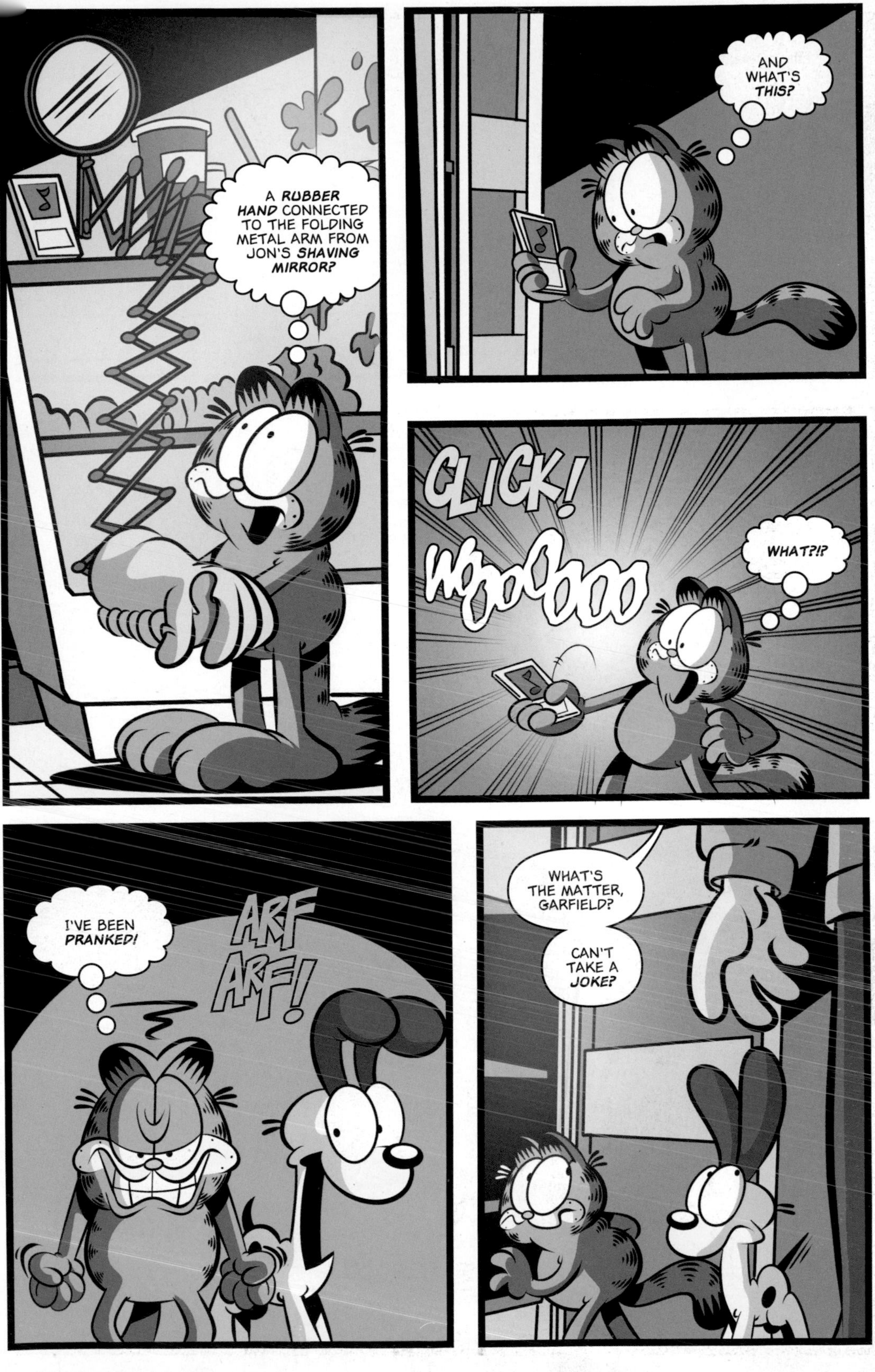
A RUBBER HAND CONNECTED TO THE FOLDING METAL ARM FROM JON'S SHAVING MIRROR?
AND WHAT'S THIS?
CLICK!
WOOOOOOOO
WHAT?!?
I'VE BEEN PRANKED!
ARF ARF!
WHAT'S THE MATTER, GARFIELD?
CAN'T TAKE A JOKE?

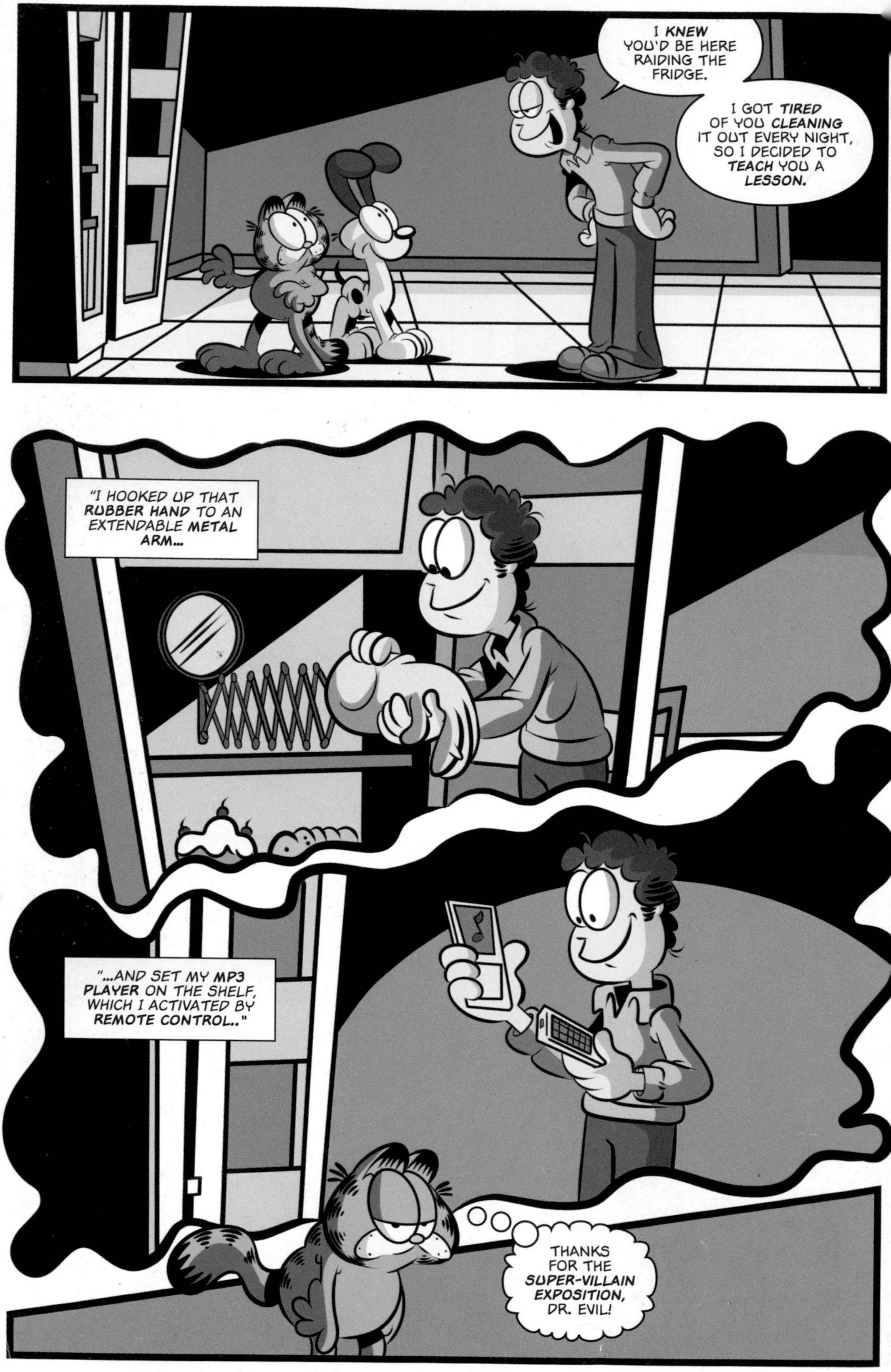
I KNEW YOU'D BE HERE RAIDING THE FRIDGE.
I GOT TIRED OF YOU CLEANING IT OUT EVERY NIGHT, SO I DECIDED TO TEACH YOU A LESSON.
"I HOOKED UP THAT RUBBER HAND TO AN EXTENDABLE METAL ARM...
"...AND SET MY MP3 PLAYER ON THE SHELF, WHICH I ACTIVATED BY REMOTE CONTROL.."
THANKS FOR THE SUPER-VILLAIN EXPOSITION, DR. EVIL!

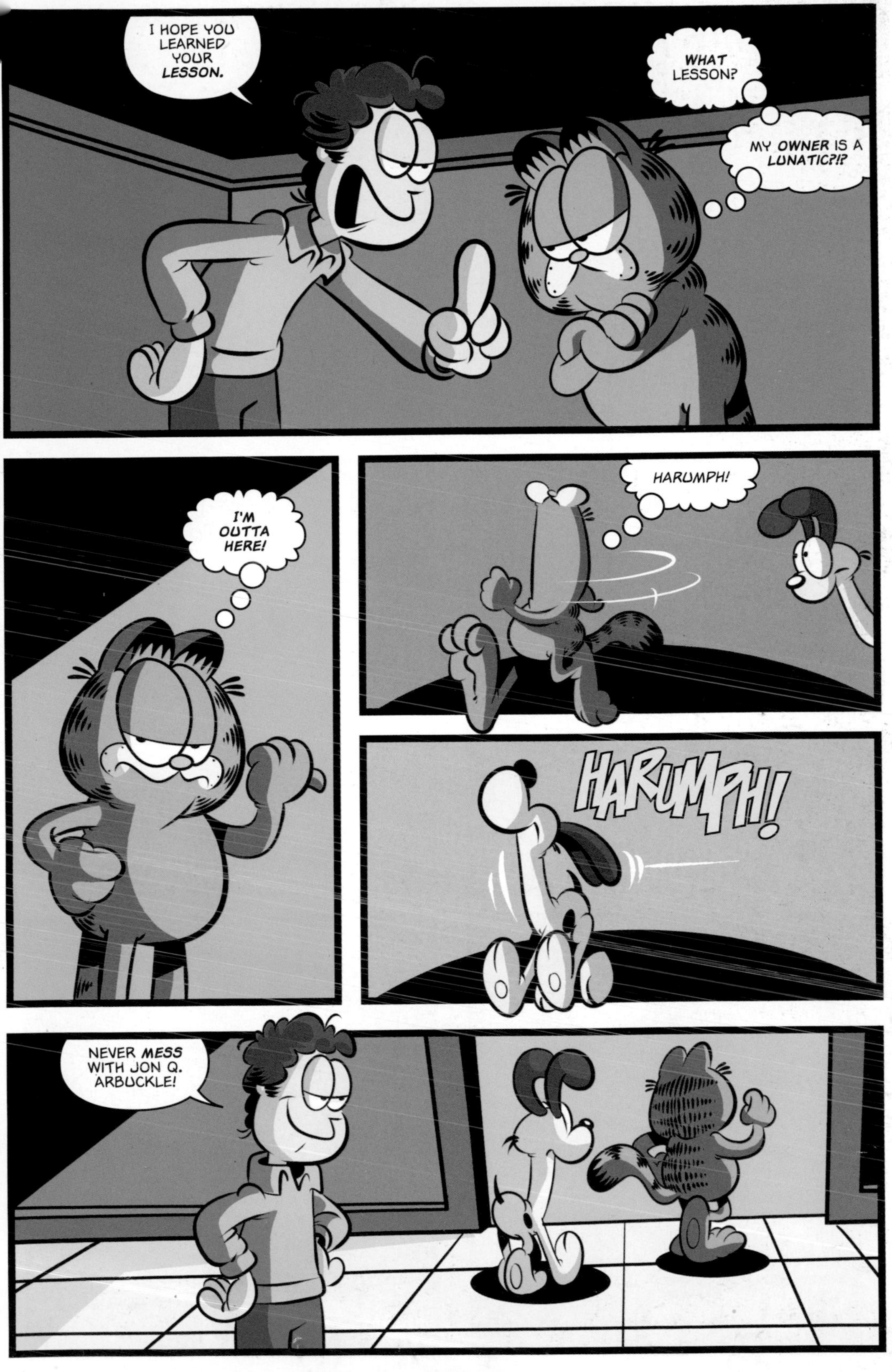
I HOPE YOU LEARNED YOUR LESSON.
WHAT LESSON?
MY OWNER IS A LUNATIC?!?
I'M OUTTA HERE!
HARUMPH!
HARUMPH!
NEVER MESS WITH JON Q. ARBUCKLE!

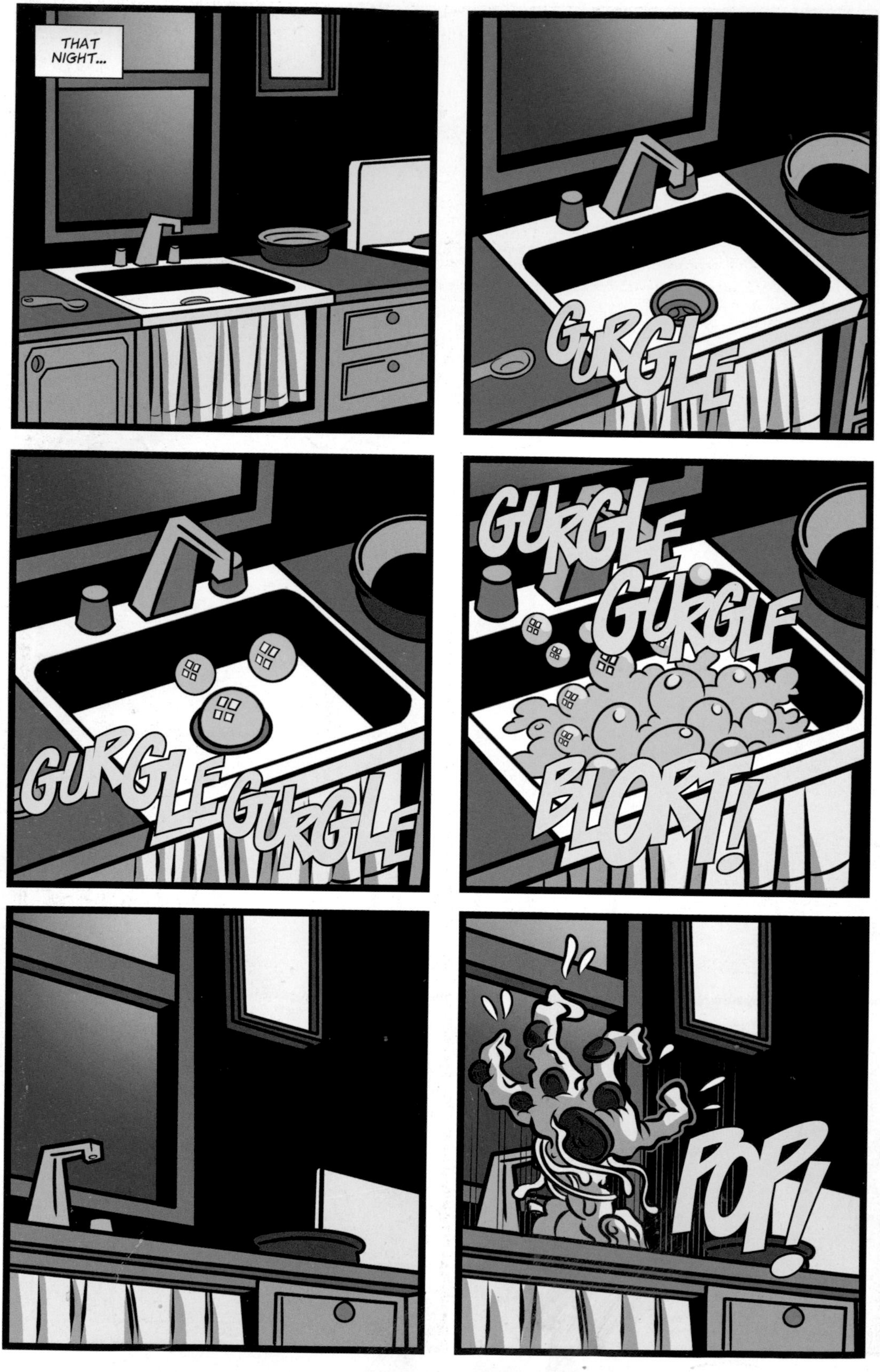
THAT NIGHT...
GURGLE
GURGLE GURGLE
GURGLE
GURGLE
BLORT!
POP!

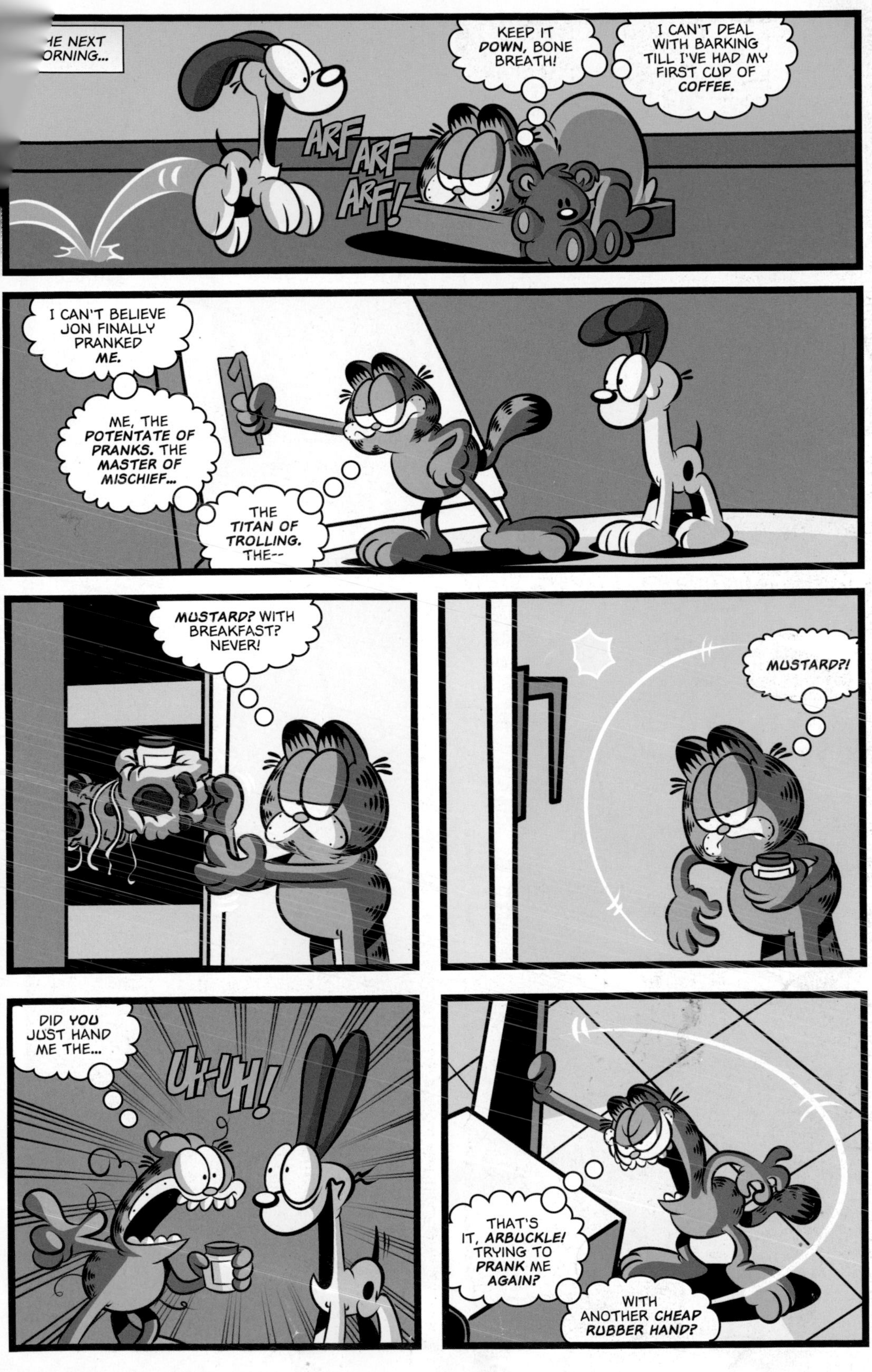
HE NEXT ORNING...
KEEP IT DOWN, BONE BREATH!
I CAN'T DEAL WITH BARKING TILL I'VE HAD MY FIRST CUP OF COFFEE.
ARF ARF ARF!
I CAN'T BELIEVE JON FINALLY PRANKED ME.
ME, THE POTENTATE OF PRANKS. THE MASTER OF MISCHIEF...
THE TITAN OF TROLLING. THE--
MUSTARD? WITH BREAKFAST? NEVER!
MUSTARD?!
DID YOU JUST HAND ME THE...
UH-UH!
THAT'S IT, ARBUCKLE! TRYING TO PRANK ME AGAIN?
WITH ANOTHER CHEAP RUBBER HAND?

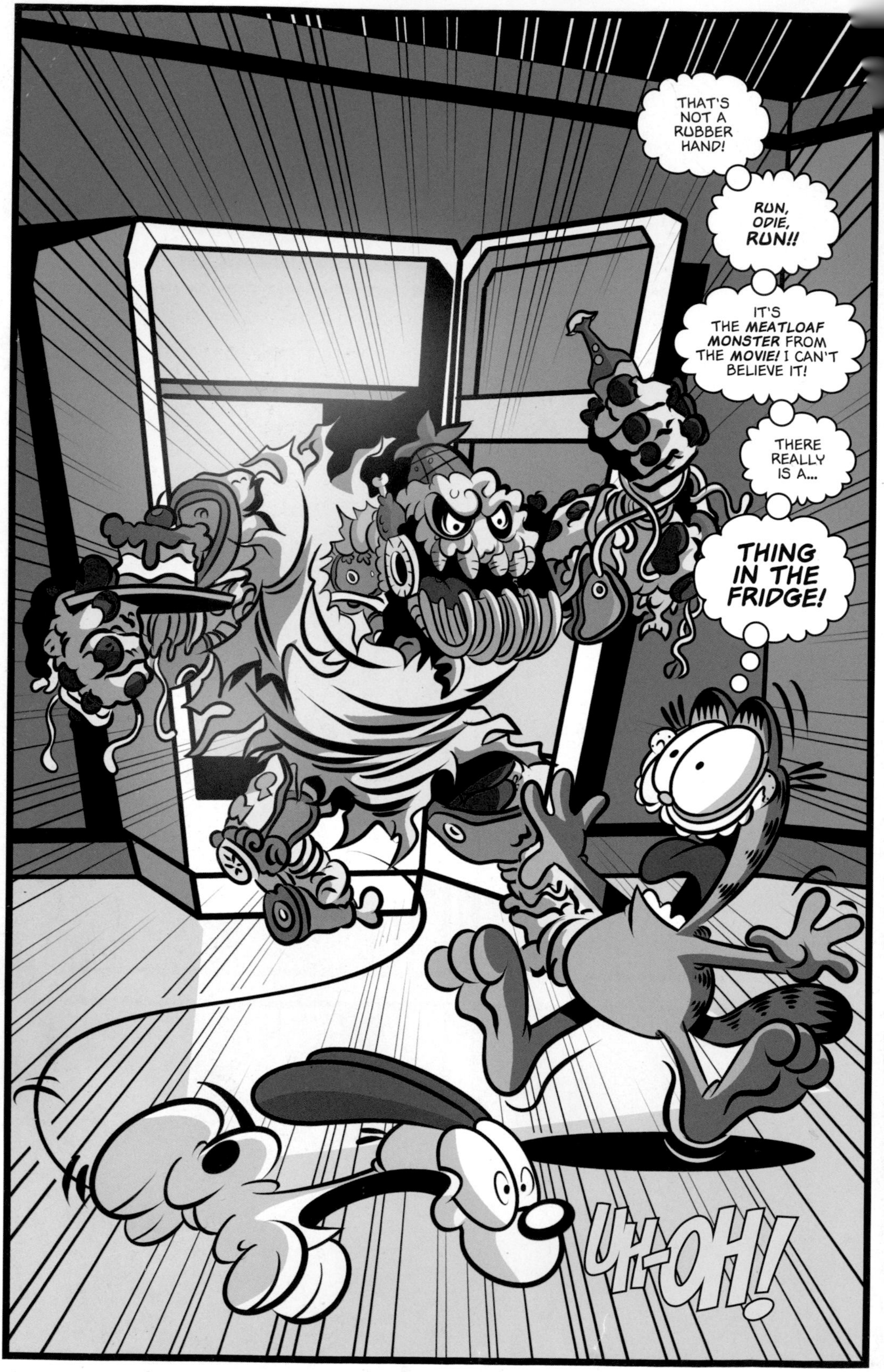

THAT'S NOT A RUBBER HAND!
RUN, ODIE, RUN!!
IT'S THE MEATLOAF MONSTER FROM THE MOVIE! I CAN'T BELIEVE IT!
THERE REALLY IS A...
THING IN THE FRIDGE!
UH-OH!

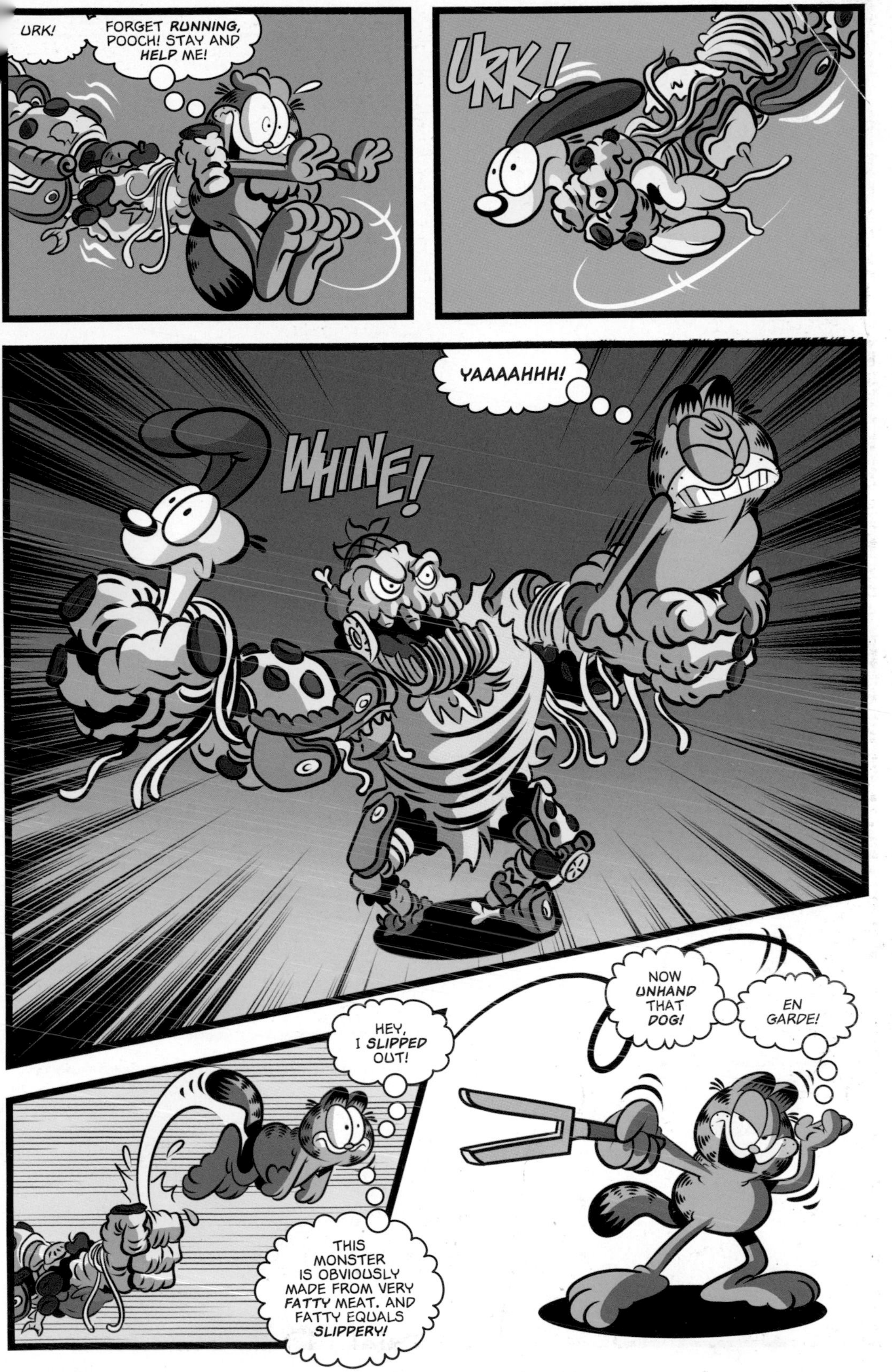
URK!
FORGET RUNNING, POOCH! STAY AND HELP ME!
URK!
YAAAAHHH!
WHINE!
HEY, I SLIPPED OUT!
THIS MONSTER IS OBVIOUSLY MADE FROM VERY FATTY MEAT. AND FATTY EQUALS SLIPPERY!
NOW UNHAND THAT DOG!
EN GARDE!

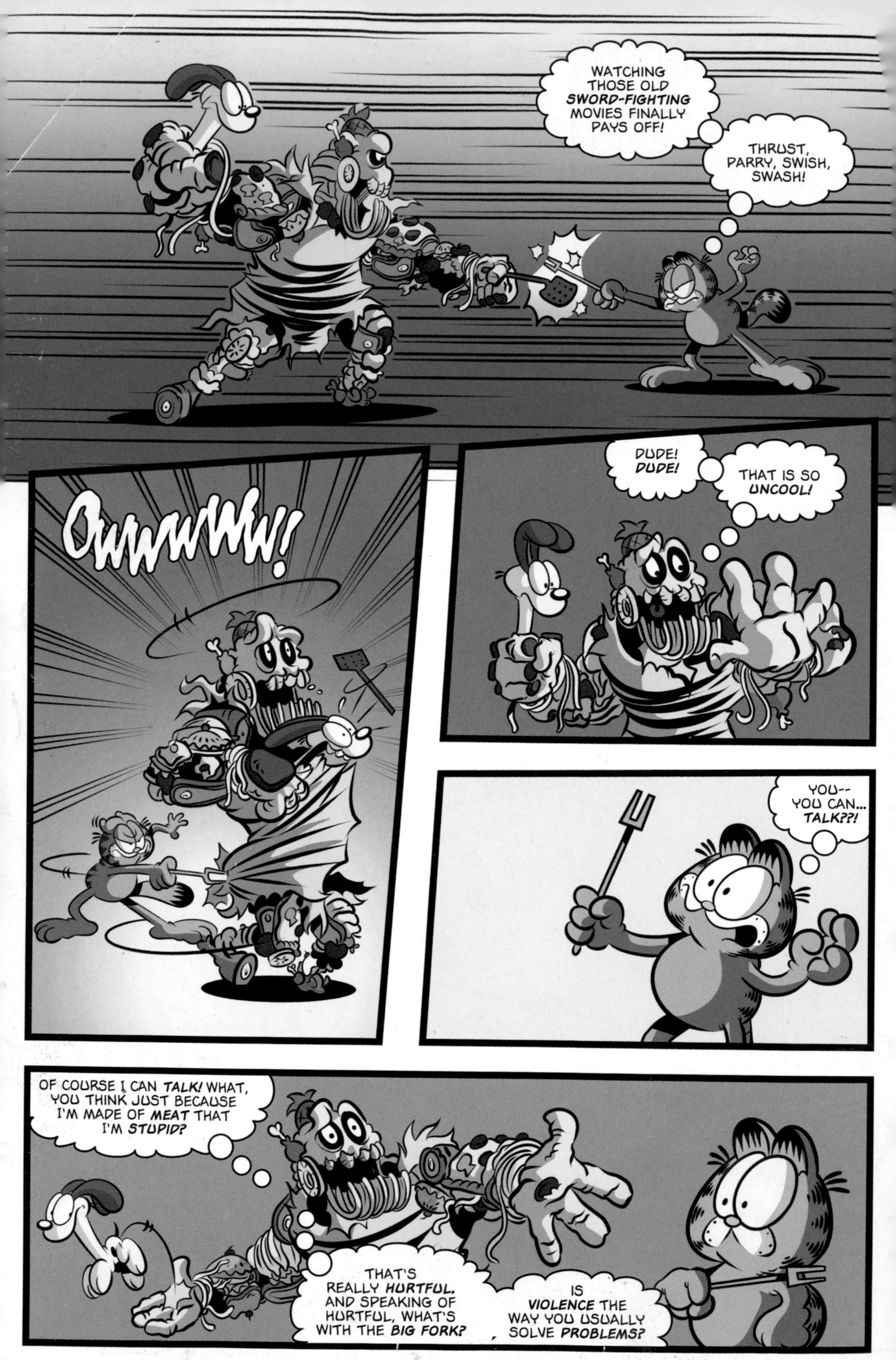
WATCHING THOSE OLD SWORD-FIGHTING MOVIES FINALLY PAYS OFF!
THRUST, PARRY, SWISH, SWASH!
OWWWWW!
DUDE! DUDE!
THAT IS SO UNCOOL!
YOU-- YOU CAN... TALK??!
OF COURSE I CAN TALK! WHAT, YOU THINK JUST BECAUSE I'M MADE OF MEAT THAT I'M STUPID?
THAT'S REALLY HURTFUL. AND SPEAKING OF HURTFUL, WHAT'S WITH THE BIG FORK?
IS VIOLENCE THE WAY YOU USUALLY SOLVE PROBLEMS?

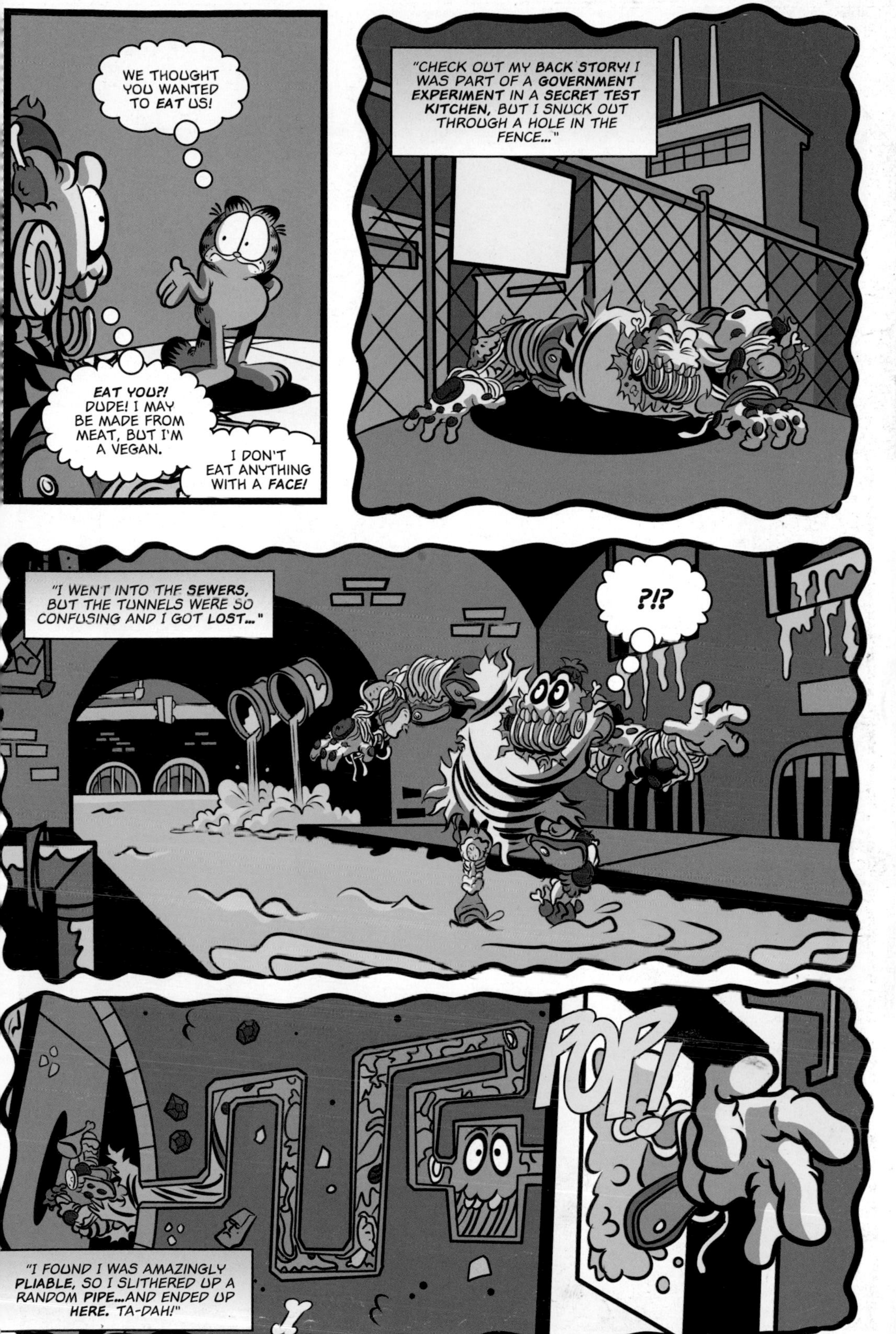
WE THOUGHT YOU WANTED TO EAT US!
EAT YOU?! DUDE! I MAY BE MADE FROM MEAT, BUT I'M A VEGAN.
I DON'T EAT ANYTHING WITH A FACE!
"CHECK OUT MY BACK STORY! I WAS PART OF A GOVERNMENT EXPERIMENT IN A SECRET TEST KITCHEN, BUT I SNUCK OUT THROUGH A HOLE IN THE FENCE..."
"I WENT INTO THE SEWERS, BUT THE TUNNELS WERE SO CONFUSING AND I GOT LOST..."
?!?
POP!
"I FOUND I WAS AMAZINGLY PLIABLE, SO I SLITHERED UP A RANDOM PIPE...AND ENDED UP HERE. TA-DAH!"

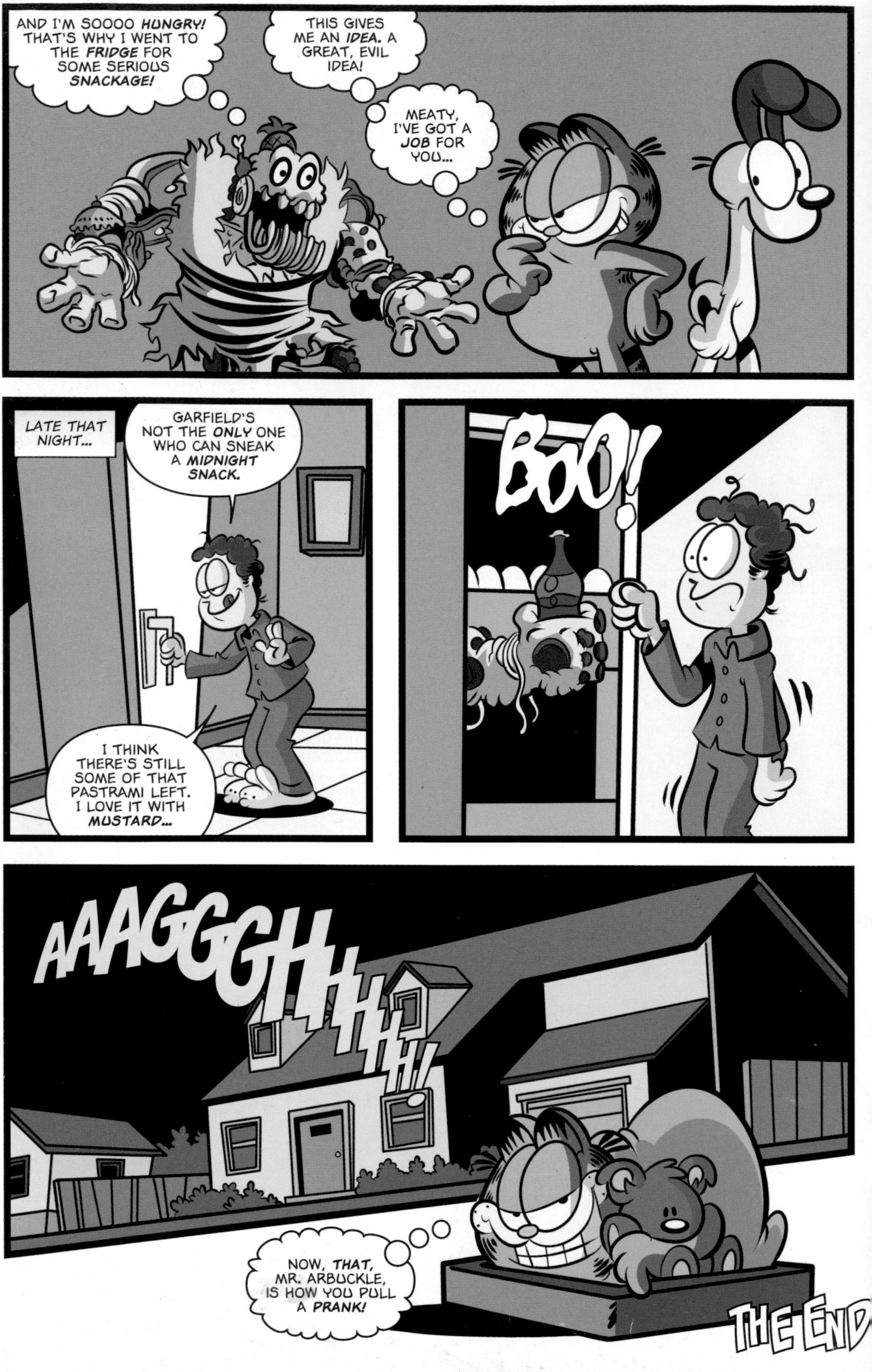

AND I'M SOOOO HUNGRY! THAT'S WHY I WENT TO THE FRIDGE FOR SOME SERIOUS SNACKAGE!
THIS GIVES ME AN IDEA. A GREAT, EVIL IDEA!
MEATY, I'VE GOT A JOB FOR YOU...
LATE THAT NIGHT...
GARFIELD'S NOT THE ONLY ONE WHO CAN SNEAK A MIDNIGHT SNACK.
I THINK THERE'S STILL SOME OF THAT PASTRAMI LEFT. I LOVE IT WITH MUSTARD...
BOO!
AAAGGGHHHHH!
NOW, THAT, MR. ARBUCKLE, IS HOW YOU PULL A PRANK!
THE END

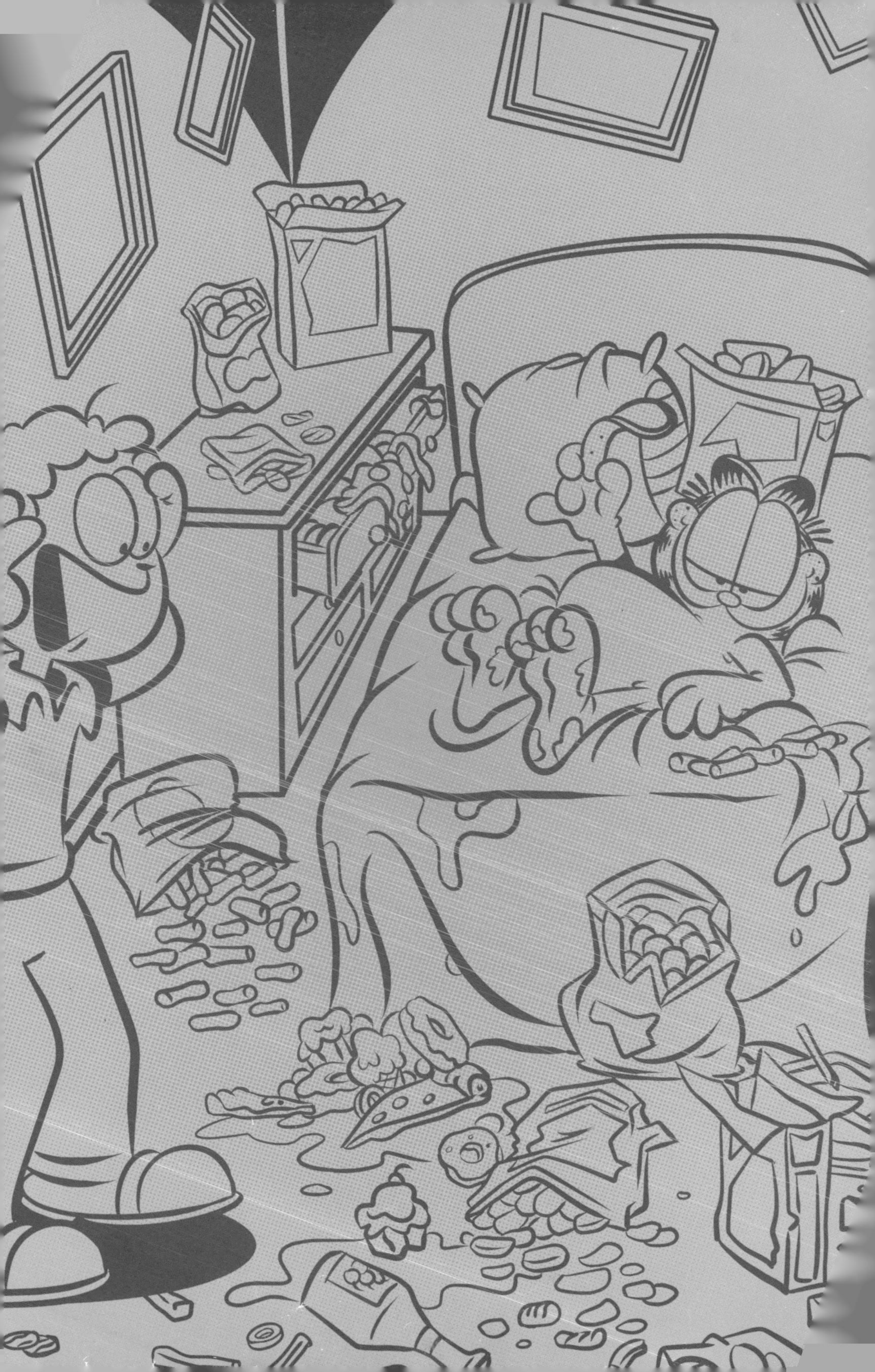

"THE EARLY JON ARBUCKLE"

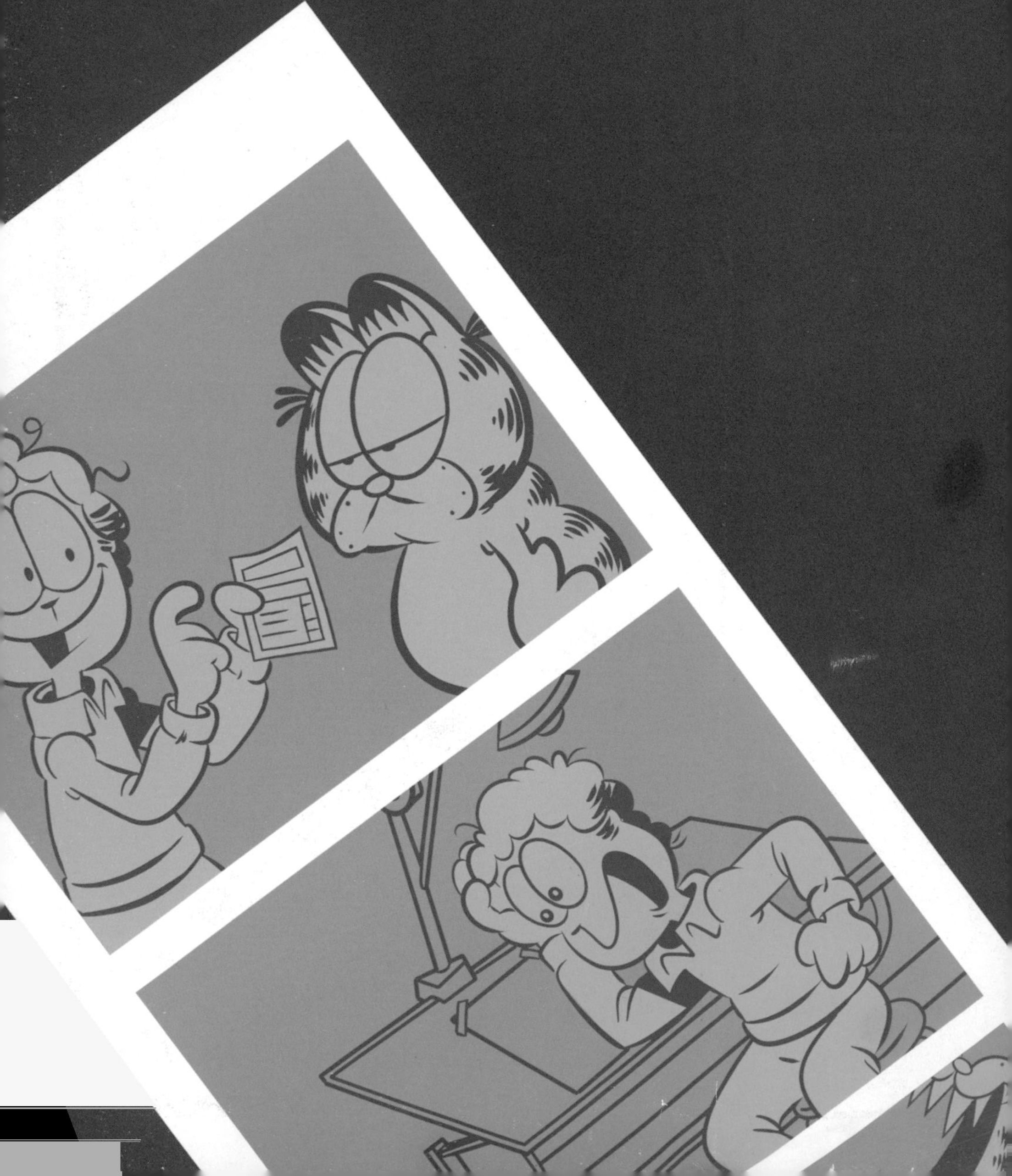

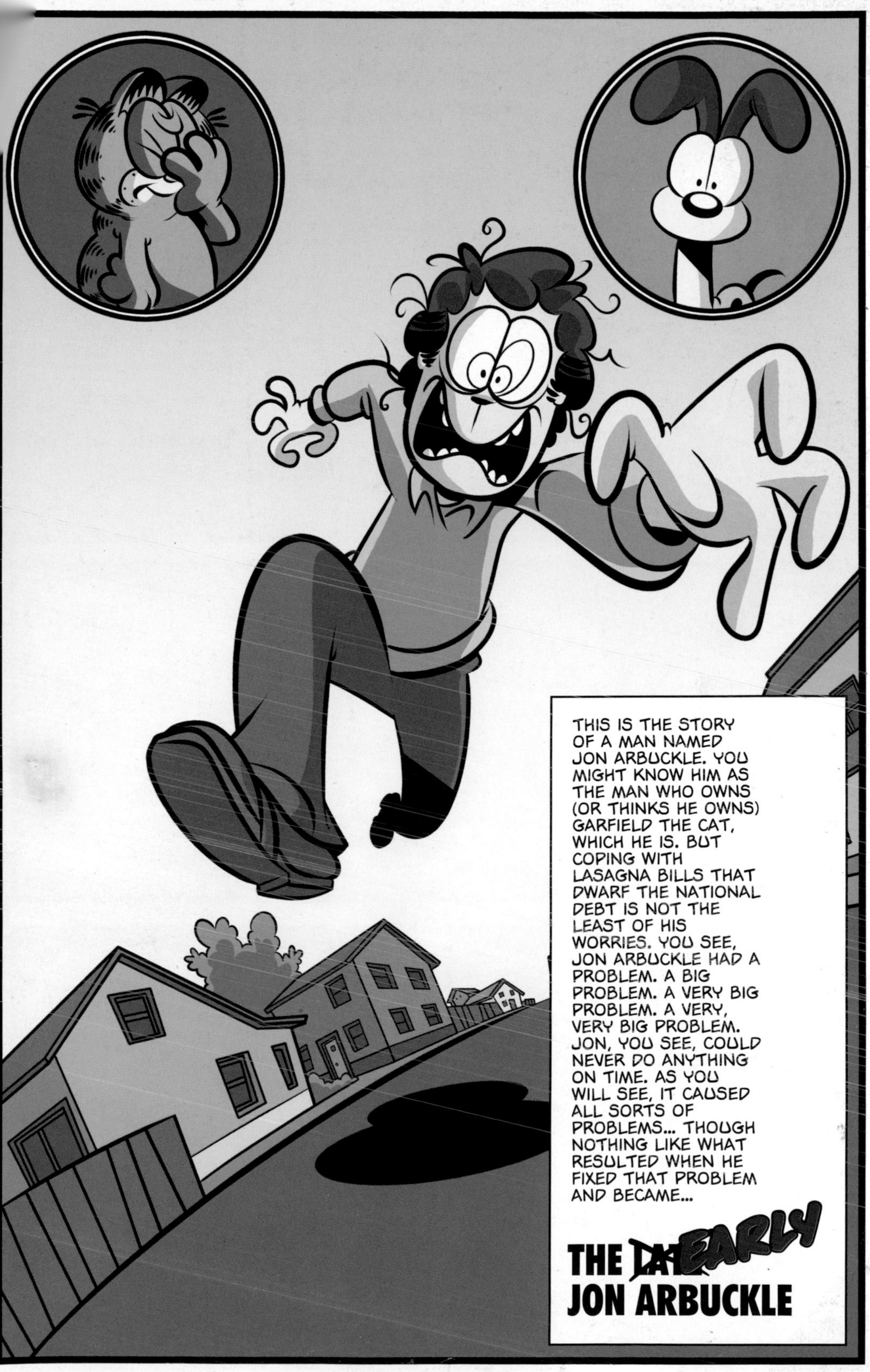

THIS IS THE STORY OF A MAN NAMED JON ARBUCKLE. YOU MIGHT KNOW HIM AS THE MAN WHO OWNS (OR THINKS HE OWNS) GARFIELD THE CAT, WHICH HE IS. BUT COPING WITH LASAGNA BILLS THAT DWARF THE NATIONAL DEBT IS NOT THE LEAST OF HIS WORRIES. YOU SEE, JON ARBUCKLE HAD A PROBLEM. A BIG PROBLEM. A VERY BIG PROBLEM. A VERY, VERY BIG PROBLEM. JON, YOU SEE, COULD NEVER DO ANYTHING ON TIME. AS YOU WILL SEE, IT CAUSED ALL SORTS OF PROBLEMS... THOUGH NOTHING LIKE WHAT RESULTED WHEN HE FIXED THAT PROBLEM AND BECAME...
THE ~~LATE~~ EARLY JON ARBUCKLE

HE WASN'T ALWAYS LIKE THIS. ONCE UPON A TIME, JON DID THINGS ON TIME. BUT SLOWLY, HE BEGAN TO GET A LITTLE LATER WITH HIS WORK...

THESE CARTOONS OF YOURS ARE FINE, ARBUCKLE, BUT YOU WERE SUPPOSED TO HAVE THEM IN ON *WEDNESDAY!*

B-B-BUT IT *IS* WEDNESDAY.

IT'S JUST *TWO WEDNESDAYS* LATER THAN THEY WERE *SUPPOSED* TO BE IN...

...AND A LITTLE LATER WITH PAYING HIS BILLS...

I SHOULD HAVE PAID *THIS ONE* THREE MONTHS AGO SO NOW I HAVE TO PAY THE $22 *LATE FEE...*

THEN I HAVE TO MAKE A TRIP TO THE BANK TO PAY THIS ONE THAT WAS DUE LAST MAY...

HOPE YOU PAID THE ELECTRIC BILL...

I KNOW WHAT *YOU'RE* WORRIED ABOUT, GARFIELD! YOU'RE WORRIED I DIDN'T PAY THE ELECTRIC BILL!

YOU READ MY MIND!

WELL, I *DID* PAY IT!

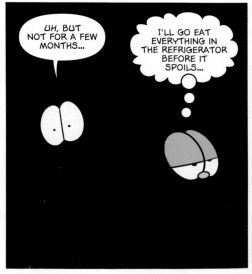

UH, BUT NOT FOR A FEW MONTHS...

I'LL GO EAT EVERYTHING IN THE REFRIGERATOR BEFORE IT SPOILS...

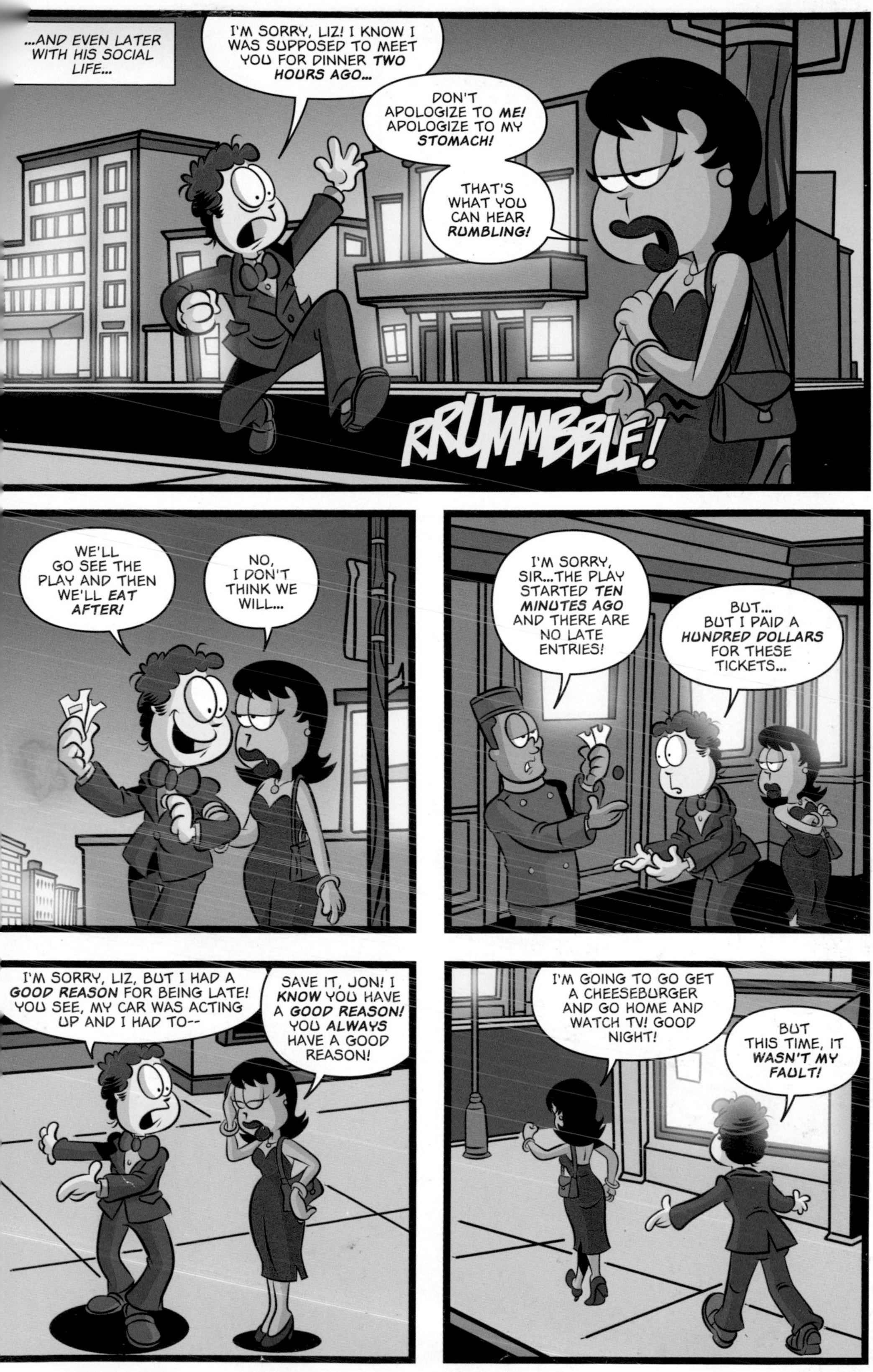
...AND EVEN LATER WITH HIS SOCIAL LIFE...
I'M SORRY, LIZ! I KNOW I WAS SUPPOSED TO MEET YOU FOR DINNER TWO HOURS AGO...
DON'T APOLOGIZE TO ME! APOLOGIZE TO MY STOMACH!
THAT'S WHAT YOU CAN HEAR RUMBLING!
RRUMMBBLE!
WE'LL GO SEE THE PLAY AND THEN WE'LL EAT AFTER!
NO, I DON'T THINK WE WILL...
I'M SORRY, SIR...THE PLAY STARTED TEN MINUTES AGO AND THERE ARE NO LATE ENTRIES!
BUT... BUT I PAID A HUNDRED DOLLARS FOR THESE TICKETS...
I'M SORRY, LIZ, BUT I HAD A GOOD REASON FOR BEING LATE! YOU SEE, MY CAR WAS ACTING UP AND I HAD TO--
SAVE IT, JON! I KNOW YOU HAVE A GOOD REASON! YOU ALWAYS HAVE A GOOD REASON!
I'M GOING TO GO GET A CHEESEBURGER AND GO HOME AND WATCH TV! GOOD NIGHT!
BUT THIS TIME, IT WASN'T MY FAULT!

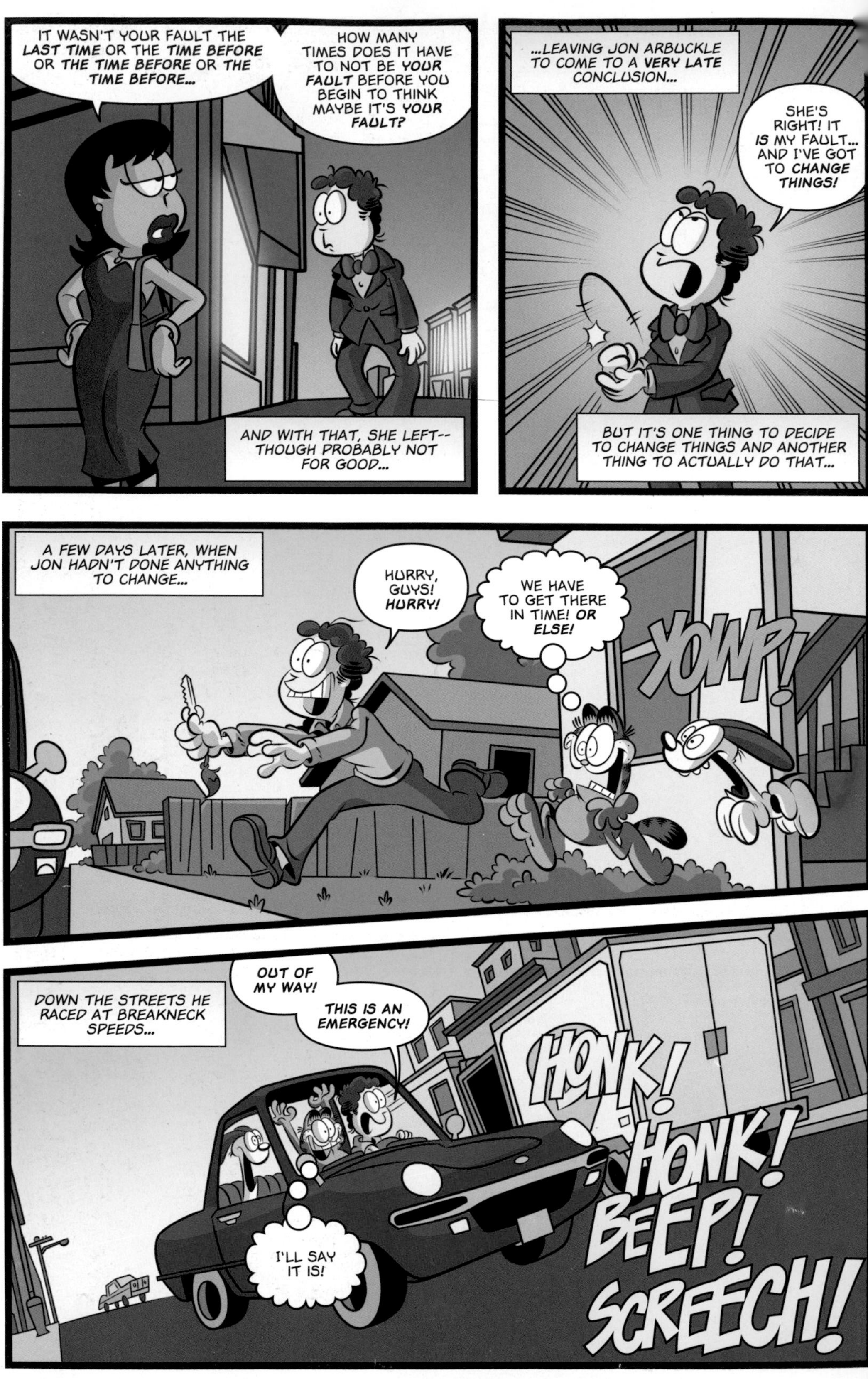
IT WASN'T YOUR FAULT THE LAST TIME OR THE TIME BEFORE OR THE TIME BEFORE OR THE TIME BEFORE...
HOW MANY TIMES DOES IT HAVE TO NOT BE YOUR FAULT BEFORE YOU BEGIN TO THINK MAYBE IT'S YOUR FAULT?
AND WITH THAT, SHE LEFT--THOUGH PROBABLY NOT FOR GOOD...
...LEAVING JON ARBUCKLE TO COME TO A VERY LATE CONCLUSION...
SHE'S RIGHT! IT IS MY FAULT... AND I'VE GOT TO CHANGE THINGS!
BUT IT'S ONE THING TO DECIDE TO CHANGE THINGS AND ANOTHER THING TO ACTUALLY DO THAT...
A FEW DAYS LATER, WHEN JON HADN'T DONE ANYTHING TO CHANGE...
HURRY, GUYS! HURRY!
WE HAVE TO GET THERE IN TIME! OR ELSE!
YOWP!
DOWN THE STREETS HE RACED AT BREAKNECK SPEEDS...
OUT OF MY WAY!
THIS IS AN EMERGENCY!
I'LL SAY IT IS!
HONK!
HONK!
BEEP!
SCREECH!

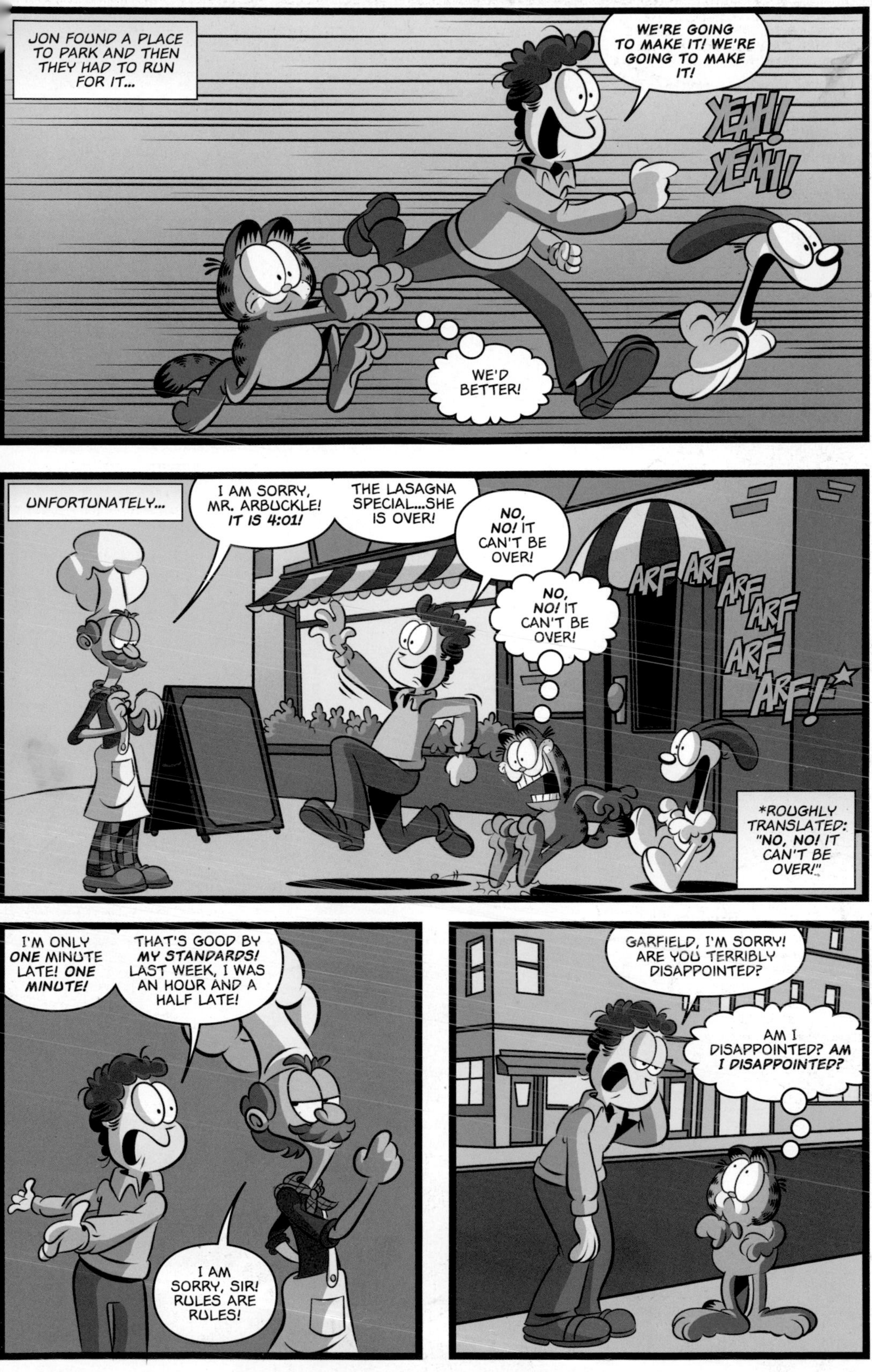

JON FOUND A PLACE TO PARK AND THEN THEY HAD TO RUN FOR IT...
WE'RE GOING TO MAKE IT! WE'RE GOING TO MAKE IT!
YEAH! YEAH!
WE'D BETTER!
UNFORTUNATELY...
I AM SORRY, MR. ARBUCKLE! IT IS 4:01!
THE LASAGNA SPECIAL...SHE IS OVER!
NO, NO! IT CAN'T BE OVER!
NO, NO! IT CAN'T BE OVER!
ARF ARF ARF ARF ARF ARF!*
*ROUGHLY TRANSLATED: "NO, NO! IT CAN'T BE OVER!"
I'M ONLY ONE MINUTE LATE! ONE MINUTE!
THAT'S GOOD BY MY STANDARDS! LAST WEEK, I WAS AN HOUR AND A HALF LATE!
I AM SORRY, SIR! RULES ARE RULES!
GARFIELD, I'M SORRY! ARE YOU TERRIBLY DISAPPOINTED?
AM I DISAPPOINTED? AM I DISAPPOINTED?

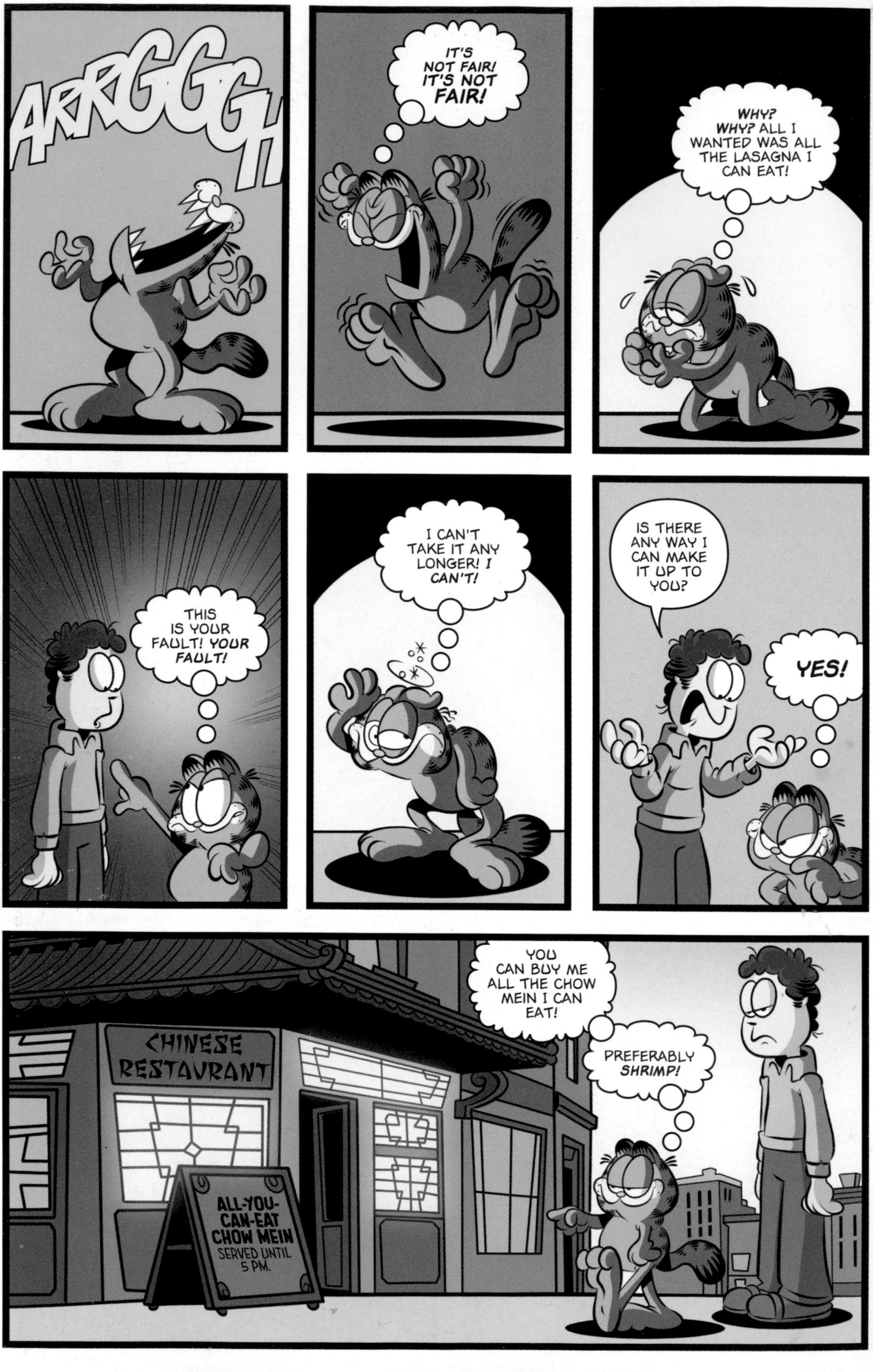
ARRGGGH
IT'S NOT FAIR! IT'S NOT FAIR!
WHY? WHY? ALL I WANTED WAS ALL THE LASAGNA I CAN EAT!
THIS IS YOUR FAULT! YOUR FAULT!
I CAN'T TAKE IT ANY LONGER! I CAN'T!
IS THERE ANY WAY I CAN MAKE IT UP TO YOU?
YES!
CHINESE RESTAURANT
ALL-YOU-CAN-EAT CHOW MEIN SERVED UNTIL 5 PM.
YOU CAN BUY ME ALL THE CHOW MEIN I CAN EAT!
PREFERABLY SHRIMP!

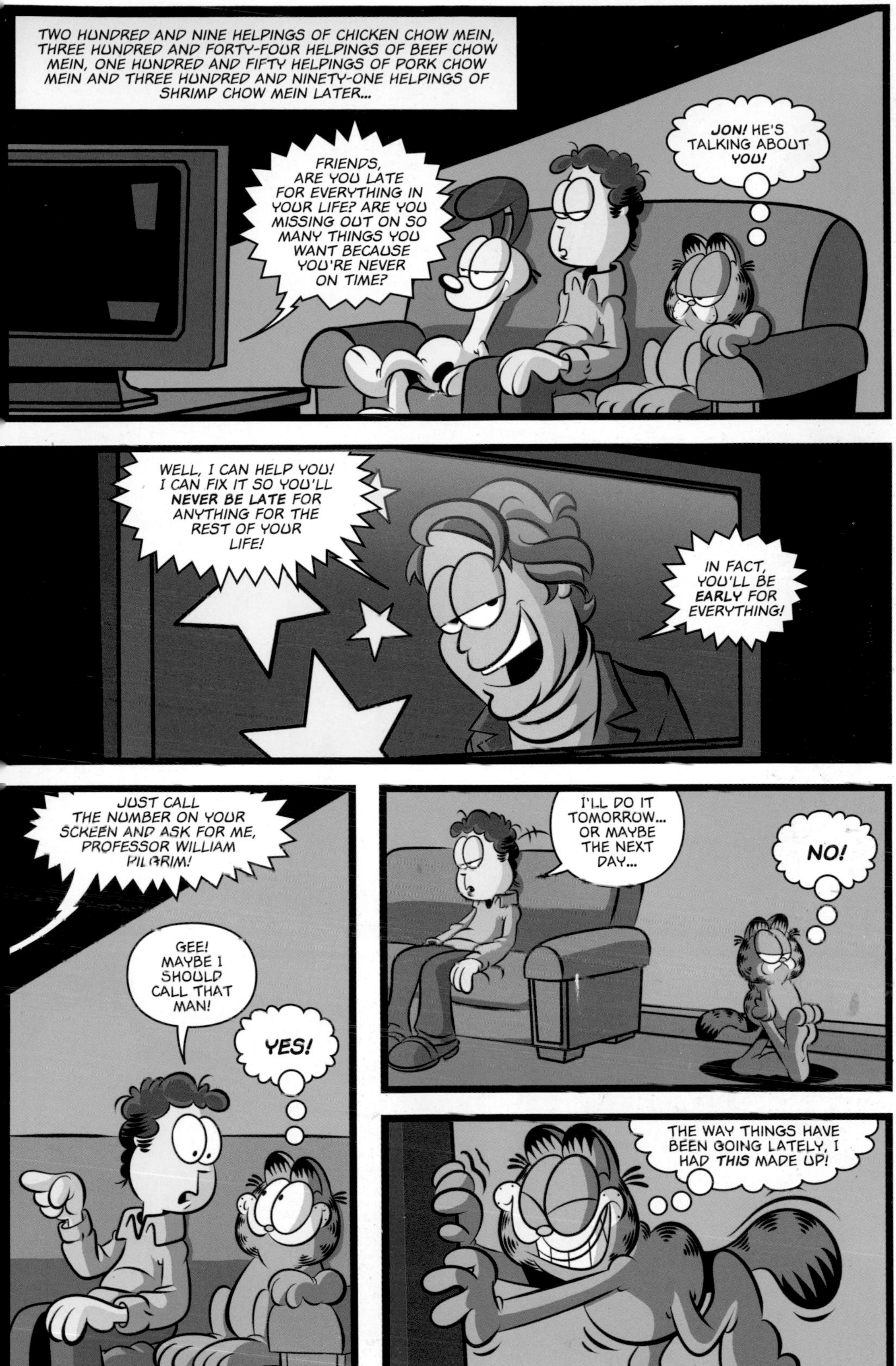
TWO HUNDRED AND NINE HELPINGS OF CHICKEN CHOW MEIN, THREE HUNDRED AND FORTY-FOUR HELPINGS OF BEEF CHOW MEIN, ONE HUNDRED AND FIFTY HELPINGS OF PORK CHOW MEIN AND THREE HUNDRED AND NINETY-ONE HELPINGS OF SHRIMP CHOW MEIN LATER...
FRIENDS, ARE YOU LATE FOR EVERYTHING IN YOUR LIFE? ARE YOU MISSING OUT ON SO MANY THINGS YOU WANT BECAUSE YOU'RE NEVER ON TIME?
JON! HE'S TALKING ABOUT YOU!
WELL, I CAN HELP YOU! I CAN FIX IT SO YOU'LL NEVER BE LATE FOR ANYTHING FOR THE REST OF YOUR LIFE!
IN FACT, YOU'LL BE EARLY FOR EVERYTHING!
JUST CALL THE NUMBER ON YOUR SCREEN AND ASK FOR ME, PROFESSOR WILLIAM PILGRIM!
GEE! MAYBE I SHOULD CALL THAT MAN!
YES!
I'LL DO IT TOMORROW... OR MAYBE THE NEXT DAY...
NO!
THE WAY THINGS HAVE BEEN GOING LATELY, I HAD THIS MADE UP!

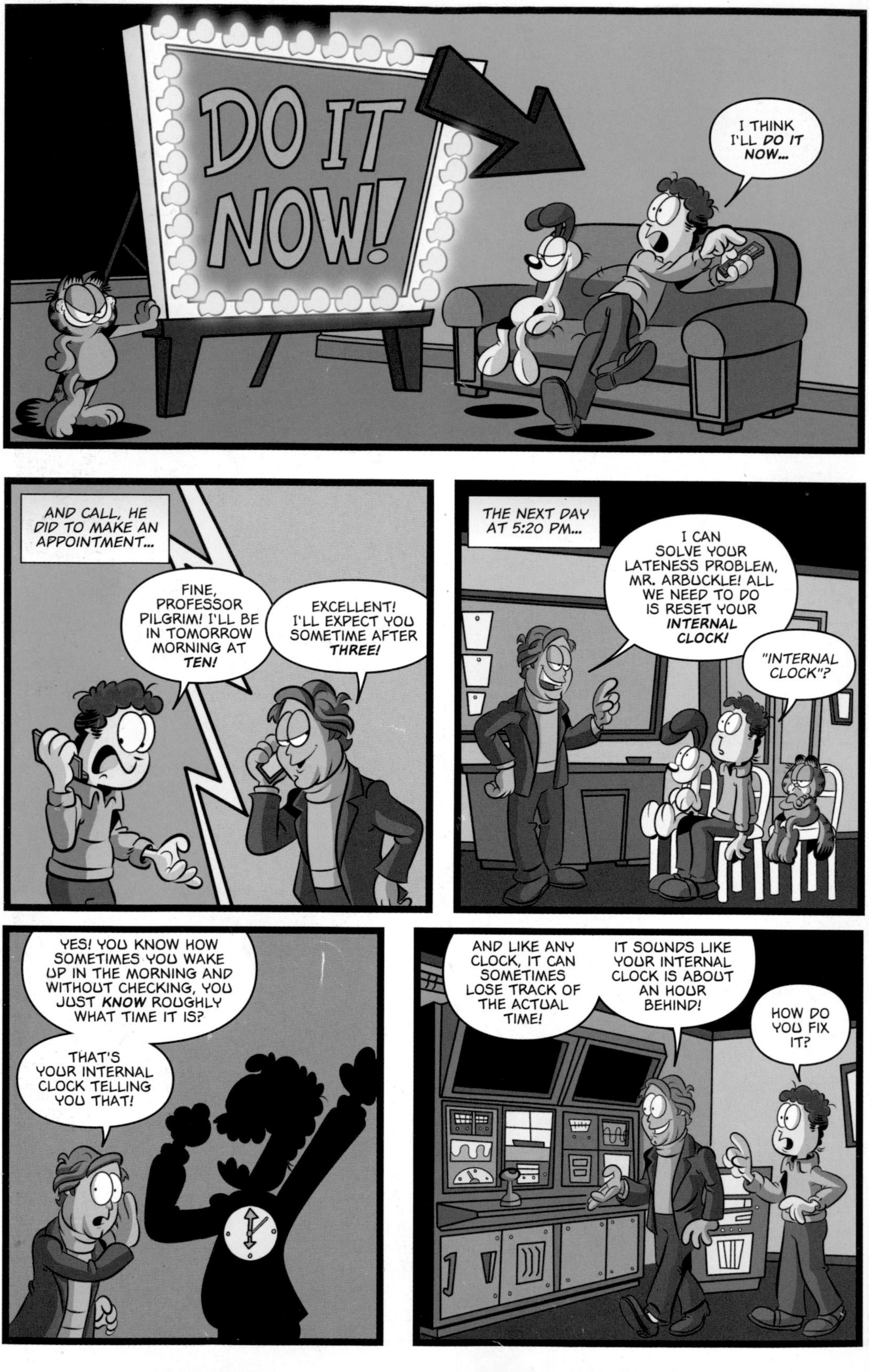
DO IT NOW!
I THINK I'LL DO IT NOW...
AND CALL, HE DID TO MAKE AN APPOINTMENT...
FINE, PROFESSOR PILGRIM! I'LL BE IN TOMORROW MORNING AT TEN!
EXCELLENT! I'LL EXPECT YOU SOMETIME AFTER THREE!
THE NEXT DAY AT 5:20 PM...
I CAN SOLVE YOUR LATENESS PROBLEM, MR. ARBUCKLE! ALL WE NEED TO DO IS RESET YOUR INTERNAL CLOCK!
"INTERNAL CLOCK"?
YES! YOU KNOW HOW SOMETIMES YOU WAKE UP IN THE MORNING AND WITHOUT CHECKING, YOU JUST KNOW ROUGHLY WHAT TIME IT IS?
THAT'S YOUR INTERNAL CLOCK TELLING YOU THAT!
AND LIKE ANY CLOCK, IT CAN SOMETIMES LOSE TRACK OF THE ACTUAL TIME!
IT SOUNDS LIKE YOUR INTERNAL CLOCK IS ABOUT AN HOUR BEHIND!
HOW DO YOU FIX IT?

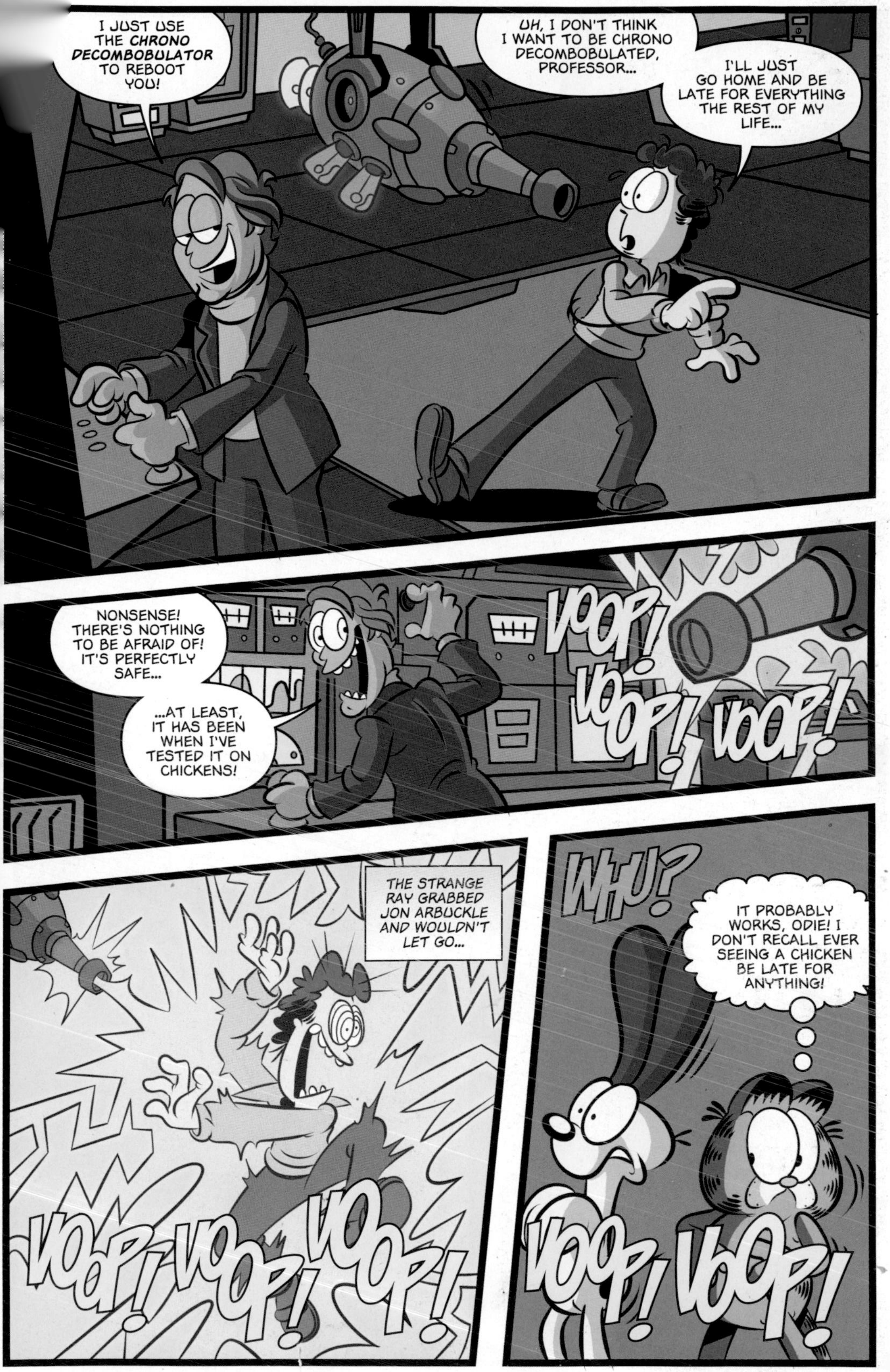
I JUST USE THE CHRONO DECOMBOBULATOR TO REBOOT YOU!
UH, I DON'T THINK I WANT TO BE CHRONO DECOMBOBULATED, PROFESSOR...
I'LL JUST GO HOME AND BE LATE FOR EVERYTHING THE REST OF MY LIFE...
NONSENSE! THERE'S NOTHING TO BE AFRAID OF! IT'S PERFECTLY SAFE...
...AT LEAST, IT HAS BEEN WHEN I'VE TESTED IT ON CHICKENS!
VOOP! VOOP! VOOP!
THE STRANGE RAY GRABBED JON ARBUCKLE AND WOULDN'T LET GO...
VOOP! VOOP! VOOP!
WHU?
IT PROBABLY WORKS, ODIE! I DON'T RECALL EVER SEEING A CHICKEN BE LATE FOR ANYTHING!
VOOP! VOOP!

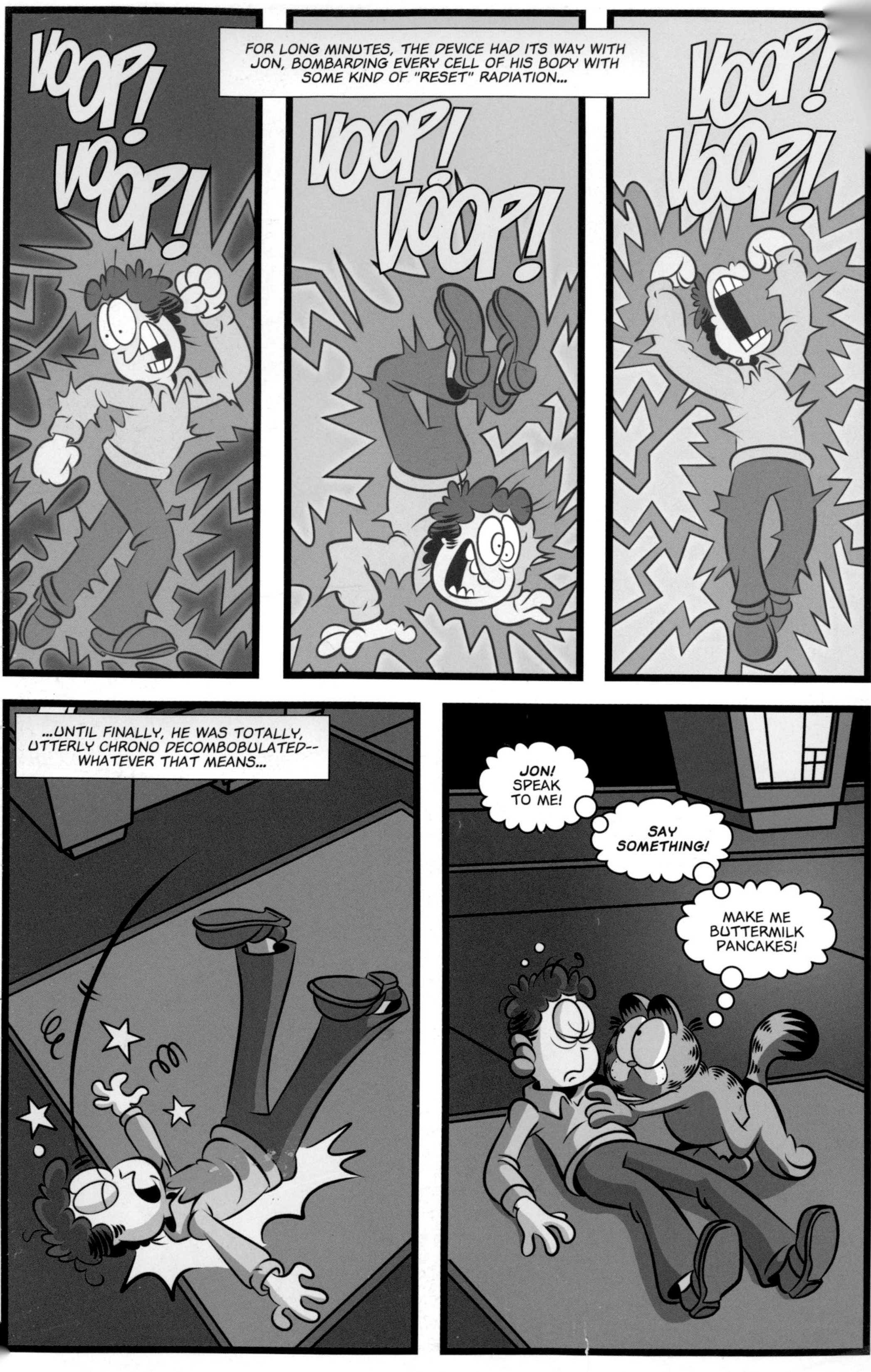
VOOP! VOOP!
FOR LONG MINUTES, THE DEVICE HAD ITS WAY WITH JON, BOMBARDING EVERY CELL OF HIS BODY WITH SOME KIND OF "RESET" RADIATION...
VOOP! VOOP!
VOOP! VOOP!
...UNTIL FINALLY, HE WAS TOTALLY, UTTERLY CHRONO DECOMBOBULATED-- WHATEVER THAT MEANS...
JON! SPEAK TO ME!
SAY SOMETHING!
MAKE ME BUTTERMILK PANCAKES!

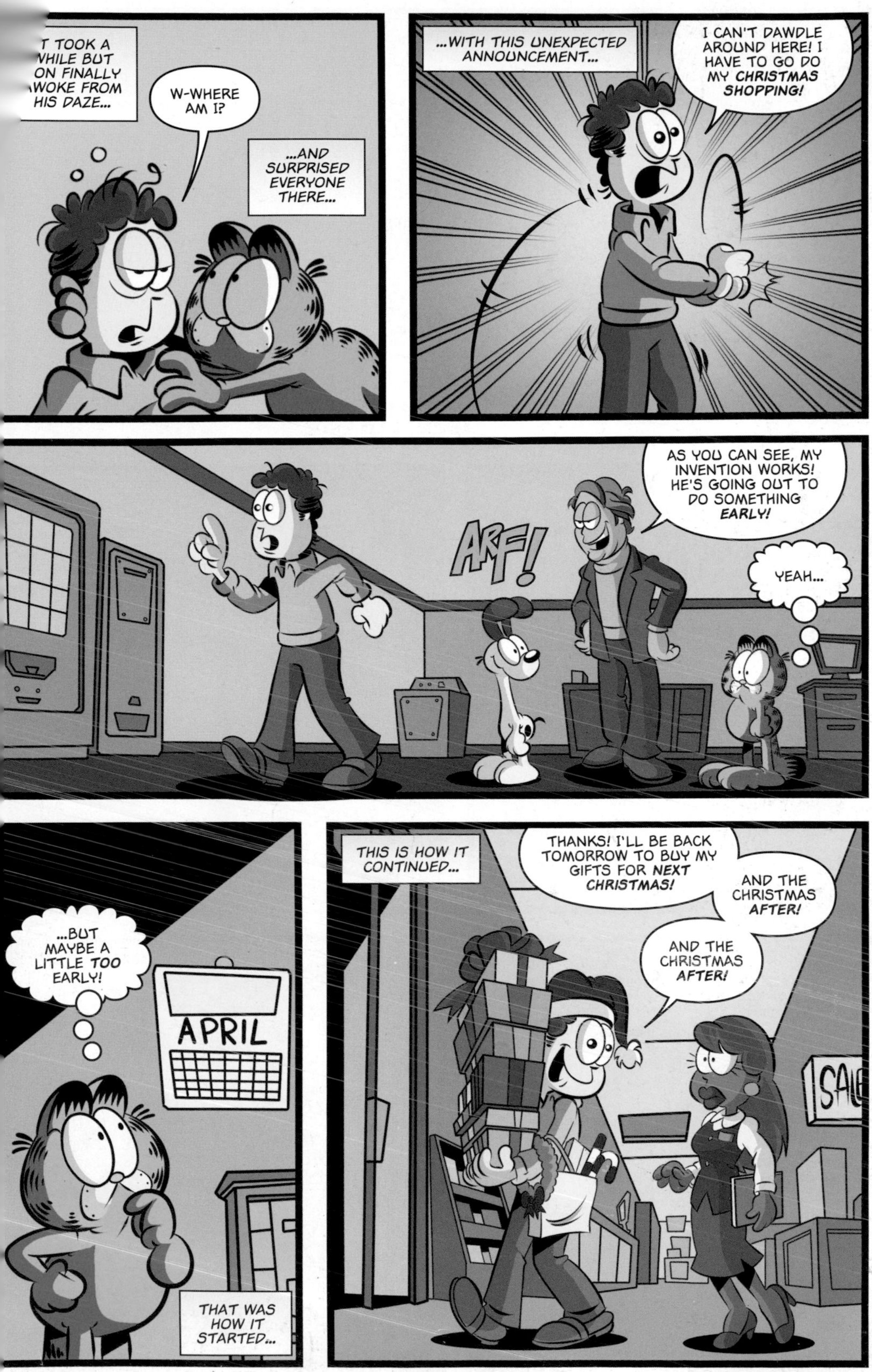

...T TOOK A ...WHILE BUT ...ON FINALLY ...WOKE FROM HIS DAZE...
W-WHERE AM I?
...AND SURPRISED EVERYONE THERE...
...WITH THIS UNEXPECTED ANNOUNCEMENT...
I CAN'T DAWDLE AROUND HERE! I HAVE TO GO DO MY CHRISTMAS SHOPPING!
AS YOU CAN SEE, MY INVENTION WORKS! HE'S GOING OUT TO DO SOMETHING EARLY!
ARF!
YEAH...
...BUT MAYBE A LITTLE TOO EARLY!
APRIL
THAT WAS HOW IT STARTED...
THIS IS HOW IT CONTINUED...
THANKS! I'LL BE BACK TOMORROW TO BUY MY GIFTS FOR NEXT CHRISTMAS!
AND THE CHRISTMAS AFTER!
AND THE CHRISTMAS AFTER!
SALE

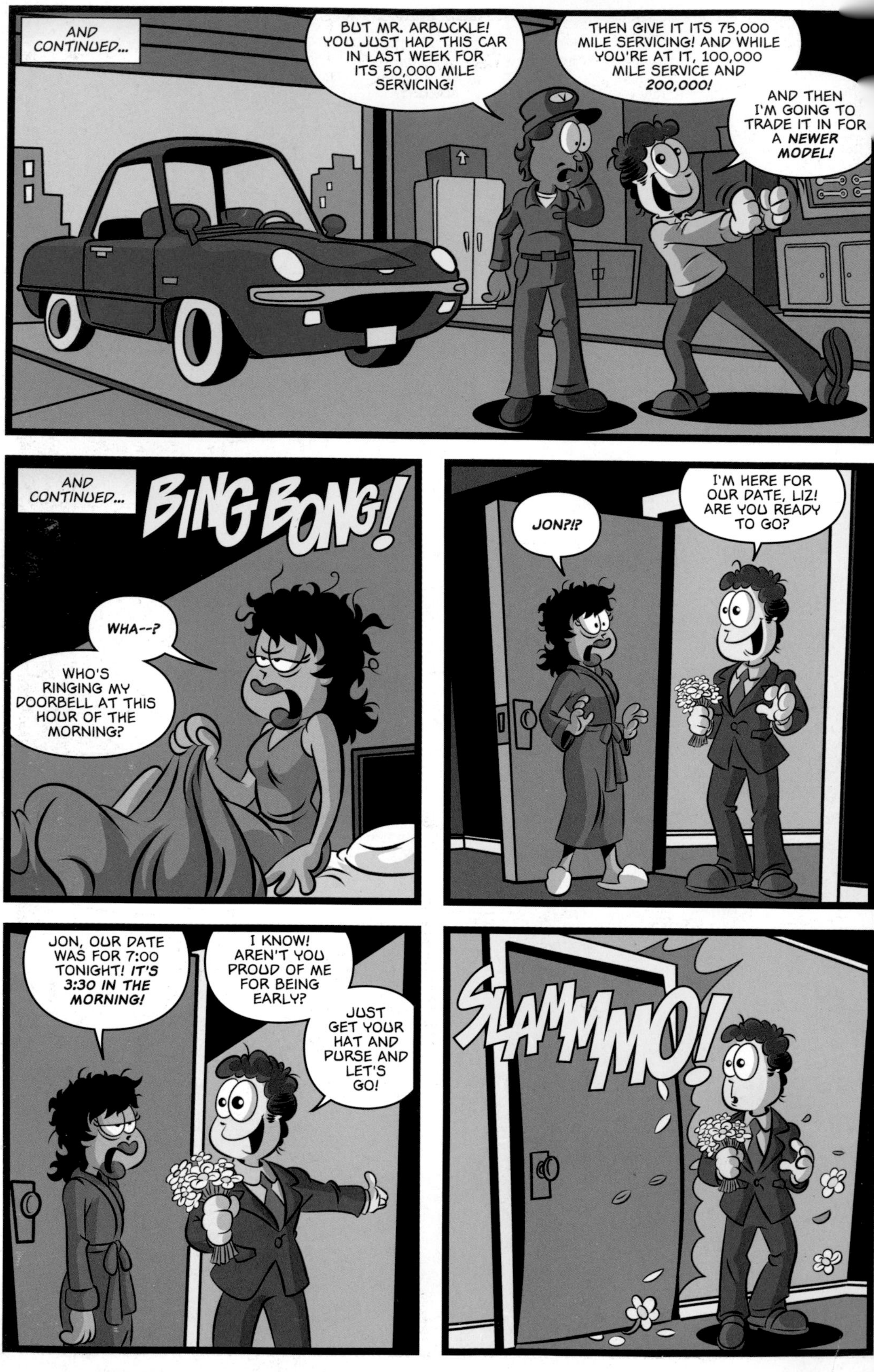
AND CONTINUED...
BUT MR. ARBUCKLE! YOU JUST HAD THIS CAR IN LAST WEEK FOR ITS 50,000 MILE SERVICING!
THEN GIVE IT ITS 75,000 MILE SERVICING! AND WHILE YOU'RE AT IT, 100,000 MILE SERVICE AND *200,000!*
AND THEN I'M GOING TO TRADE IT IN FOR A *NEWER MODEL!*
AND CONTINUED...
BING BONG!
WHA--?
WHO'S RINGING MY DOORBELL AT THIS HOUR OF THE MORNING?
JON?!?
I'M HERE FOR OUR DATE, LIZ! ARE YOU READY TO GO?
JON, OUR DATE WAS FOR 7:00 TONIGHT! *IT'S 3:30 IN THE MORNING!*
I KNOW! AREN'T YOU PROUD OF ME FOR BEING EARLY?
JUST GET YOUR HAT AND PURSE AND LET'S GO!
SLAMMMO!

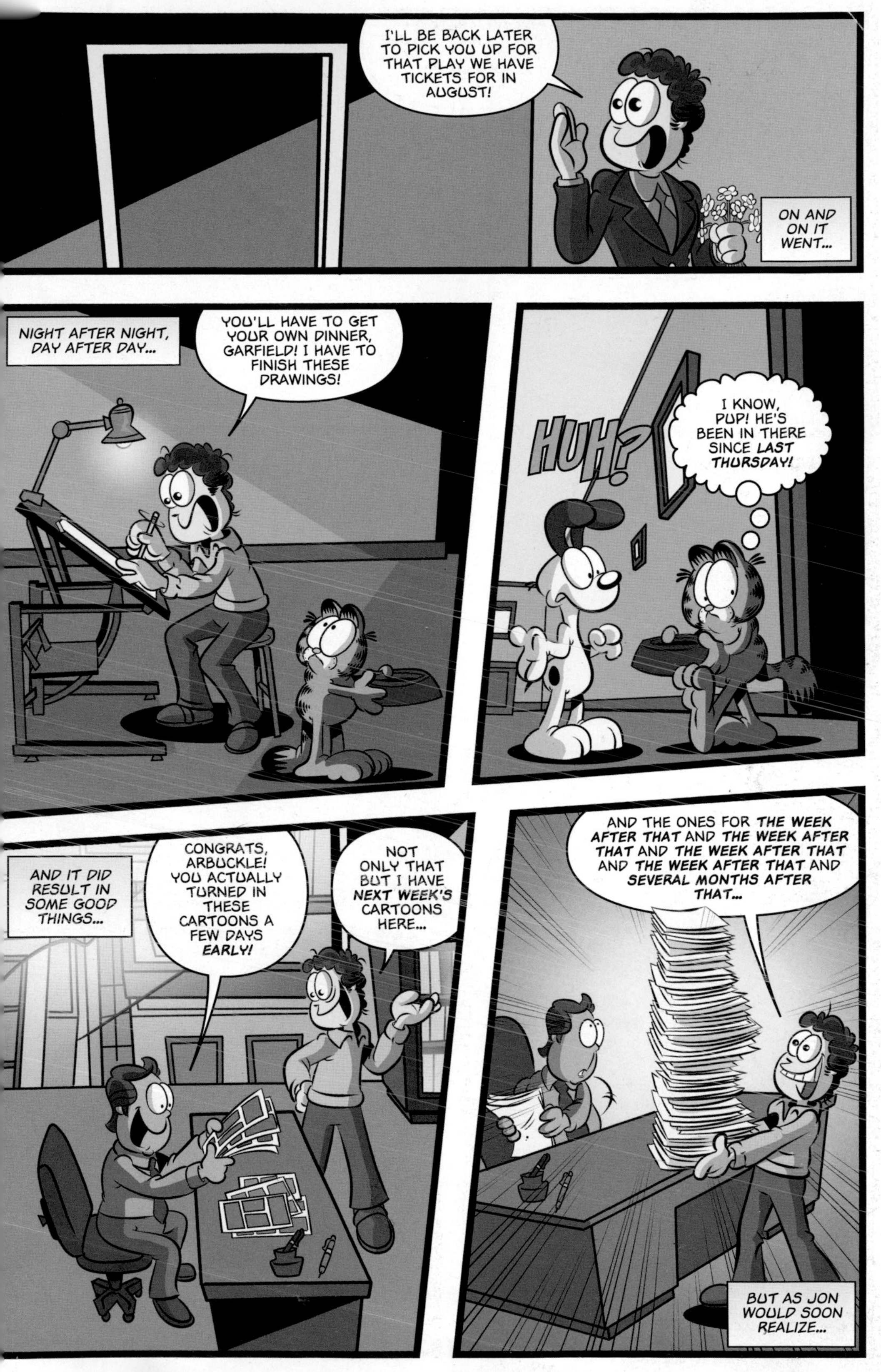
I'LL BE BACK LATER TO PICK YOU UP FOR THAT PLAY WE HAVE TICKETS FOR IN AUGUST!
ON AND ON IT WENT...
NIGHT AFTER NIGHT, DAY AFTER DAY...
YOU'LL HAVE TO GET YOUR OWN DINNER, GARFIELD! I HAVE TO FINISH THESE DRAWINGS!
HUH?
I KNOW, PUP! HE'S BEEN IN THERE SINCE LAST THURSDAY!
AND IT DID RESULT IN SOME GOOD THINGS...
CONGRATS, ARBUCKLE! YOU ACTUALLY TURNED IN THESE CARTOONS A FEW DAYS EARLY!
NOT ONLY THAT BUT I HAVE NEXT WEEK'S CARTOONS HERE...
AND THE ONES FOR THE WEEK AFTER THAT AND THE WEEK AFTER THAT AND THE WEEK AFTER THAT AND THE WEEK AFTER THAT AND SEVERAL MONTHS AFTER THAT...
BUT AS JON WOULD SOON REALIZE...

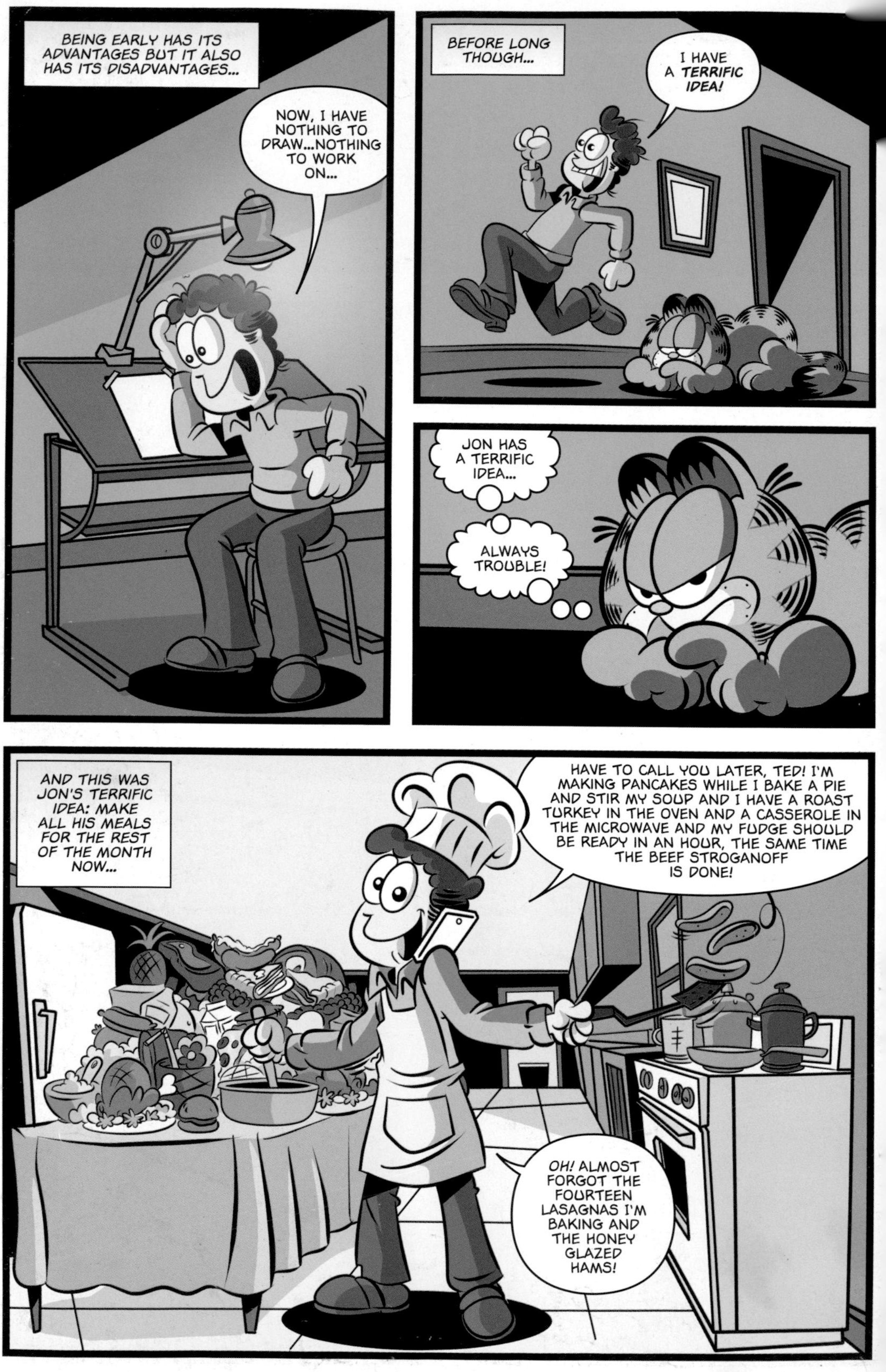
BEING EARLY HAS ITS ADVANTAGES BUT IT ALSO HAS ITS DISADVANTAGES...
NOW, I HAVE NOTHING TO DRAW...NOTHING TO WORK ON...
BEFORE LONG THOUGH...
I HAVE A TERRIFIC IDEA!
JON HAS A TERRIFIC IDEA...
ALWAYS TROUBLE!
AND THIS WAS JON'S TERRIFIC IDEA: MAKE ALL HIS MEALS FOR THE REST OF THE MONTH NOW...
HAVE TO CALL YOU LATER, TED! I'M MAKING PANCAKES WHILE I BAKE A PIE AND STIR MY SOUP AND I HAVE A ROAST TURKEY IN THE OVEN AND A CASSEROLE IN THE MICROWAVE AND MY FUDGE SHOULD BE READY IN AN HOUR, THE SAME TIME THE BEEF STROGANOFF IS DONE!
OH! ALMOST FORGOT THE FOURTEEN LASAGNAS I'M BAKING AND THE HONEY GLAZED HAMS!

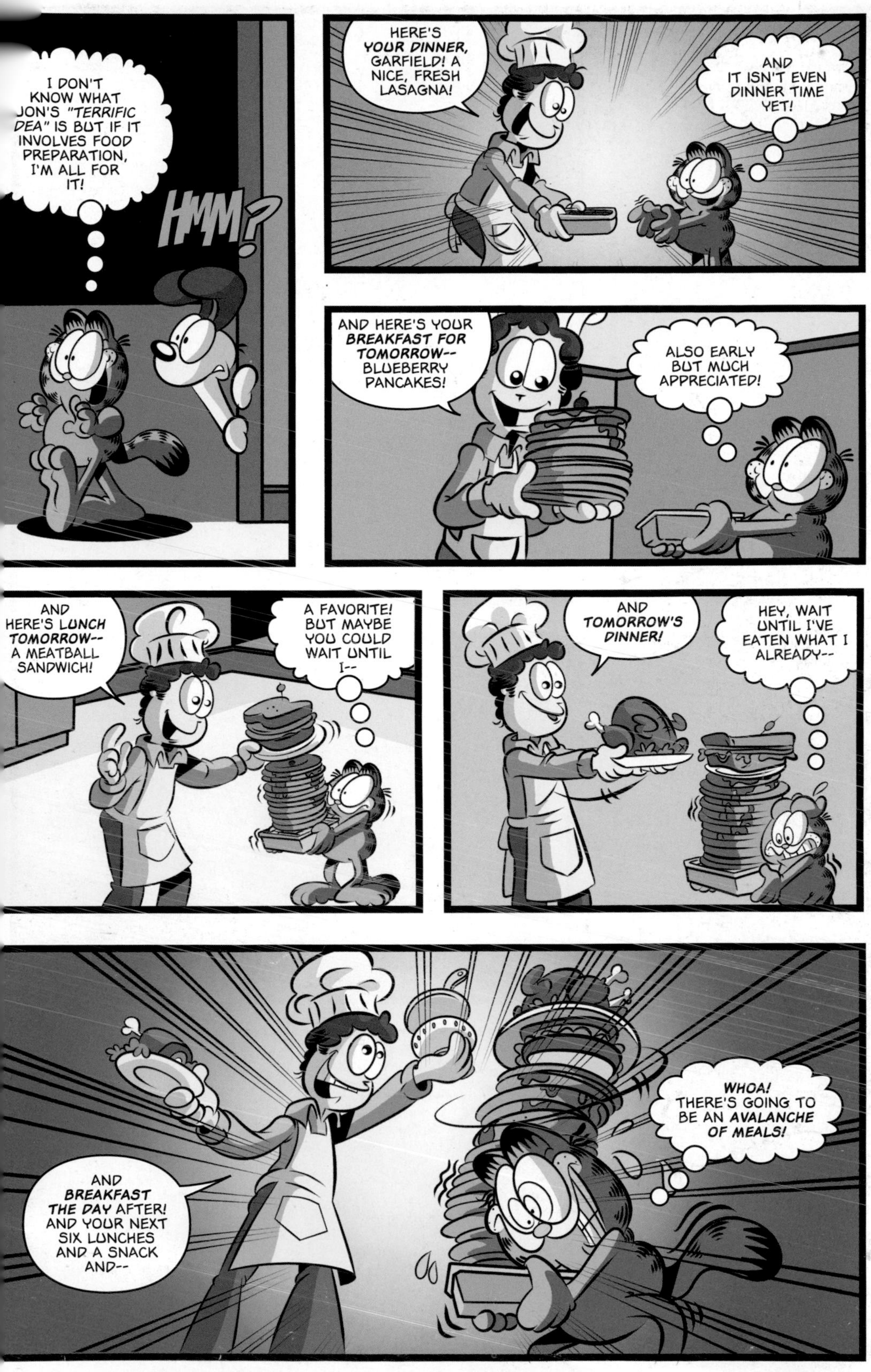

I DON'T KNOW WHAT JON'S "TERRIFIC IDEA" IS BUT IF IT INVOLVES FOOD PREPARATION, I'M ALL FOR IT!
HMM?
HERE'S YOUR DINNER, GARFIELD! A NICE, FRESH LASAGNA!
AND IT ISN'T EVEN DINNER TIME YET!
AND HERE'S YOUR BREAKFAST FOR TOMORROW-- BLUEBERRY PANCAKES!
ALSO EARLY BUT MUCH APPRECIATED!
AND HERE'S LUNCH TOMORROW-- A MEATBALL SANDWICH!
A FAVORITE! BUT MAYBE YOU COULD WAIT UNTIL I--
AND TOMORROW'S DINNER!
HEY, WAIT UNTIL I'VE EATEN WHAT I ALREADY--
WHOA! THERE'S GOING TO BE AN AVALANCHE OF MEALS!
AND BREAKFAST THE DAY AFTER! AND YOUR NEXT SIX LUNCHES AND A SNACK AND--

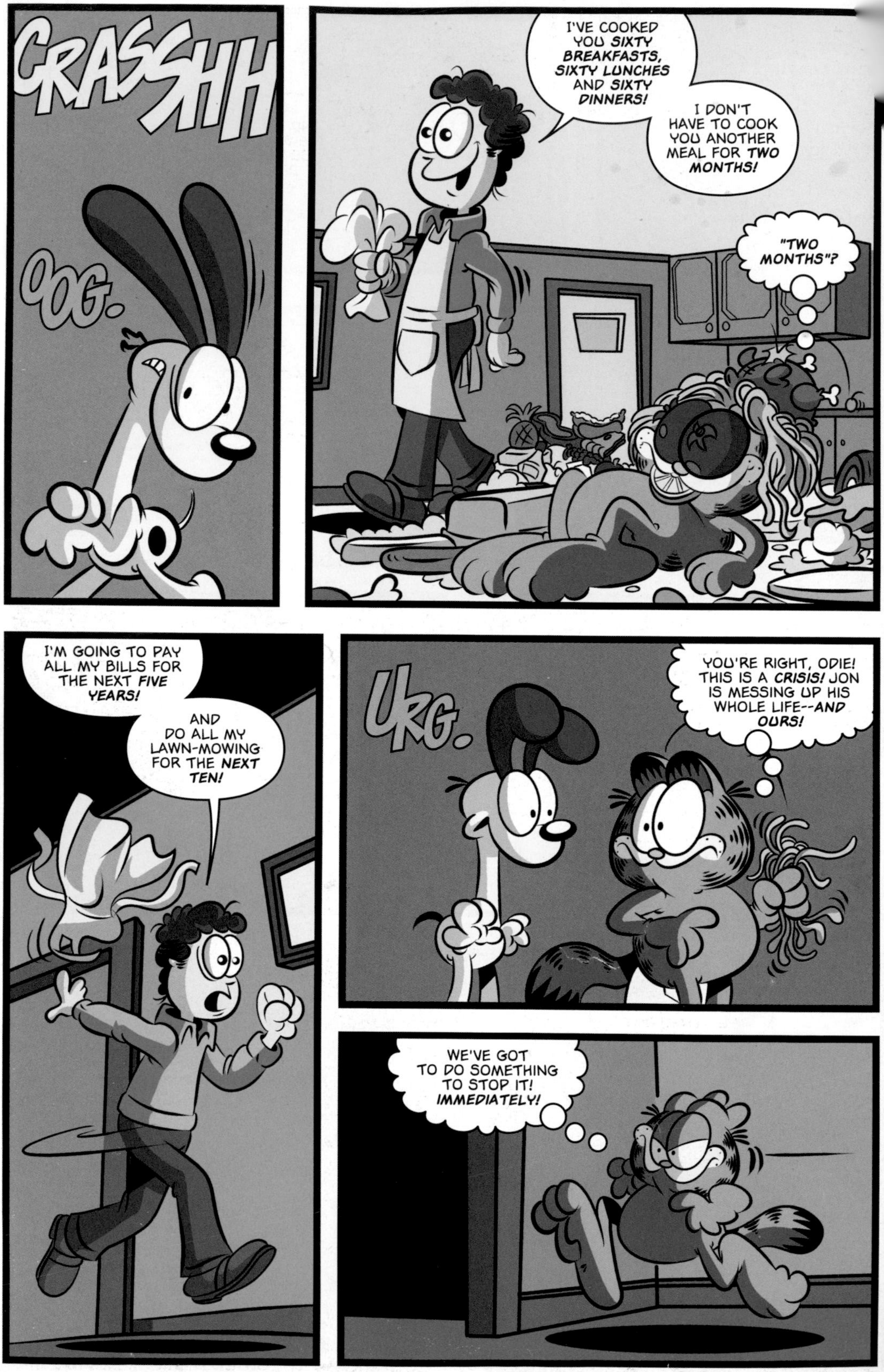
CRASSHH
OOG.
I'VE COOKED YOU SIXTY BREAKFASTS, SIXTY LUNCHES AND SIXTY DINNERS!
I DON'T HAVE TO COOK YOU ANOTHER MEAL FOR TWO MONTHS!
"TWO MONTHS"?
I'M GOING TO PAY ALL MY BILLS FOR THE NEXT FIVE YEARS!
AND DO ALL MY LAWN-MOWING FOR THE NEXT TEN!
URG.
YOU'RE RIGHT, ODIE! THIS IS A CRISIS! JON IS MESSING UP HIS WHOLE LIFE--AND OURS!
WE'VE GOT TO DO SOMETHING TO STOP IT! IMMEDIATELY!

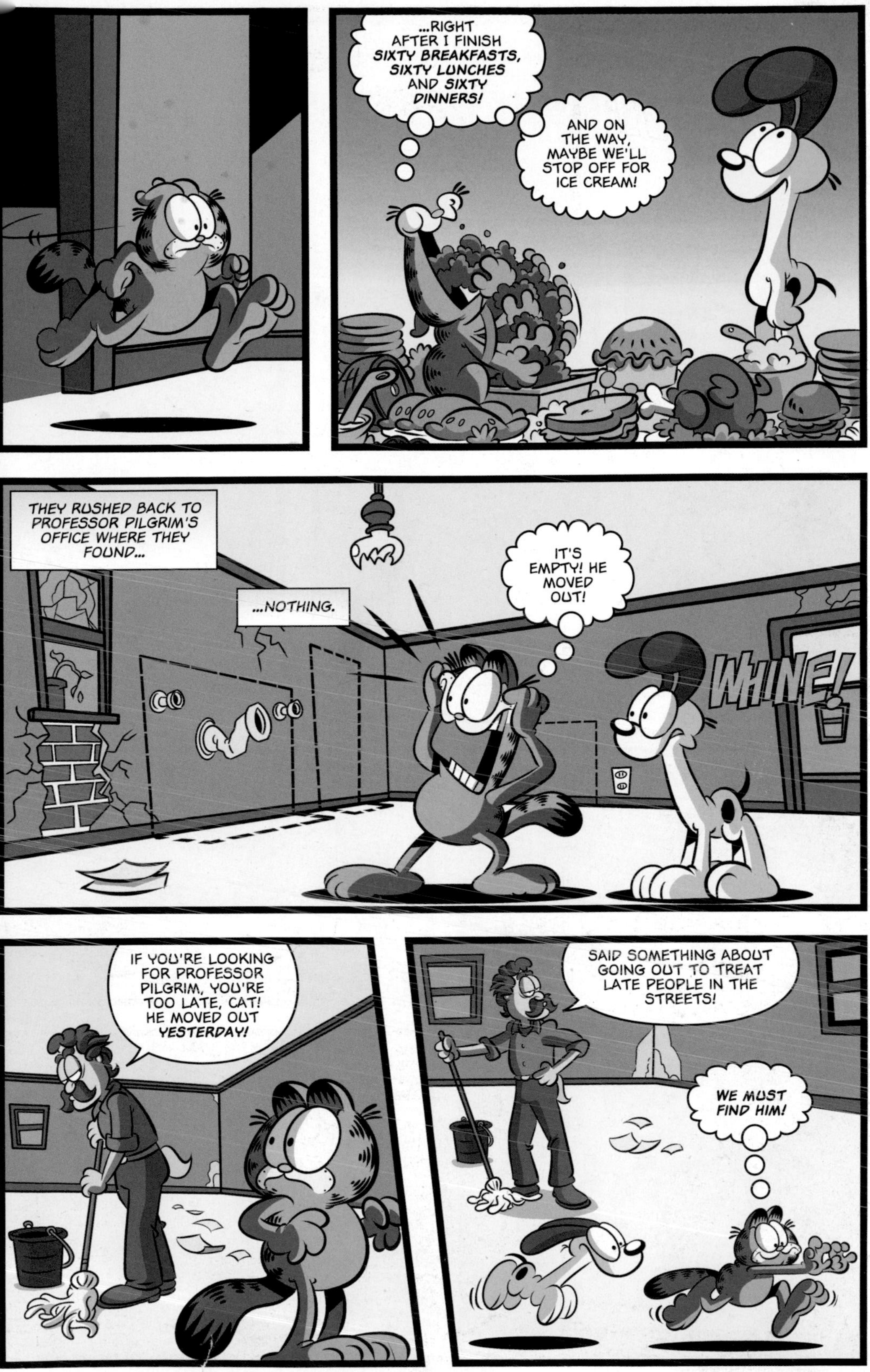

...RIGHT AFTER I FINISH SIXTY BREAKFASTS, SIXTY LUNCHES AND SIXTY DINNERS!
AND ON THE WAY, MAYBE WE'LL STOP OFF FOR ICE CREAM!
THEY RUSHED BACK TO PROFESSOR PILGRIM'S OFFICE WHERE THEY FOUND...
...NOTHING.
IT'S EMPTY! HE MOVED OUT!
WHINE!
IF YOU'RE LOOKING FOR PROFESSOR PILGRIM, YOU'RE TOO LATE, CAT! HE MOVED OUT YESTERDAY!
SAID SOMETHING ABOUT GOING OUT TO TREAT LATE PEOPLE IN THE STREETS!
WE MUST FIND HIM!

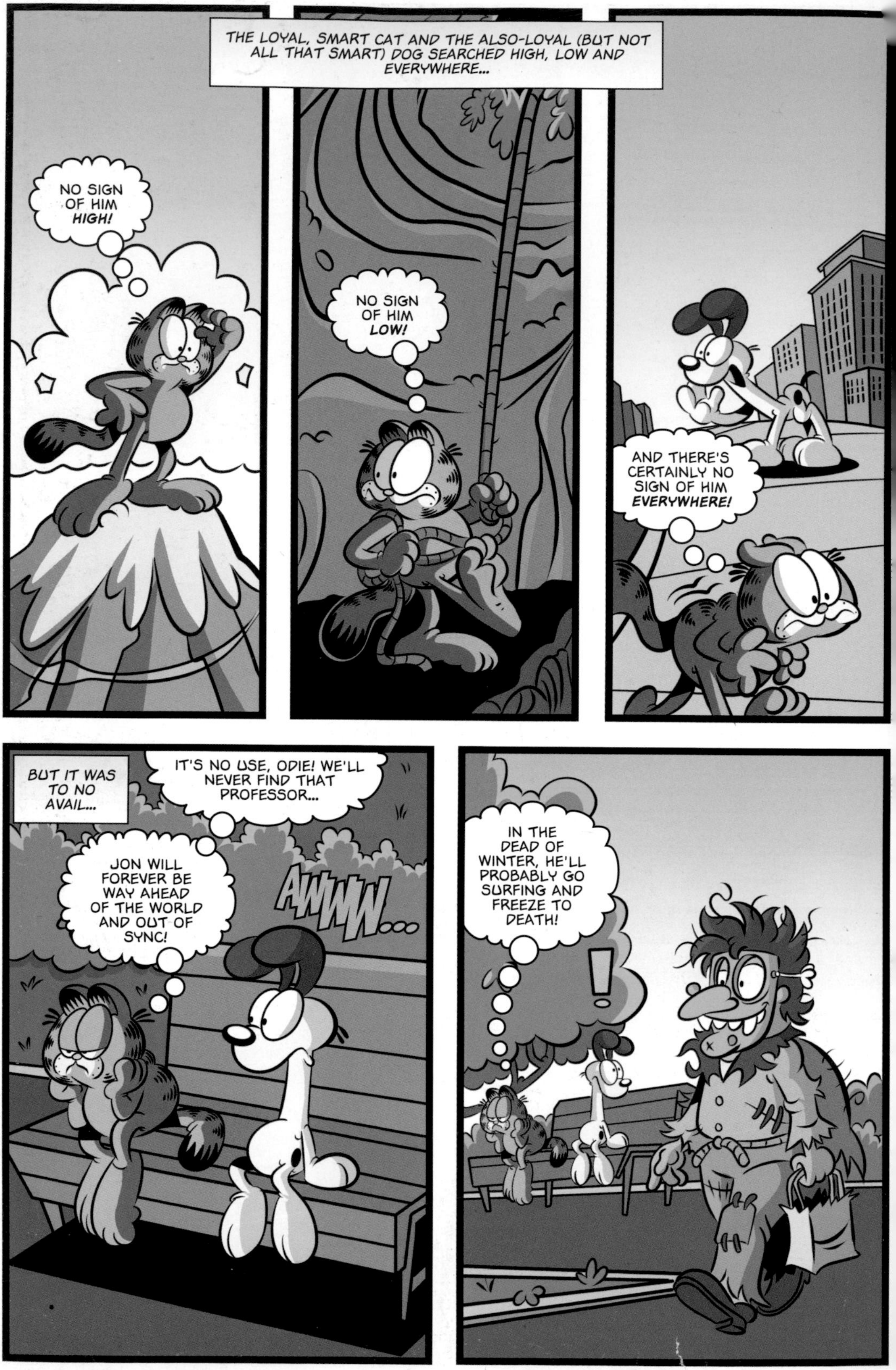
THE LOYAL, SMART CAT AND THE ALSO-LOYAL (BUT NOT ALL THAT SMART) DOG SEARCHED HIGH, LOW AND EVERYWHERE...
NO SIGN OF HIM HIGH!
NO SIGN OF HIM LOW!
AND THERE'S CERTAINLY NO SIGN OF HIM EVERYWHERE!
BUT IT WAS TO NO AVAIL...
IT'S NO USE, ODIE! WE'LL NEVER FIND THAT PROFESSOR...
JON WILL FOREVER BE WAY AHEAD OF THE WORLD AND OUT OF SYNC!
AWWW...
IN THE DEAD OF WINTER, HE'LL PROBABLY GO SURFING AND FREEZE TO DEATH!
!

ARF ARF! ARF ARF ARF ARF ARF ARF ARF ARF ARF ARF ARF ARF ARF ARF ARF!

DON'T YOU ARF AT ME, PUP! SO WHAT IF THERE'S A GUY TRICK-OR-TREATING SIX MONTHS EARLY! I DON'T CARE IF HE--

"SIX MONTHS EARLY"?

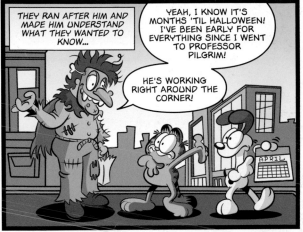

THEY RAN AFTER HIM AND MADE HIM UNDERSTAND WHAT THEY WANTED TO KNOW...

YEAH, I KNOW IT'S MONTHS 'TIL HALLOWEEN! I'VE BEEN EARLY FOR EVERYTHING SINCE I WENT TO PROFESSOR PILGRIM!

HE'S WORKING RIGHT AROUND THE CORNER!

COME ON, ODIE! HE'S RIGHT AROUND THE CORNER!

YEAH! YEAH!

THE PROFESSOR WASN'T AROUND THE CORNER BUT SANTA CLAUS WAS...

YEAH, THE PROFESSOR'S MACHINE HAS MADE ME EARLY FOR EVERYTHING! HE'S RIGHT OUTSIDE THE BUS DEPOT!

BUS DEPOT! GOT IT!

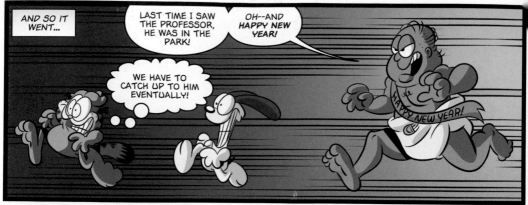

AND SO IT WENT...

LAST TIME I SAW THE PROFESSOR, HE WAS IN THE PARK!

OH--AND HAPPY NEW YEAR!

WE HAVE TO CATCH UP TO HIM EVENTUALLY!

HAPPY NEW YEAR!

AND SURE ENOUGH...

WHAT ARE YOU TRYING TO TELL ME, CAT? SOMETHING IS WRONG WITH YOUR FRIEND I CHRONO DECOMBOBULATED?

COME ON! SEE FOR YOURSELF!

WAIT! LET ME BRING MY PORTABLE CHRONO DECOMBOBULATOR ALONG!

IT DIDN'T TAKE LONG FOR THE PROFESSOR TO REALIZE WHAT A SHAMBLES JON HAD MADE OF HIS LIFE...

I JUST FINISHED WRITING MY DIARY FOR THE NEXT EIGHT YEARS!

I CAN'T WAIT TO READ IT AND FIND OUT WHAT'S GOING TO HAPPEN TO ME!

OH, DEAR! OH, DEAR! OH, DEAR!

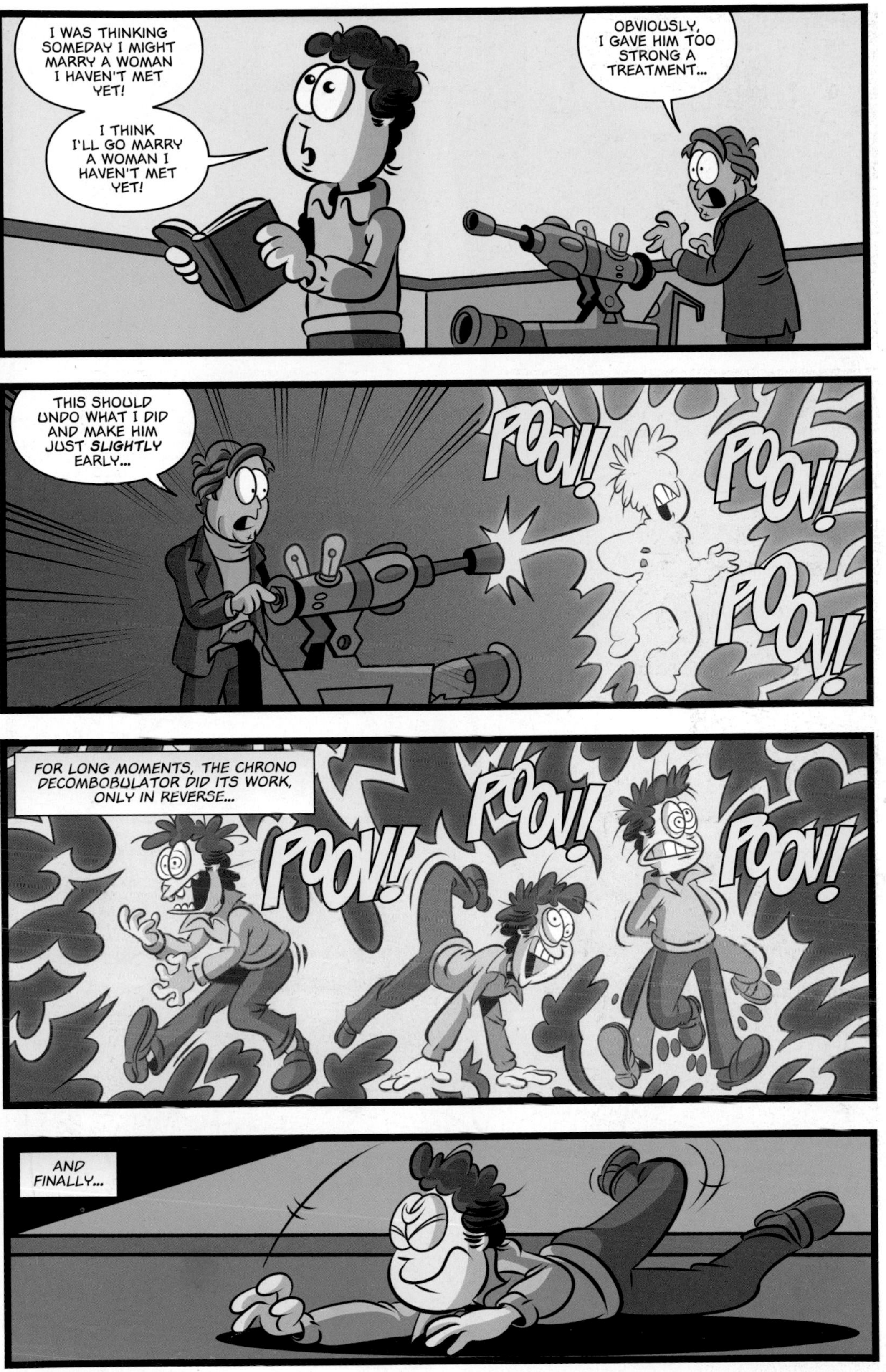
I WAS THINKING SOMEDAY I MIGHT MARRY A WOMAN I HAVEN'T MET YET!
I THINK I'LL GO MARRY A WOMAN I HAVEN'T MET YET!
OBVIOUSLY, I GAVE HIM TOO STRONG A TREATMENT...
THIS SHOULD UNDO WHAT I DID AND MAKE HIM JUST SLIGHTLY EARLY...
POOV!
POOV!
POOV!
FOR LONG MOMENTS, THE CHRONO DECOMBOBULATOR DID ITS WORK, ONLY IN REVERSE...
POOV!
POOV!
POOV!
AND FINALLY...

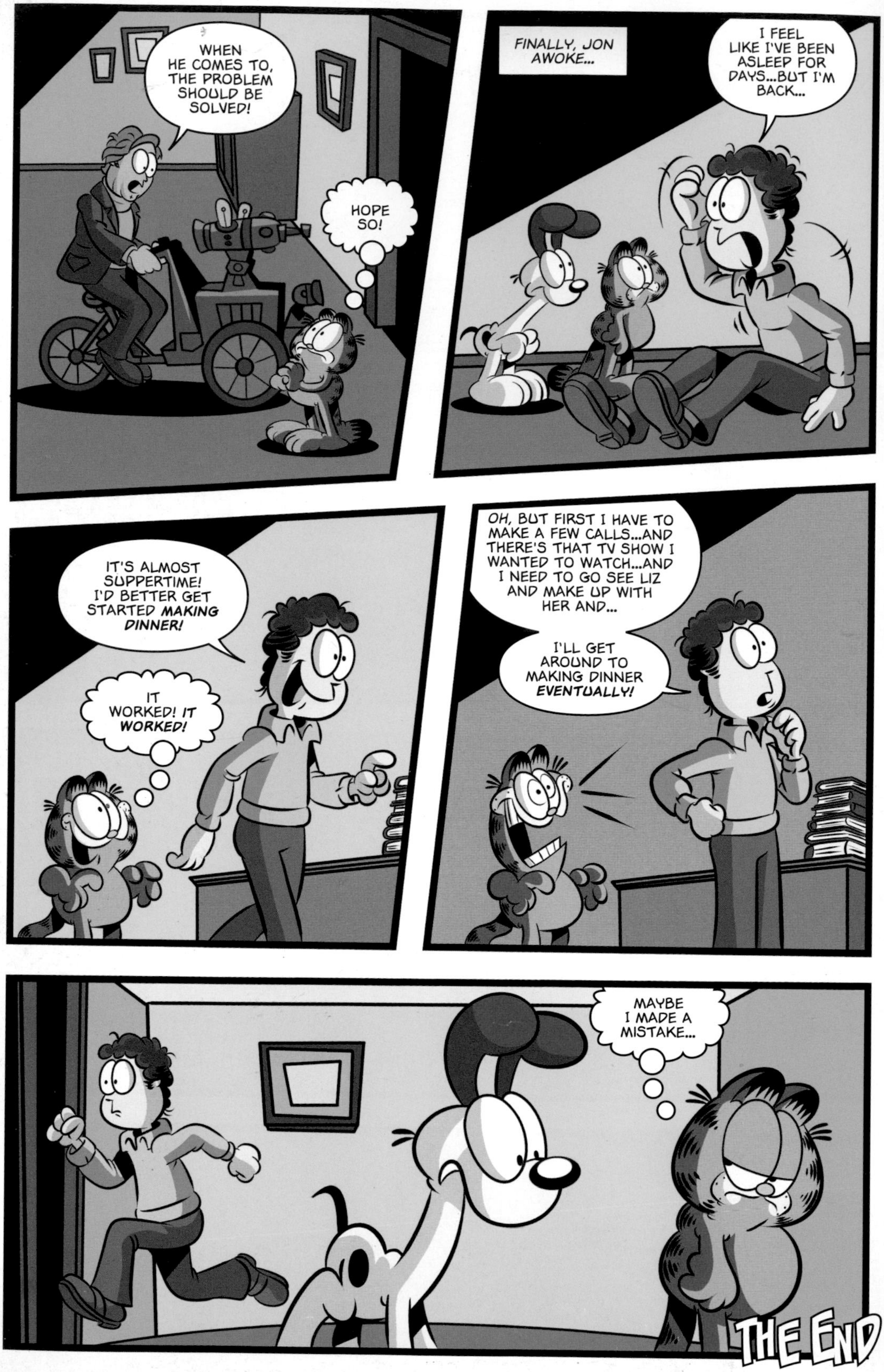
WHEN HE COMES TO, THE PROBLEM SHOULD BE SOLVED!
HOPE SO!
FINALLY, JON AWOKE...
I FEEL LIKE I'VE BEEN ASLEEP FOR DAYS...BUT I'M BACK...
IT'S ALMOST SUPPERTIME! I'D BETTER GET STARTED MAKING DINNER!
IT WORKED! IT WORKED!
OH, BUT FIRST I HAVE TO MAKE A FEW CALLS...AND THERE'S THAT TV SHOW I WANTED TO WATCH...AND I NEED TO GO SEE LIZ AND MAKE UP WITH HER AND...
I'LL GET AROUND TO MAKING DINNER EVENTUALLY!
MAYBE I MADE A MISTAKE...
THE END

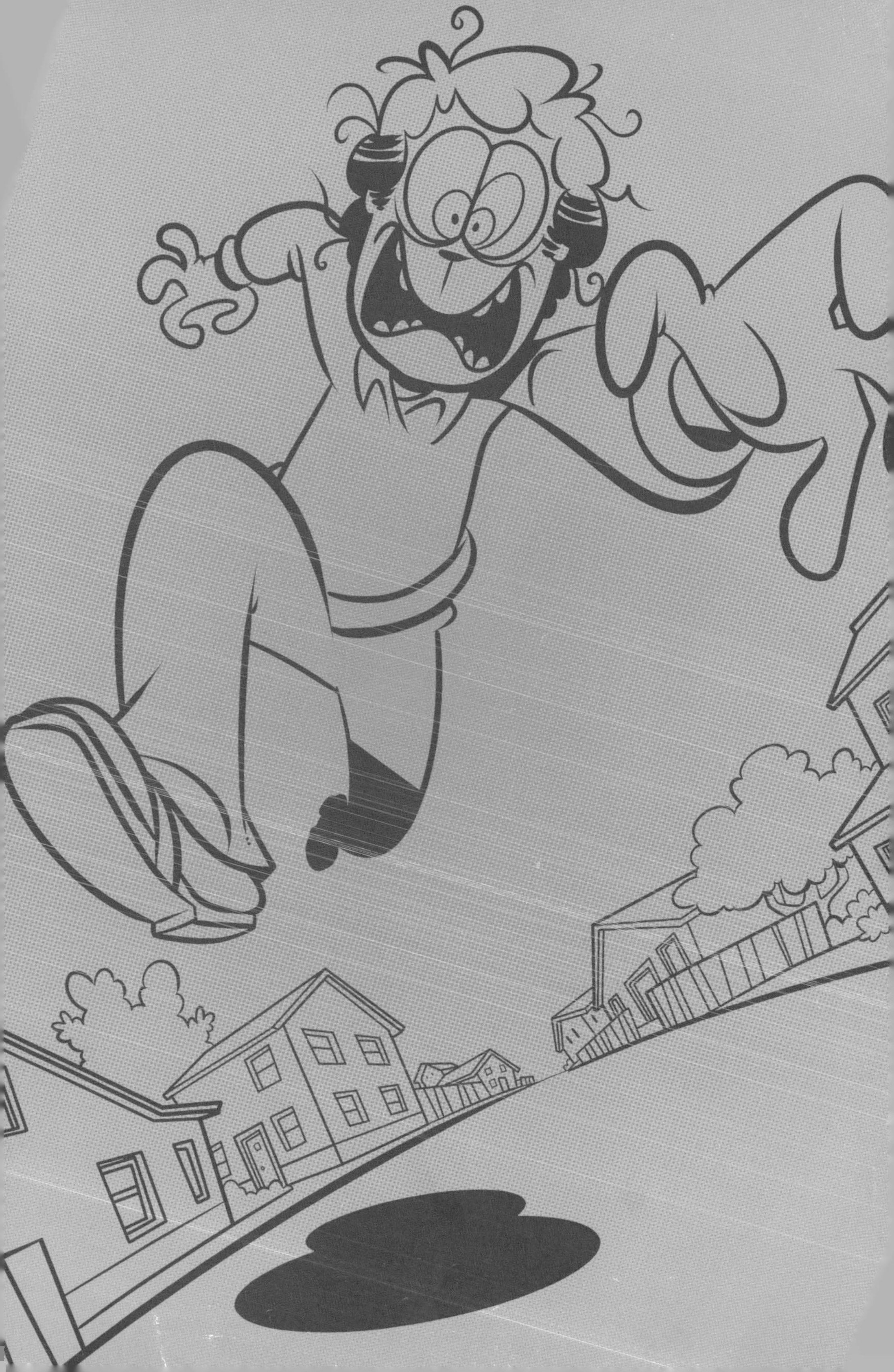

"ONLY HUMAN"

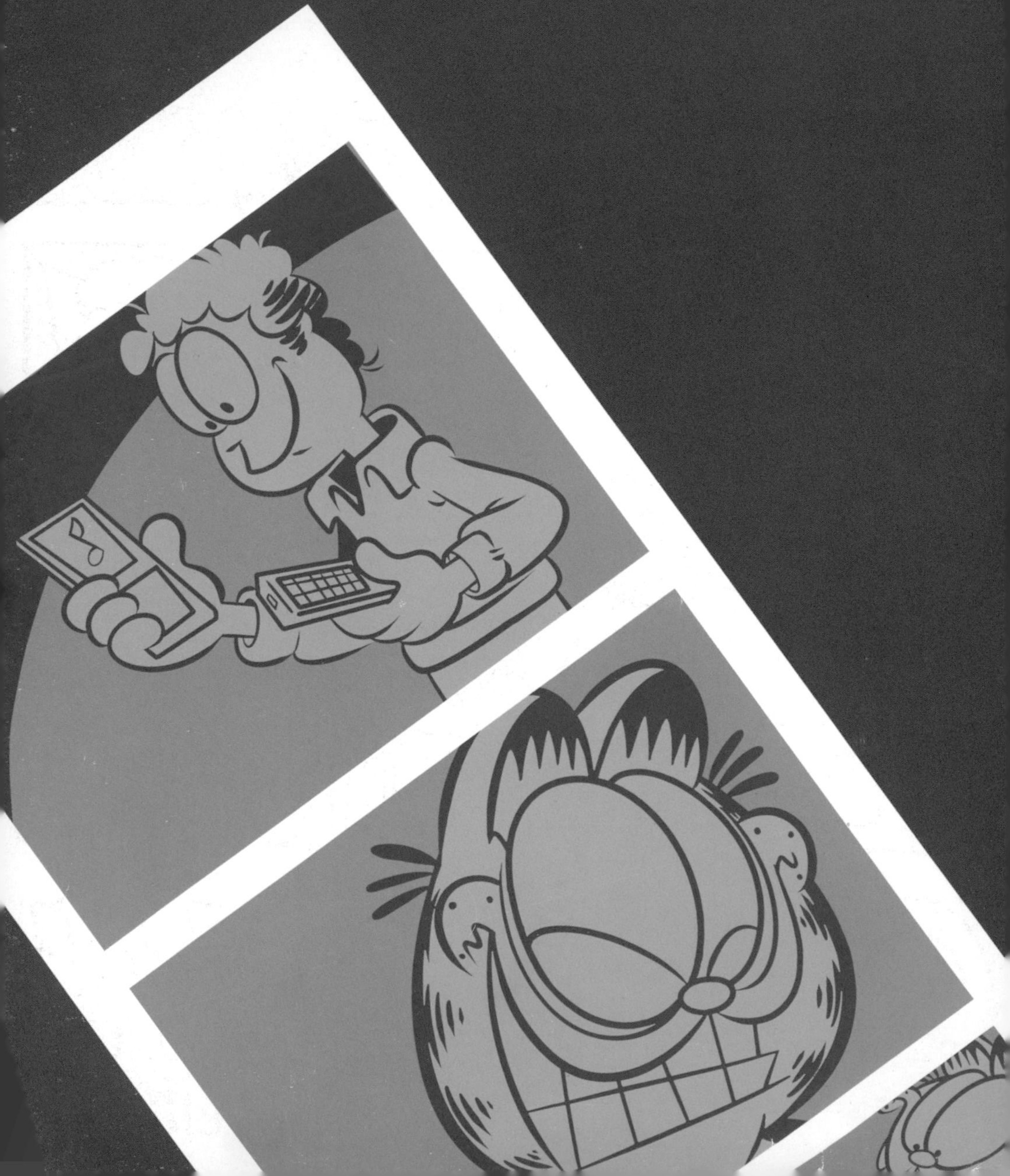

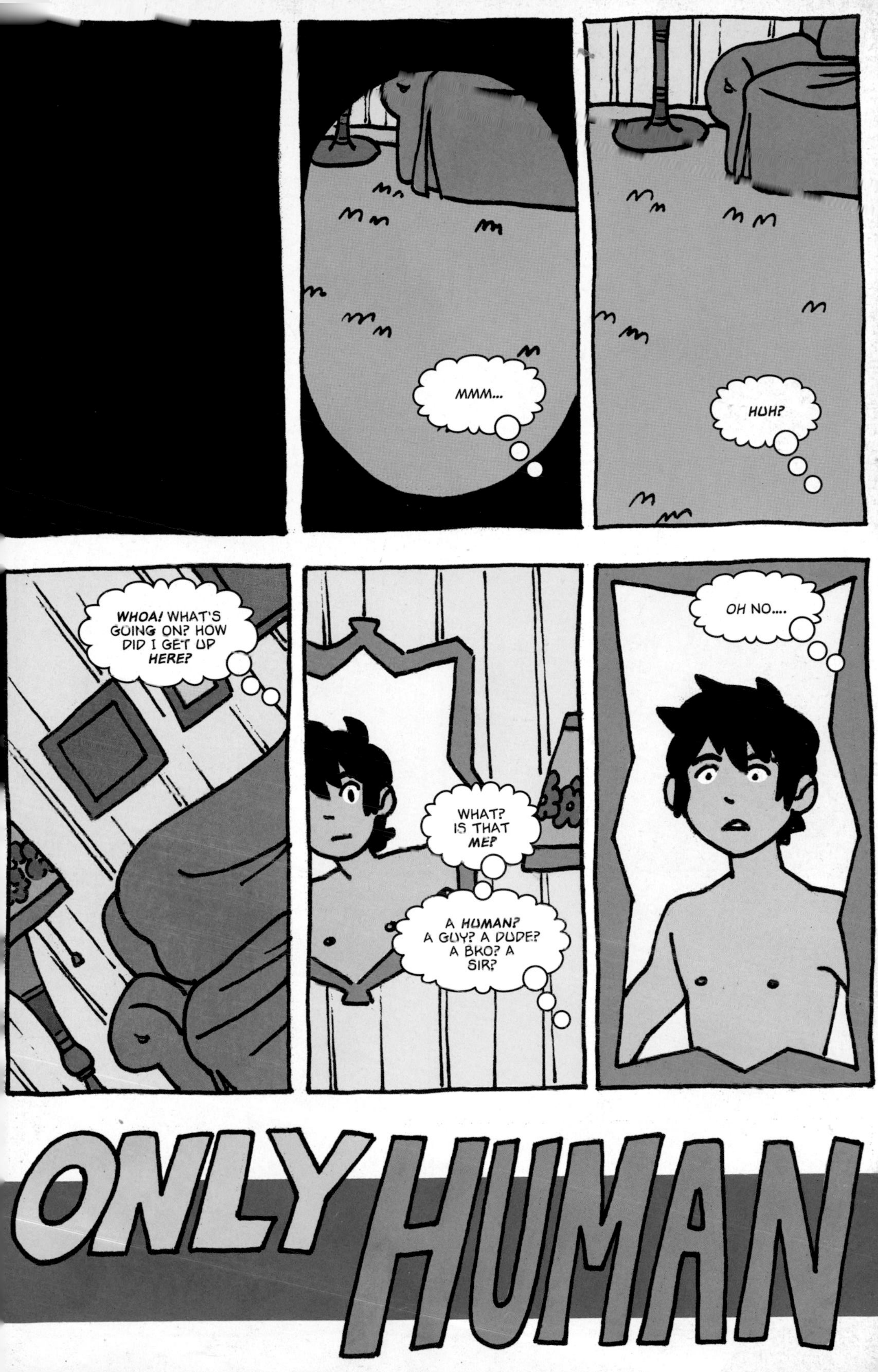
MMM...
HUH?
WHOA! WHAT'S GOING ON? HOW DID I GET UP HERE?
WHAT? IS THAT ME?
A HUMAN? A GUY? A DUDE? A BRO? A SIR?
OH NO....
ONLY HUMAN

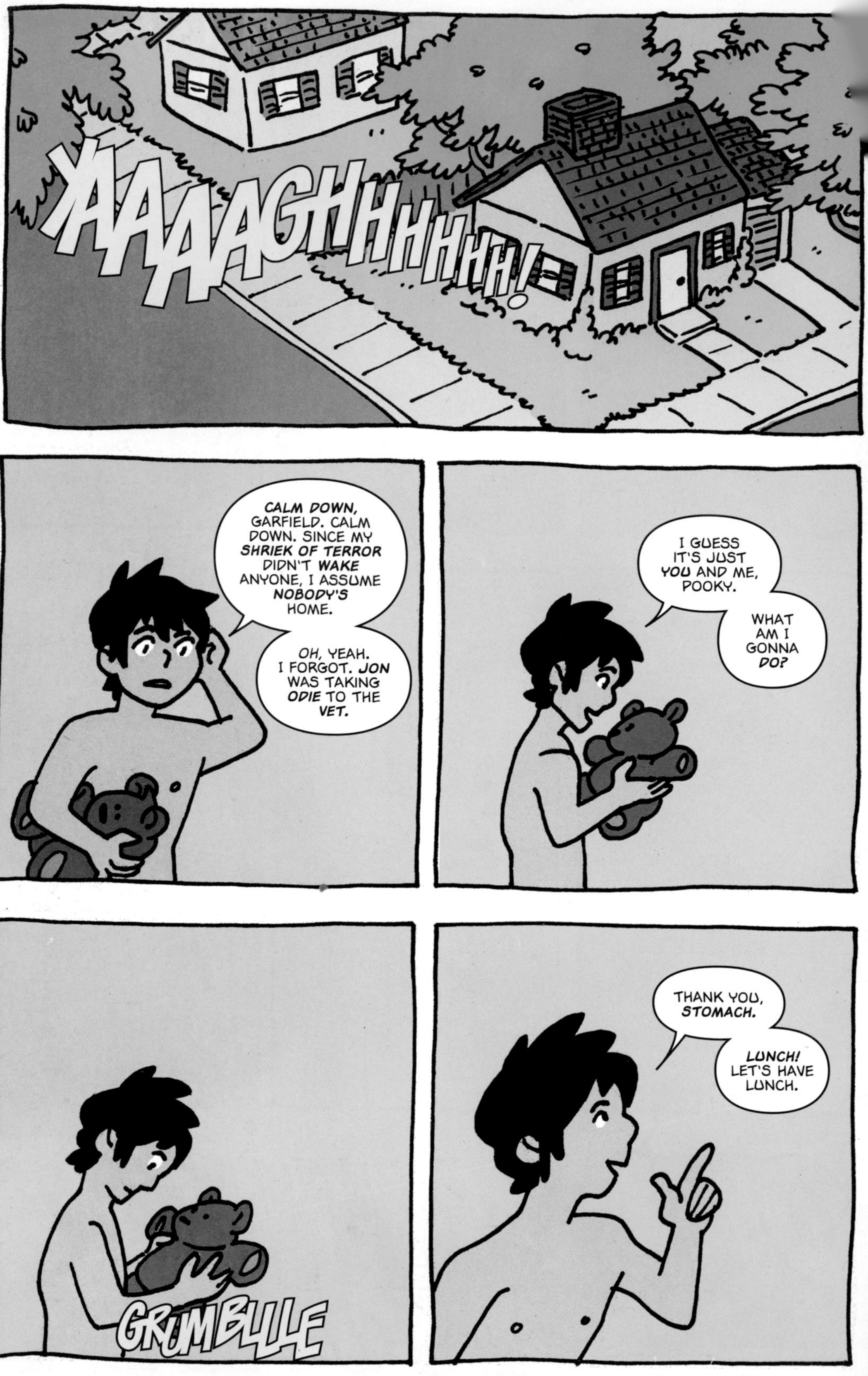
YAAAAGHHHHHH!
CALM DOWN, GARFIELD. CALM DOWN. SINCE MY SHRIEK OF TERROR DIDN'T WAKE ANYONE, I ASSUME NOBODY'S HOME.
OH, YEAH. I FORGOT. JON WAS TAKING ODIE TO THE VET.
I GUESS IT'S JUST YOU AND ME, POOKY.
WHAT AM I GONNA DO?
GRUMBLLLE
THANK YOU, STOMACH.
LUNCH! LET'S HAVE LUNCH.

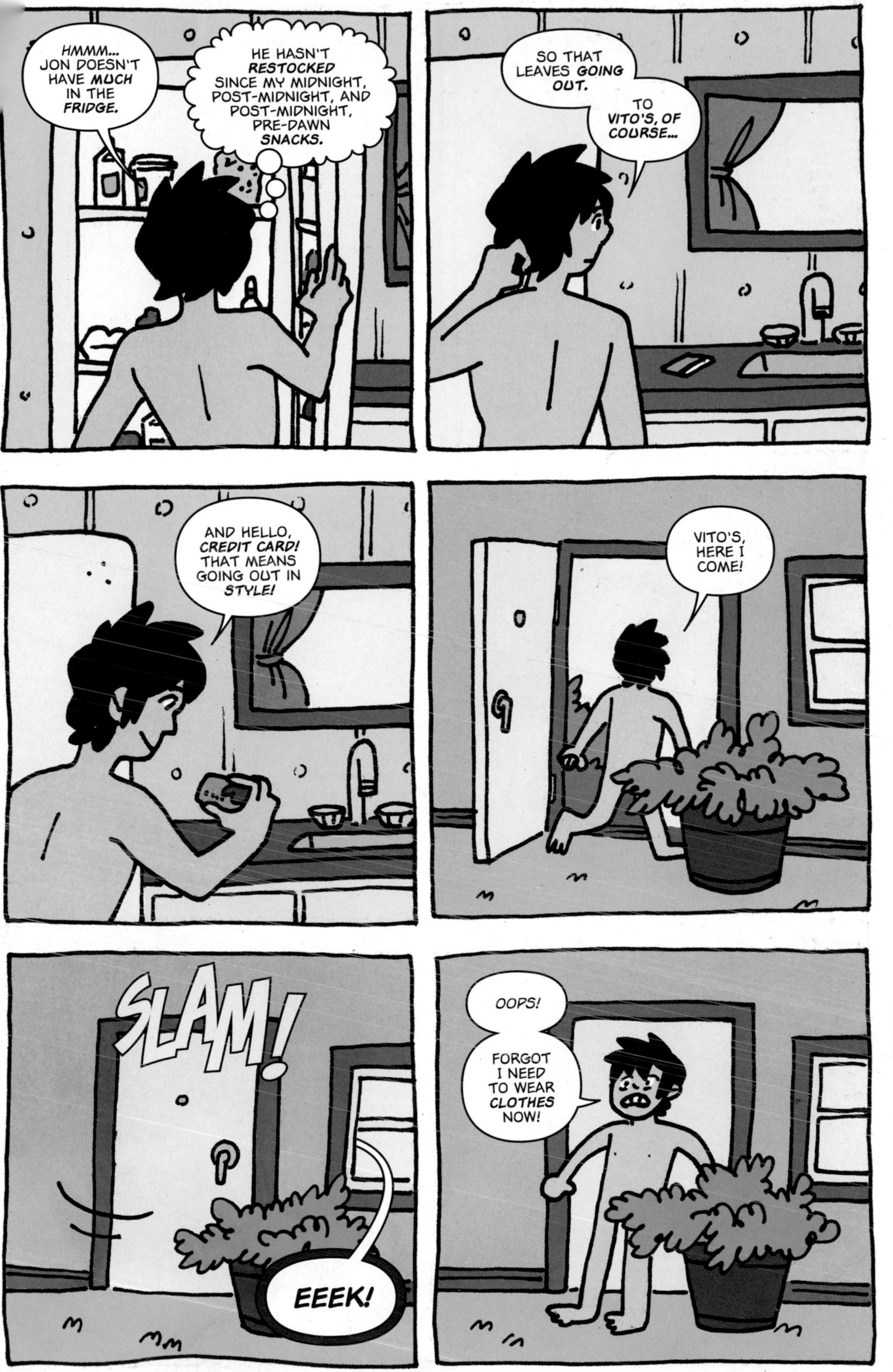
HMMM... JON DOESN'T HAVE MUCH IN THE FRIDGE.
HE HASN'T RESTOCKED SINCE MY MIDNIGHT, POST-MIDNIGHT, AND POST-MIDNIGHT, PRE-DAWN SNACKS.
SO THAT LEAVES GOING OUT.
TO VITO'S, OF COURSE...
AND HELLO, CREDIT CARD! THAT MEANS GOING OUT IN STYLE!
VITO'S, HERE I COME!
SLAM!
EEEK!
OOPS!
FORGOT I NEED TO WEAR CLOTHES NOW!

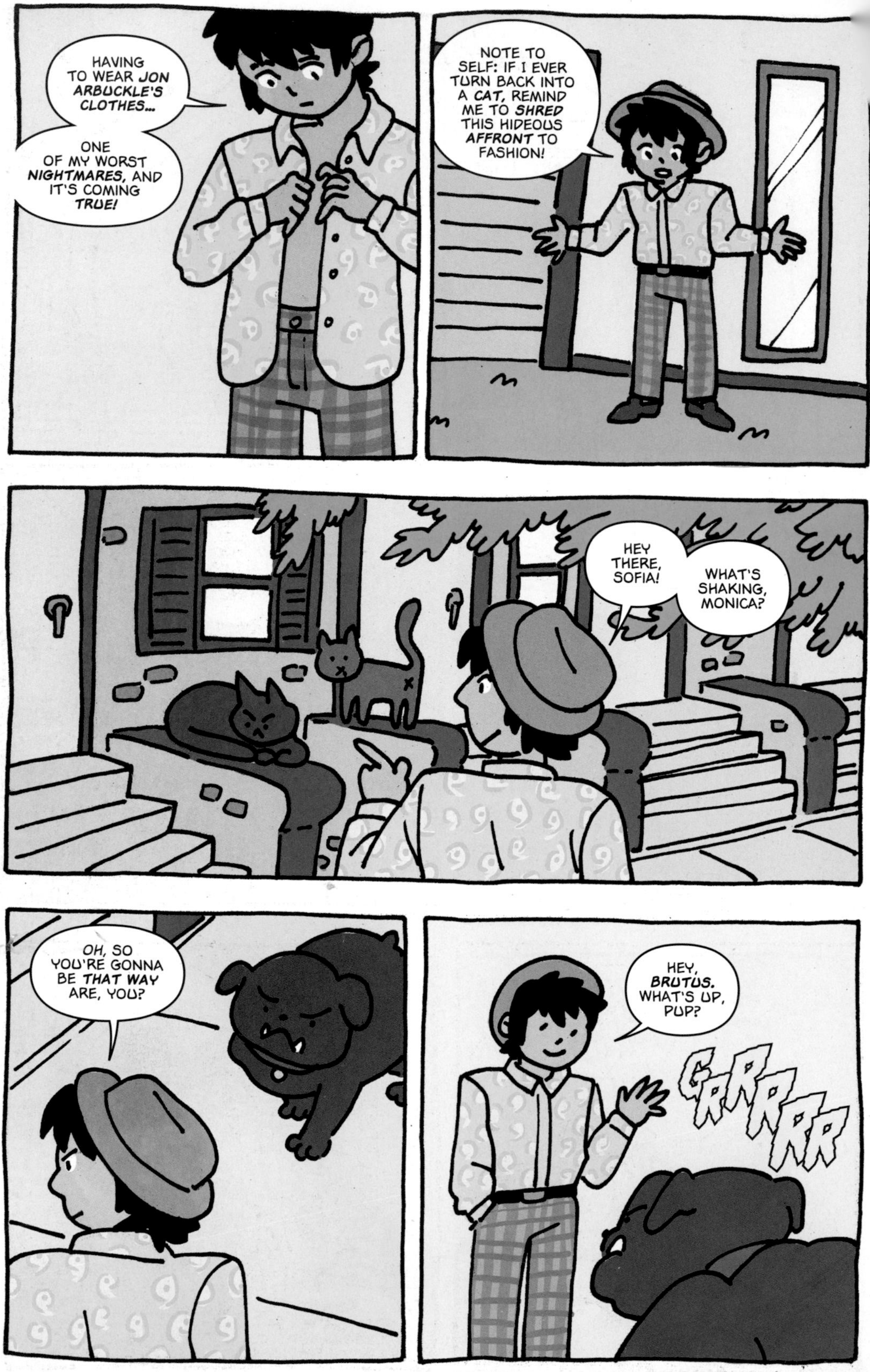
HAVING TO WEAR JON ARBUCKLE'S CLOTHES...
ONE OF MY WORST NIGHTMARES, AND IT'S COMING TRUE!
NOTE TO SELF: IF I EVER TURN BACK INTO A CAT, REMIND ME TO SHRED THIS HIDEOUS AFFRONT TO FASHION!
HEY THERE, SOFIA!
WHAT'S SHAKING, MONICA?
OH, SO YOU'RE GONNA BE THAT WAY ARE, YOU?
HEY, BRUTUS. WHAT'S UP, PUP?
GRRRRR

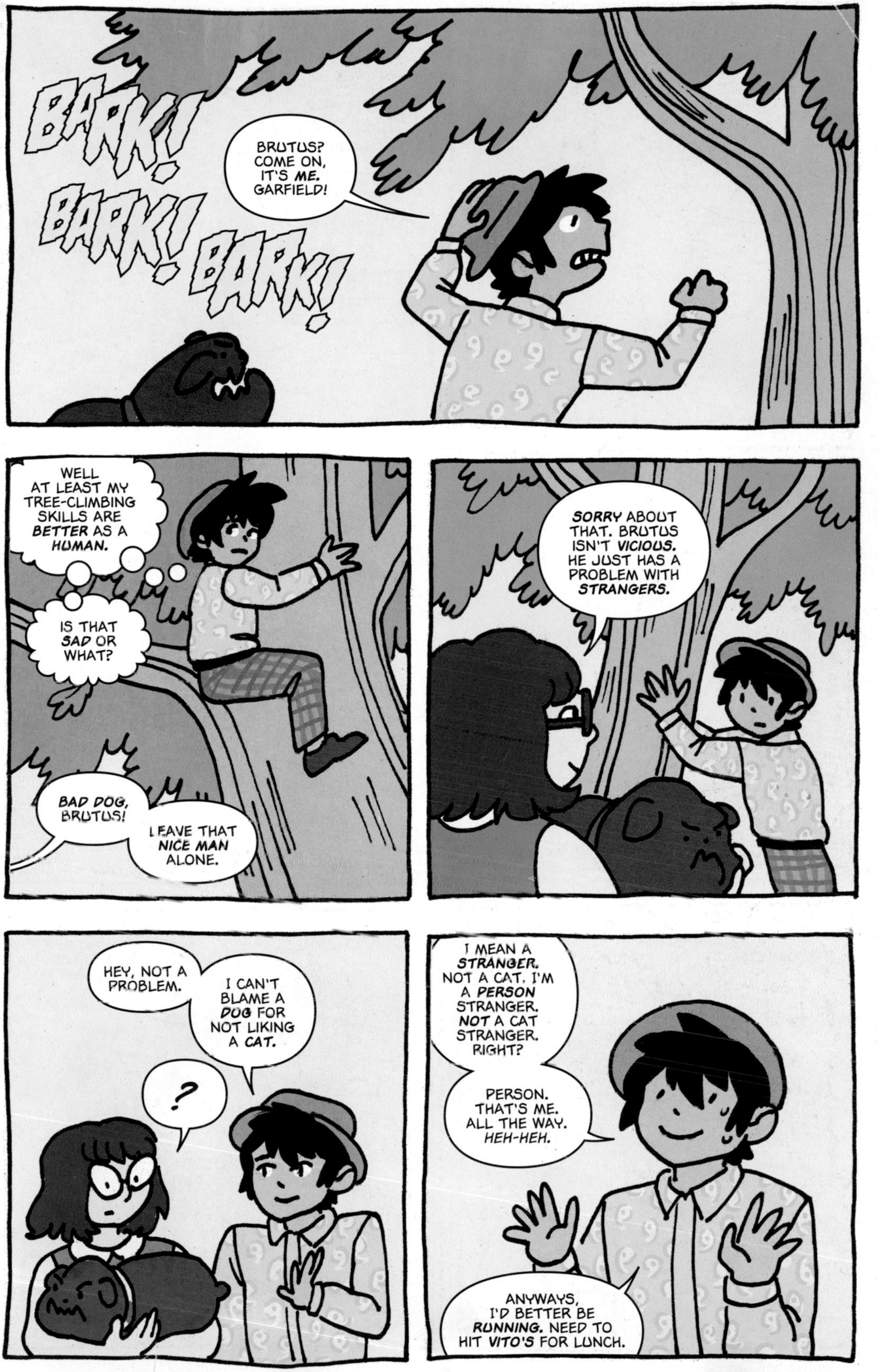
BARK! BARK! BARK!
BRUTUS? COME ON, IT'S ME. GARFIELD!
WELL AT LEAST MY TREE-CLIMBING SKILLS ARE BETTER AS A HUMAN.
IS THAT SAD OR WHAT?
BAD DOG, BRUTUS!
LEAVE THAT NICE MAN ALONE.
SORRY ABOUT THAT. BRUTUS ISN'T VICIOUS. HE JUST HAS A PROBLEM WITH STRANGERS.
HEY, NOT A PROBLEM.
I CAN'T BLAME A DOG FOR NOT LIKING A CAT.
?
I MEAN A STRANGER. NOT A CAT. I'M A PERSON STRANGER. NOT A CAT STRANGER. RIGHT?
PERSON. THAT'S ME. ALL THE WAY. HEH-HEH.
ANYWAYS, I'D BETTER BE RUNNING. NEED TO HIT VITO'S FOR LUNCH.

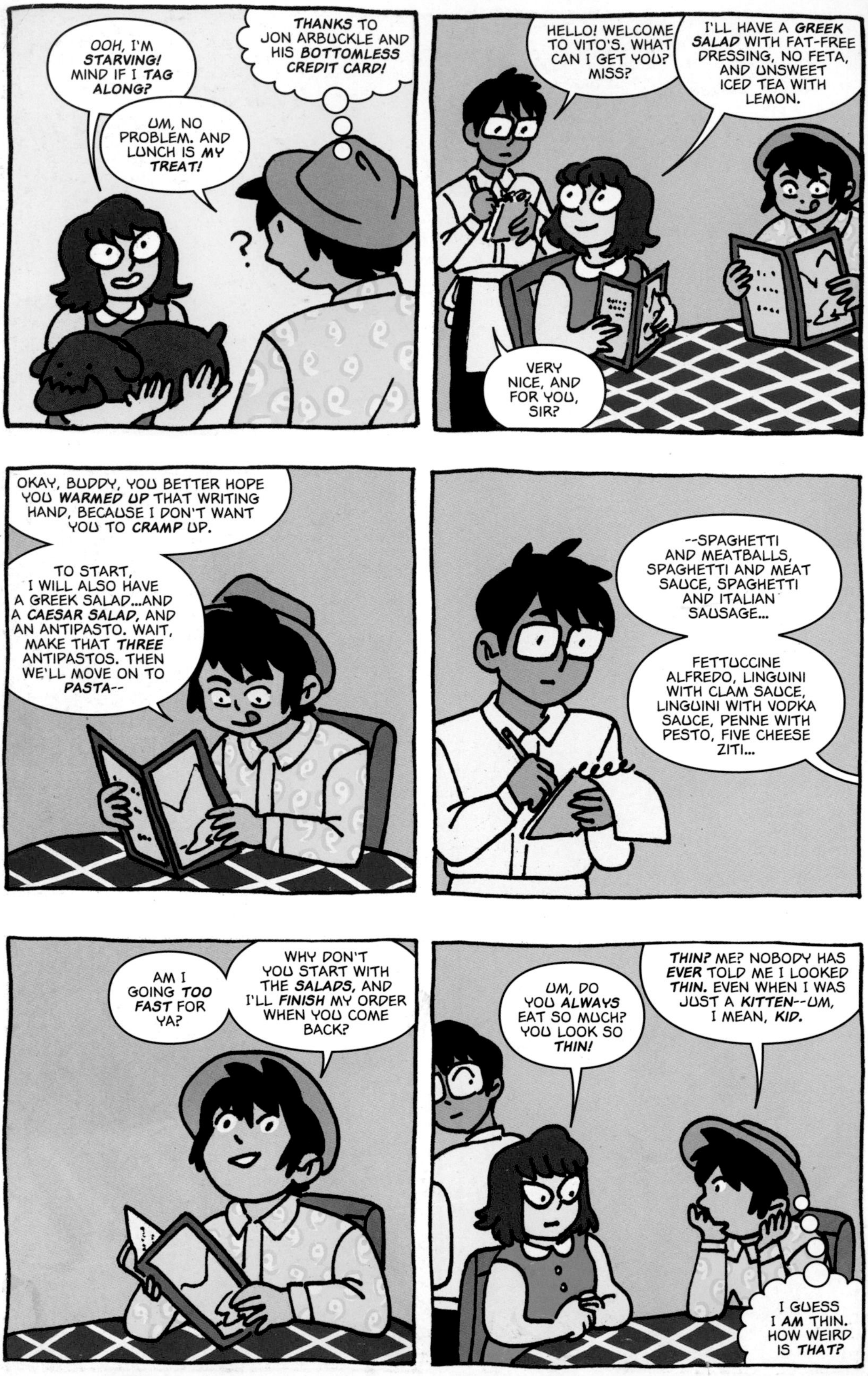
OOH, I'M STARVING! MIND IF I TAG ALONG?
UM, NO PROBLEM. AND LUNCH IS MY TREAT!
THANKS TO JON ARBUCKLE AND HIS BOTTOMLESS CREDIT CARD!
?
HELLO! WELCOME TO VITO'S. WHAT CAN I GET YOU? MISS?
I'LL HAVE A GREEK SALAD WITH FAT-FREE DRESSING, NO FETA, AND UNSWEET ICED TEA WITH LEMON.
VERY NICE, AND FOR YOU, SIR?
OKAY, BUDDY, YOU BETTER HOPE YOU WARMED UP THAT WRITING HAND, BECAUSE I DON'T WANT YOU TO CRAMP UP.
TO START, I WILL ALSO HAVE A GREEK SALAD...AND A CAESAR SALAD, AND AN ANTIPASTO. WAIT, MAKE THAT THREE ANTIPASTOS. THEN WE'LL MOVE ON TO PASTA--
--SPAGHETTI AND MEATBALLS, SPAGHETTI AND MEAT SAUCE, SPAGHETTI AND ITALIAN SAUSAGE...
FETTUCCINE ALFREDO, LINGUINI WITH CLAM SAUCE, LINGUINI WITH VODKA SAUCE, PENNE WITH PESTO, FIVE CHEESE ZITI...
AM I GOING TOO FAST FOR YA?
WHY DON'T YOU START WITH THE SALADS, AND I'LL FINISH MY ORDER WHEN YOU COME BACK?
UM, DO YOU ALWAYS EAT SO MUCH? YOU LOOK SO THIN!
THIN? ME? NOBODY HAS EVER TOLD ME I LOOKED THIN. EVEN WHEN I WAS JUST A KITTEN--UM, I MEAN, KID.
I GUESS I AM THIN. HOW WEIRD IS THAT?

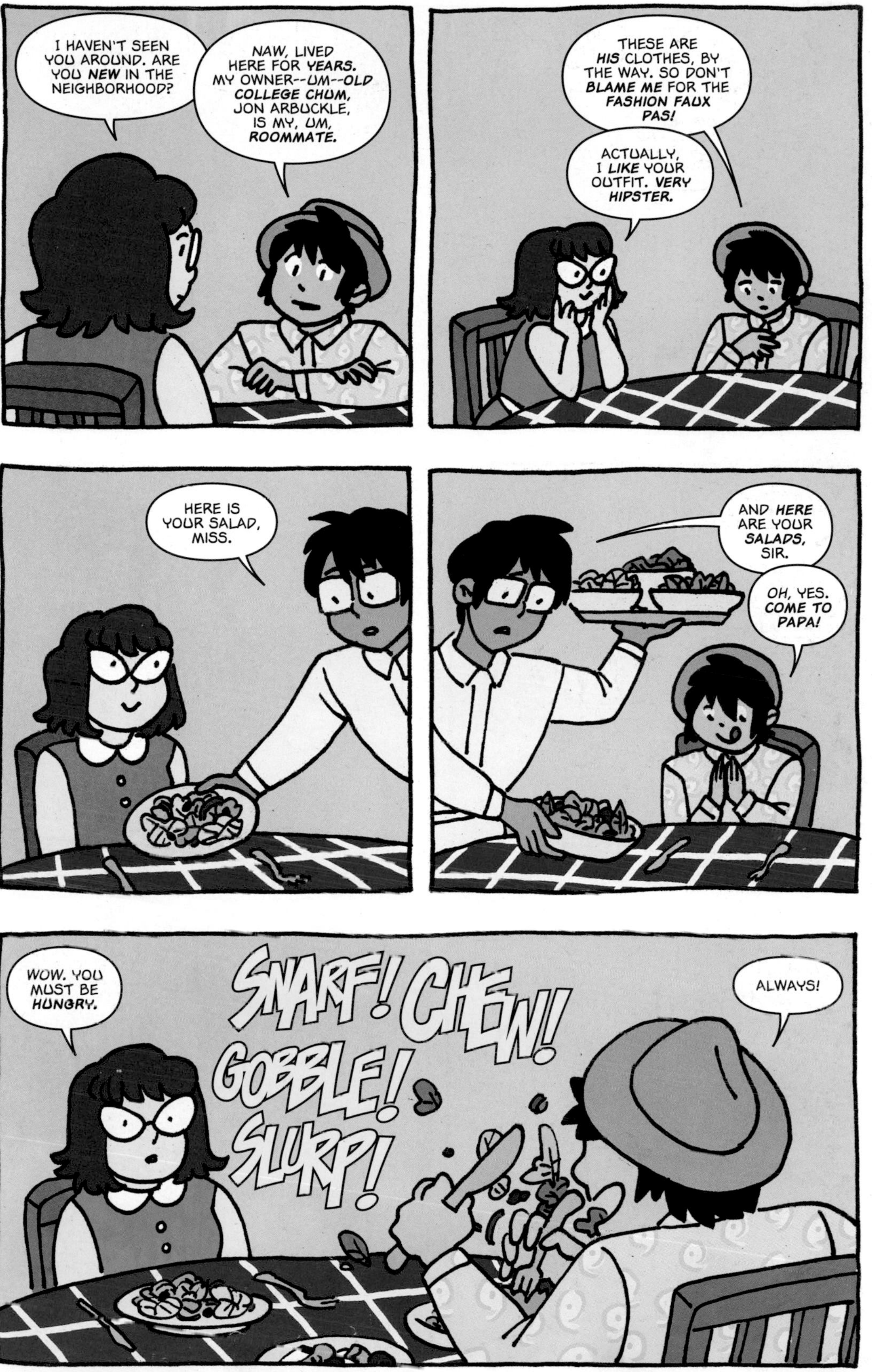
I HAVEN'T SEEN YOU AROUND. ARE YOU NEW IN THE NEIGHBORHOOD?
NAW, LIVED HERE FOR YEARS. MY OWNER--UM--OLD COLLEGE CHUM, JON ARBUCKLE, IS MY, UM, ROOMMATE.
THESE ARE HIS CLOTHES, BY THE WAY. SO DON'T BLAME ME FOR THE FASHION FAUX PAS!
ACTUALLY, I LIKE YOUR OUTFIT. VERY HIPSTER.
HERE IS YOUR SALAD, MISS.
AND HERE ARE YOUR SALADS, SIR.
OH, YES. COME TO PAPA!
WOW. YOU MUST BE HUNGRY.
SNARF! CHEW! GOBBLE! SLURP!
ALWAYS!

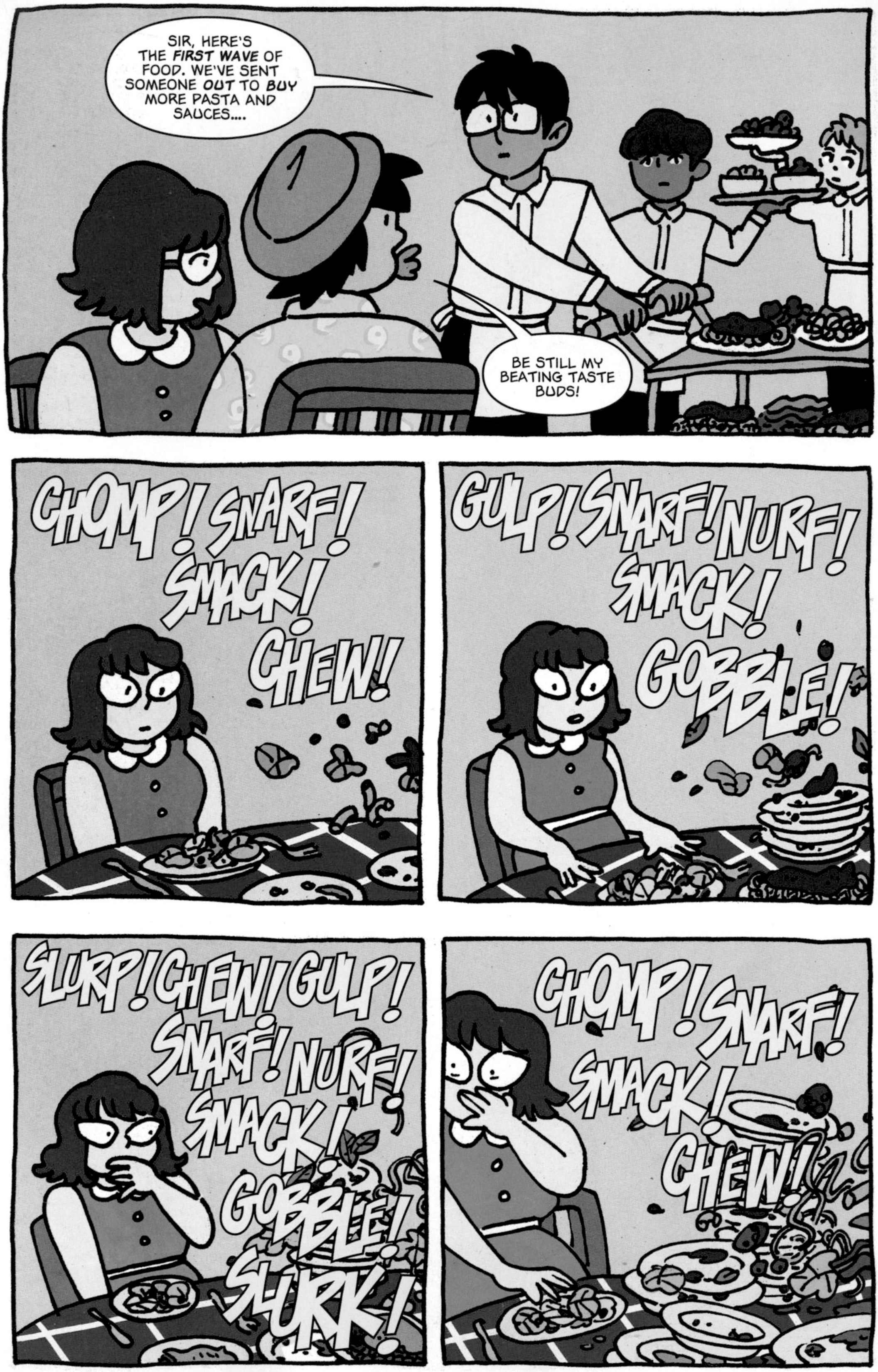
SIR, HERE'S THE FIRST WAVE OF FOOD. WE'VE SENT SOMEONE OUT TO BUY MORE PASTA AND SAUCES....
BE STILL MY BEATING TASTE BUDS!
CHOMP! SNARF! SMACK! CHEW!
GULP! SNARF! NURF! SMACK! GOBBLE!
SLURP! CHEW! GULP! SNARF! NURF! SMACK! GOBBLE! SLURK!
CHOMP! SNARF! SMACK! CHEW!

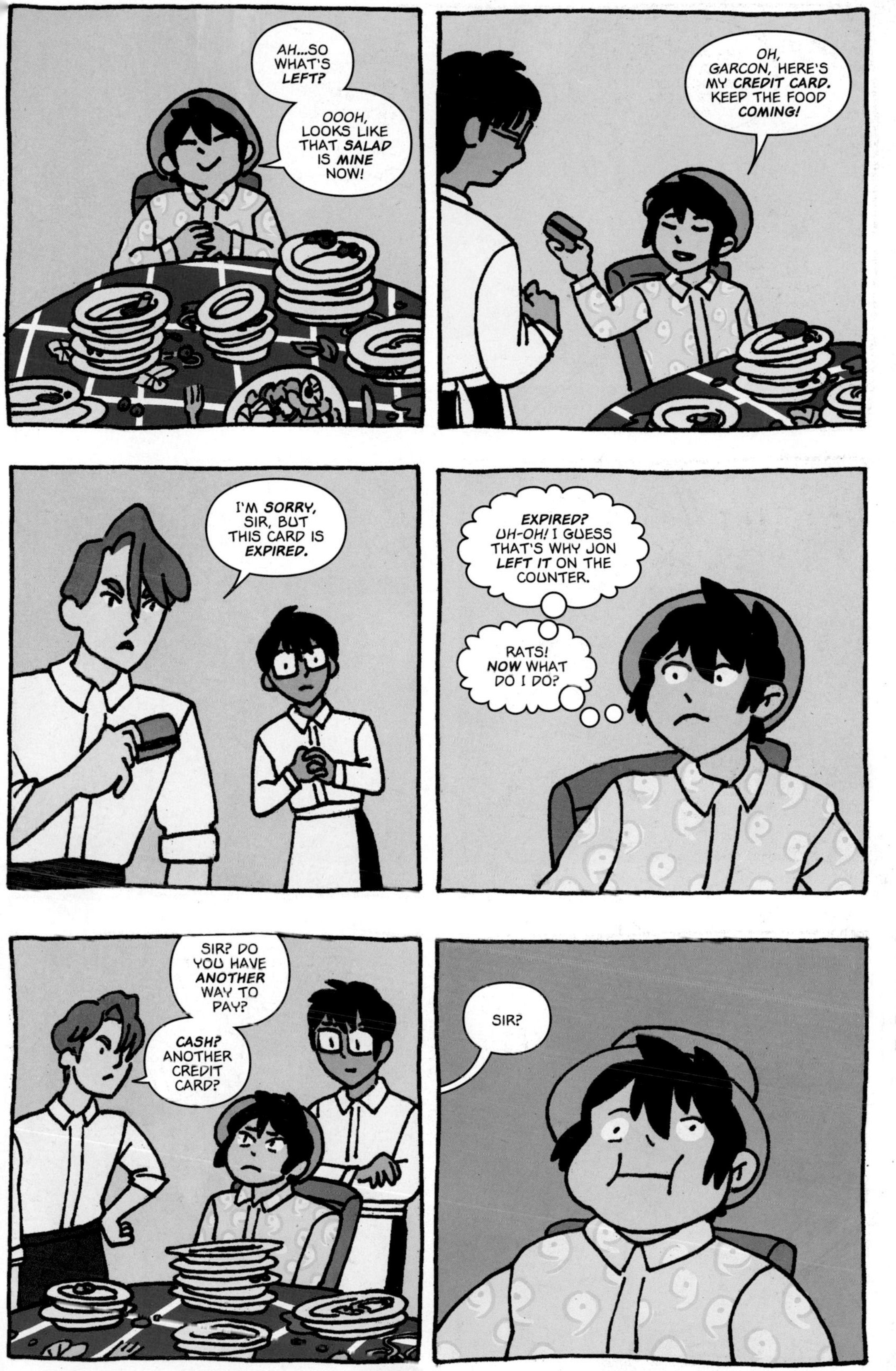
AH...SO WHAT'S LEFT?
OOOH, LOOKS LIKE THAT SALAD IS MINE NOW!
OH, GARCON, HERE'S MY CREDIT CARD. KEEP THE FOOD COMING!
I'M SORRY, SIR, BUT THIS CARD IS EXPIRED.
EXPIRED? UH-OH! I GUESS THAT'S WHY JON LEFT IT ON THE COUNTER.
RATS! NOW WHAT DO I DO?
SIR? DO YOU HAVE ANOTHER WAY TO PAY?
CASH? ANOTHER CREDIT CARD?
SIR?

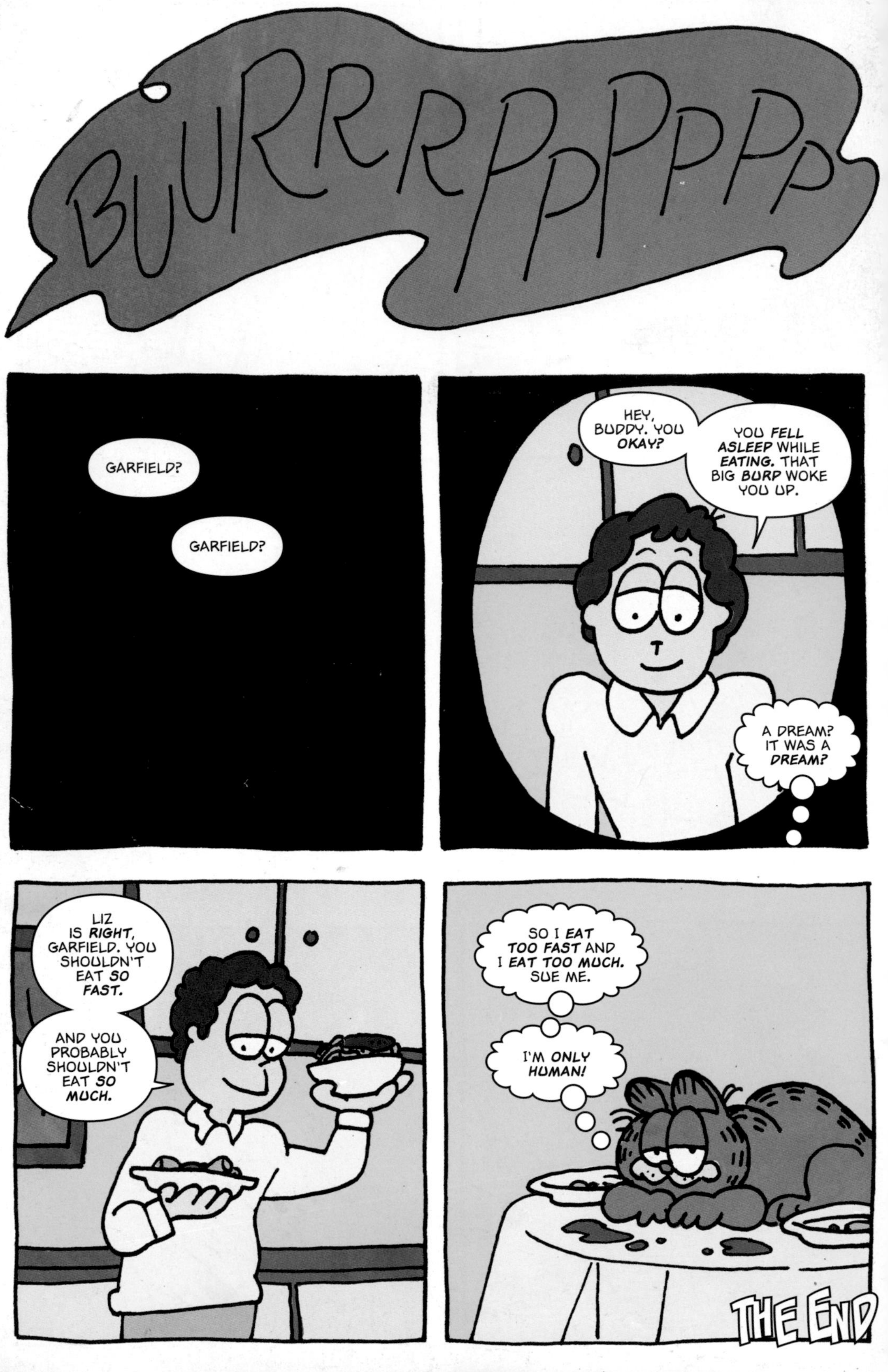

BUURRRRPPPPPPP
GARFIELD?
GARFIELD?
HEY, BUDDY. YOU **OKAY?**
YOU **FELL ASLEEP** WHILE **EATING.** THAT BIG **BURP** WOKE YOU UP.
A DREAM? IT WAS A **DREAM?**
LIZ IS **RIGHT,** GARFIELD. YOU SHOULDN'T EAT **SO FAST.**
AND YOU PROBABLY SHOULDN'T EAT **SO MUCH.**
SO I **EAT TOO FAST** AND I **EAT TOO MUCH.** SUE ME.
I'M **ONLY HUMAN!**
THE END

Fridge Funnies

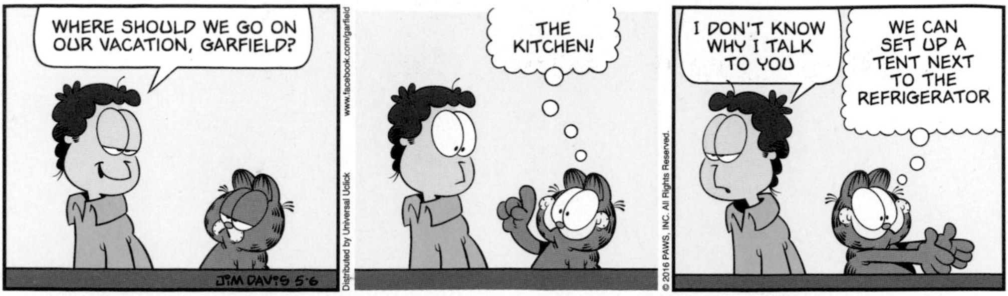

WHERE SHOULD WE GO ON OUR VACATION, GARFIELD?
JIM DAVIS 5-6
www.facebook.com/garfield
Distributed by Universal Uclick
THE KITCHEN!
© 2016 PAWS, INC. All Rights Reserved.
I DON'T KNOW WHY I TALK TO YOU
WE CAN SET UP A TENT NEXT TO THE REFRIGERATOR

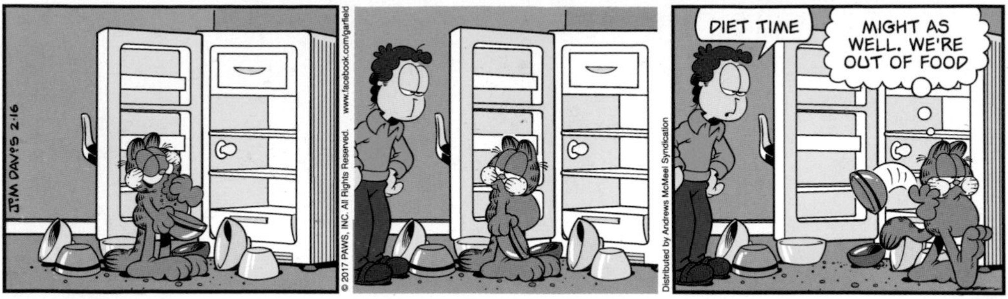

JIM DAVIS 2-16
© 2017 PAWS, INC. All Rights Reserved.
www.facebook.com/garfield
Distributed by Andrews McMeel Syndication
DIET TIME
MIGHT AS WELL. WE'RE OUT OF FOOD

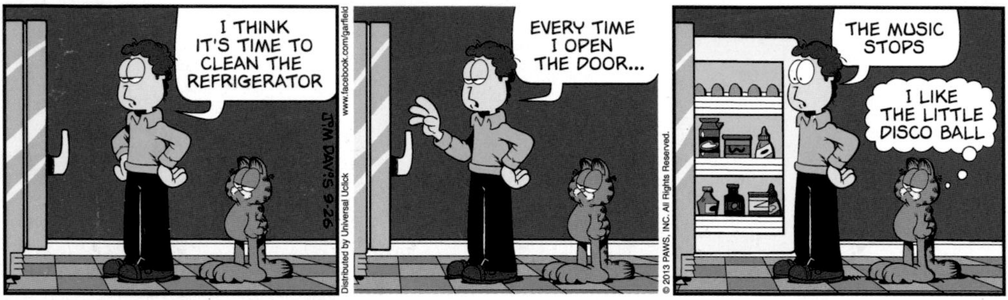

I THINK IT'S TIME TO CLEAN THE REFRIGERATOR
JIM DAVIS 9-26
www.facebook.com/garfield
Distributed by Universal Uclick
EVERY TIME I OPEN THE DOOR...
© 2013 PAWS, INC. All Rights Reserved.
THE MUSIC STOPS
I LIKE THE LITTLE DISCO BALL

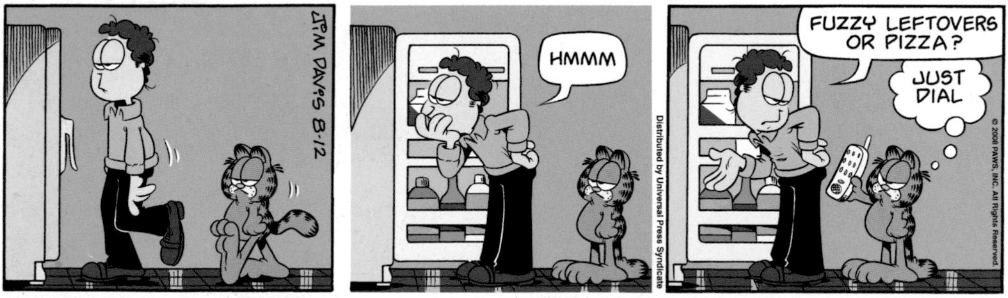

JIM DAVIS 8-12
HMMM
Distributed by Universal Press Syndicate
FUZZY LEFTOVERS OR PIZZA?
JUST DIAL
© 2008 PAWS, INC. All Rights Reserved.

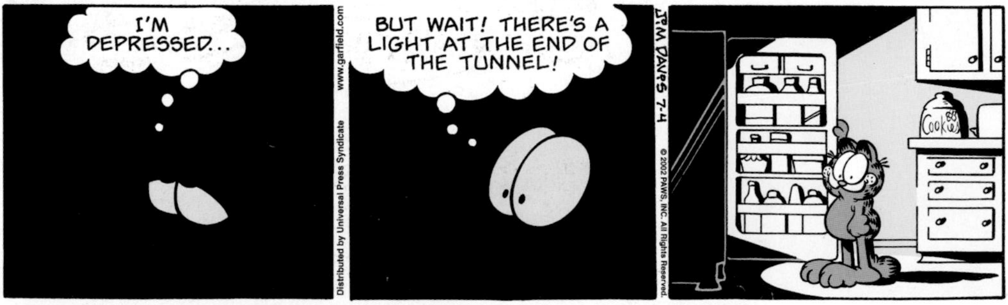

I'M DEPRESSED...
www.garfield.com
Distributed by Universal Press Syndicate
BUT WAIT! THERE'S A LIGHT AT THE END OF THE TUNNEL!
JIM DAVIS 7-4
© 2002 PAWS, INC. All Rights Reserved.
COOKIES

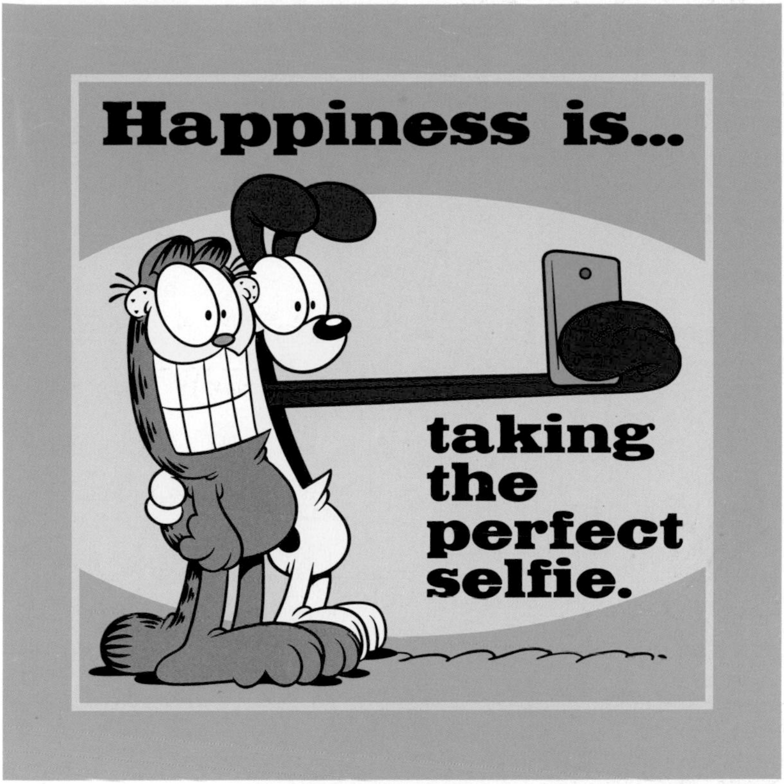
Happiness is...
taking the perfect selfie.

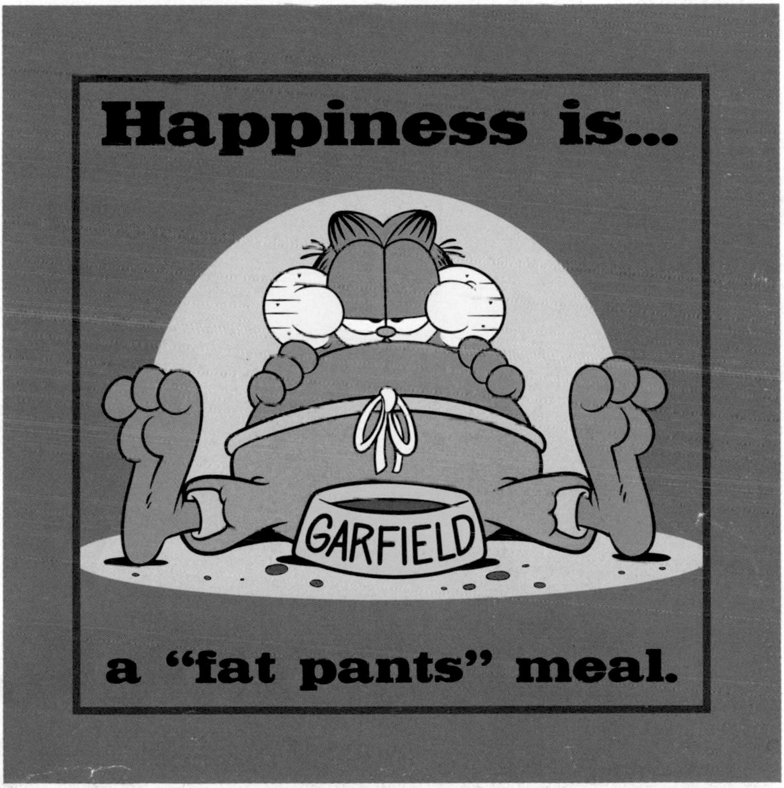
Happiness is...
GARFIELD
a "fat pants" meal.

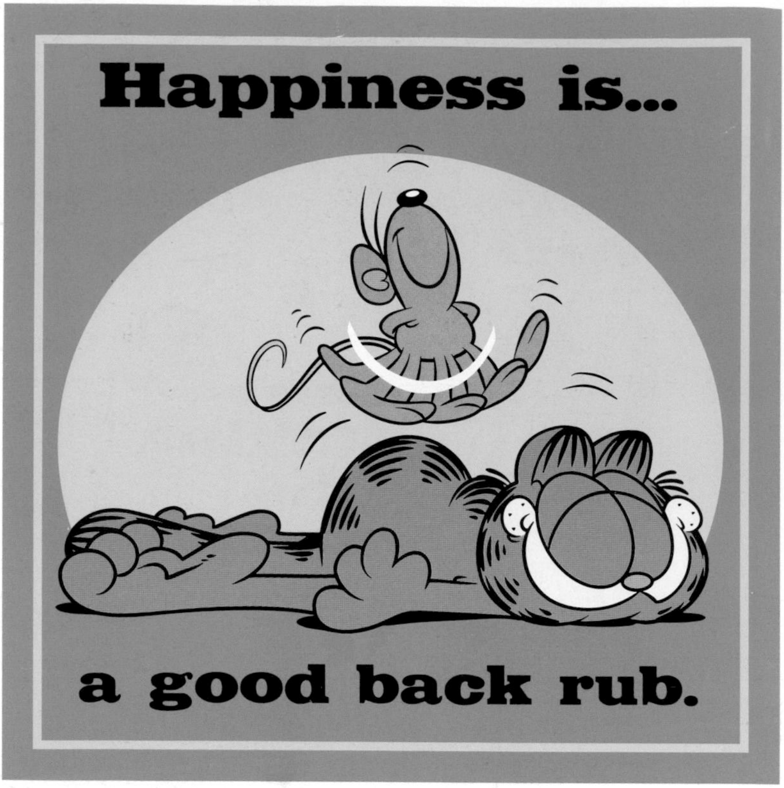
Happiness is...
a good back rub.

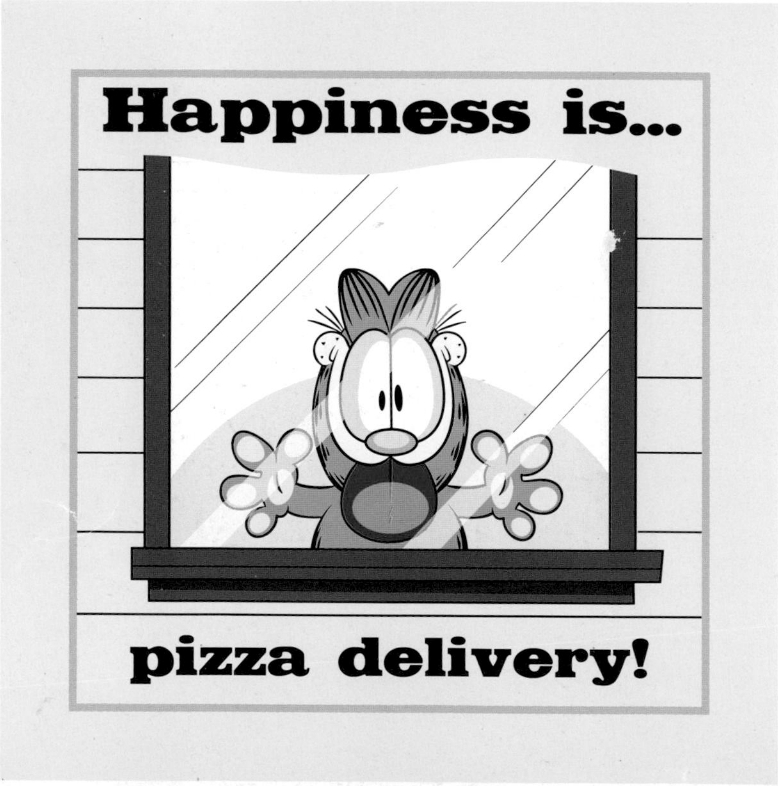
Happiness is...
pizza delivery!

Creature Comforts

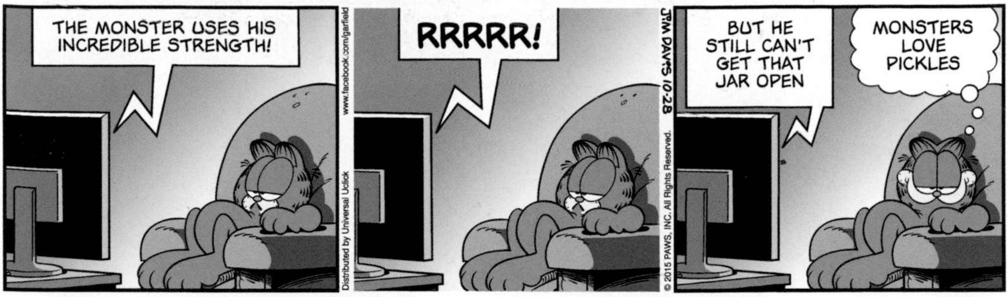
THE MONSTER USES HIS INCREDIBLE STRENGTH!
RRRRR!
BUT HE STILL CAN'T GET THAT JAR OPEN
MONSTERS LOVE PICKLES
JIM DAVIS 10-28
Distributed by Universal Uclick www.facebook.com/garfield
© 2015 PAWS, INC. All Rights Reserved.

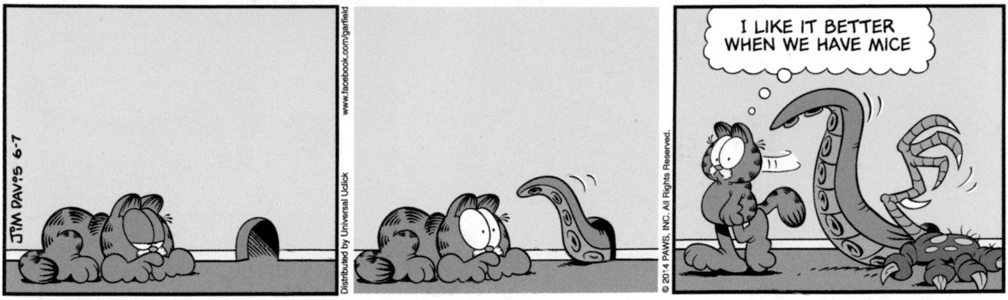
JIM DAVIS 6-7
I LIKE IT BETTER WHEN WE HAVE MICE
Distributed by Universal Uclick www.facebook.com/garfield
© 2014 PAWS, INC. All Rights Reserved.

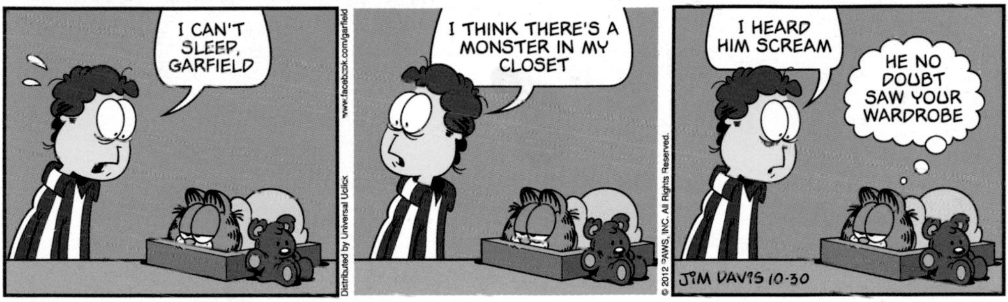
I CAN'T SLEEP, GARFIELD
I THINK THERE'S A MONSTER IN MY CLOSET
I HEARD HIM SCREAM
HE NO DOUBT SAW YOUR WARDROBE
JIM DAVIS 10-30
Distributed by Universal Uclick www.facebook.com/garfield
© 2012 PAWS, INC. All Rights Reserved.

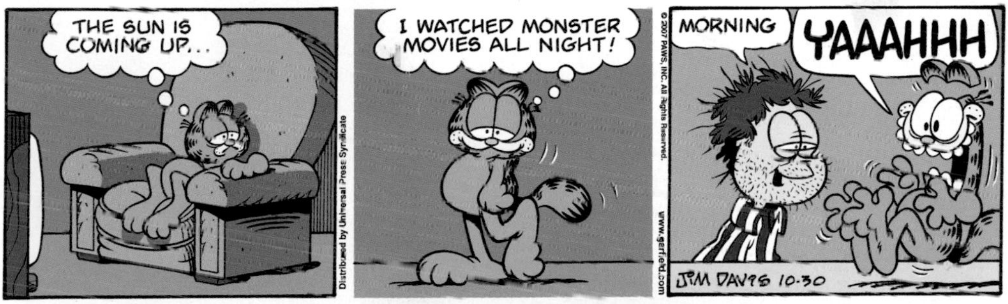
THE SUN IS COMING UP...
I WATCHED MONSTER MOVIES ALL NIGHT!
MORNING
YAAAHHH
JIM DAVIS 10-30
Distributed by Universal Press Syndicate
© 2007 PAWS, INC. All Rights Reserved. www.garfield.com

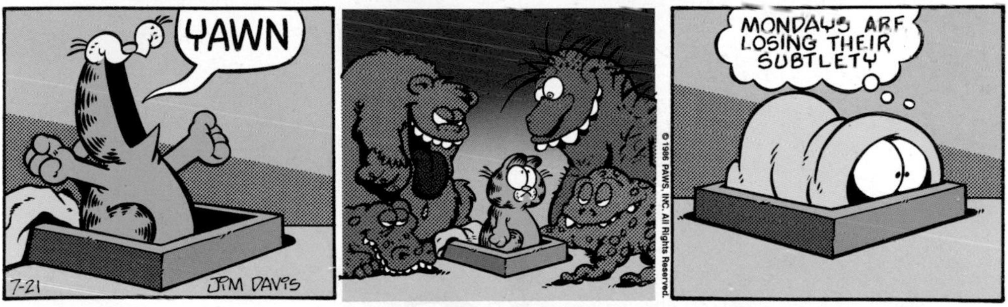
YAWN
MONDAYS ARE LOSING THEIR SUBTLETY
7-21 JIM DAVIS
© 1986 PAWS, INC. All Rights Reserved.

Classic 80s Garfield

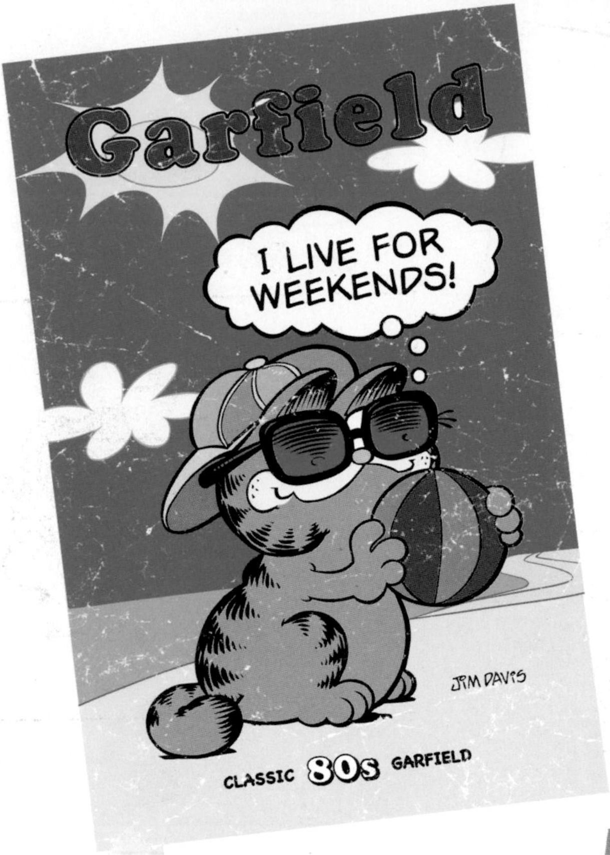
Garfield
I LIVE FOR WEEKENDS!
JIM DAVIS
CLASSIC 80s GARFIELD

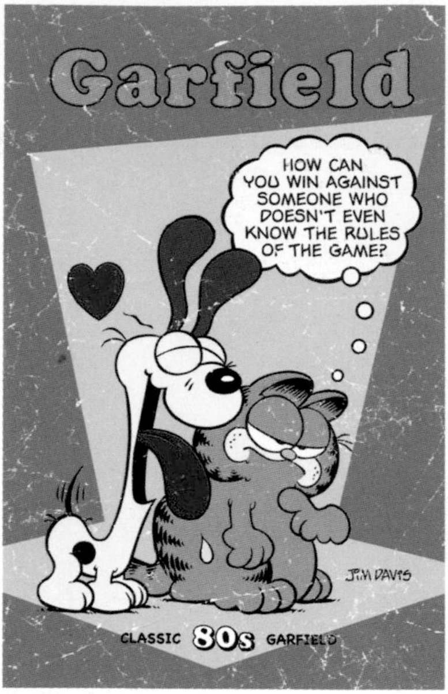
Garfield
HOW CAN YOU WIN AGAINST SOMEONE WHO DOESN'T EVEN KNOW THE RULES OF THE GAME?
JIM DAVIS
CLASSIC 80s GARFIELD

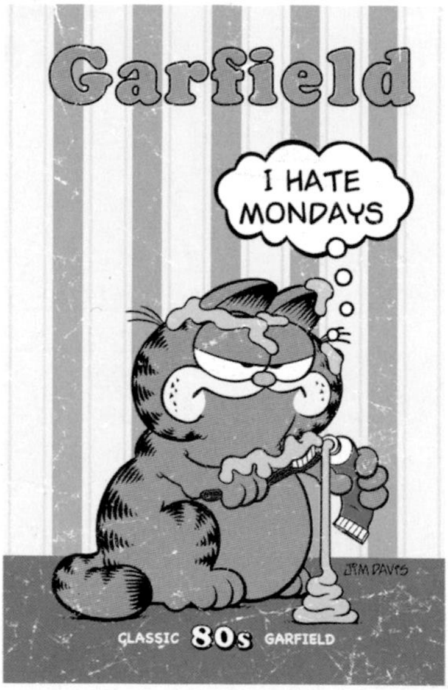
Garfield
I HATE MONDAYS
JIM DAVIS
CLASSIC 80s GARFIELD

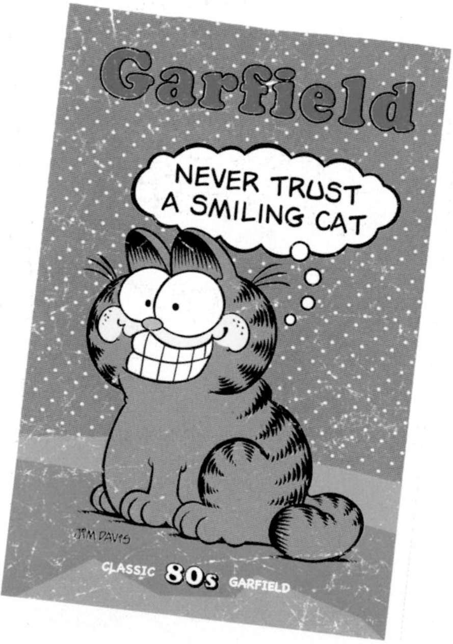
Garfield
NEVER TRUST A SMILING CAT
JIM DAVIS
CLASSIC 80s GARFIELD